SHOOT OUT

THE BALTIMORE BANNERS (BOOK 7)

LISA B. KAMPS

D1528158

Lisa B. Kamps

SHOOT OUT
The Baltimore Banners
Book 7

Lisa B. Kamps

SHOOT OUT

SHOOT OUT
Copyright © 2016 by Elizabeth Belbot Kamps

Cover and logo design by Jay Aheer of Simply Defined Art
http://www.jayscoversbydesign.com/

Lisa B. Kamps

Lisa B. Kamps

DEDICATION

For Christine Tovey and Logan Hernandez. Thanks so much for the continuing words of encouragement, feedback, and unending support. Your words mean so much more than you realize!

SHOOT OUT

Contents

SHOOT OUT

Lisa B. Kamps

Other titles by this author

THE BALTIMORE BANNERS

Crossing The Line, Book 1
Game Over, Book 2
Blue Ribbon Summer, Book 3
Body Check, Book 4
Break Away, Book 5
Playmaker (A Baltimore Banners Intermission novella)
Delay of Game, Book 6
Shoot Out, Book 7
The Baltimore Banners 1st Period Trilogy (Books 1-3)
On Thin Ice, Book 8

FIREHOUSE FOURTEEN

Once Burned, Book 1
Playing With Fire, Book 2
Breaking Protocol, Book 3

STAND-ALONE TITLES

Emeralds and Gold: A Treasury of Irish Short Stories
(*anthology*)
Finding Dr. Right, Silhouette Special Edition
Time To Heal

Lisa B. Kamps

Chapter One

"You have the most gorgeous eyes."

Mat Herron tried to smile but wasn't sure if his mouth actually moved or not. Hell, he wasn't sure of anything right now, not with the numbing effects of the alcohol he'd been drinking. All he knew was that he should leave. If he had any sense at all, he would leave. This was a bad idea, this entire night. He should have known better, should have never listened to his teammates, should have never even come on this trip.

Yeah, he could tell himself that all he wanted but it would be a lie. Wasn't he the one who said he was turning over a new leaf? Taking a break from everyone else's drama and living his own life? No more Saint Mat—and damn Derek Caulton for even starting that damn nickname. Besides, skipping out on the trip wasn't an option. Although why in the hell his teammate, Jean-Pierre Larocque, thought it would be a good idea to have a pre-wedding getaway in New Orleans, in early June, was anyone's guess. Probably because his fiancée, Emily, wanted to see New Orleans.

And JP would do anything for Emily.

So here he was, in some crowded bar on Bourbon Street drinking a too-sweet and too-potent bright green drink even though he should have stopped drinking two hours ago. No, more than two hours ago. This drink was his third. Fifth. Maybe. Hell, he didn't know, he'd lost track hours ago. All he knew was that the woman grinning up at him, complimenting his eyes, was a friend of Derek's girlfriend, Bridget. He couldn't remember her name, wasn't even sure if he knew it. At this point in time, he was lucky if he could keep his teammates' names straight, let alone their girlfriends' names.

Was the girl staring up at him in the wedding party? Maybe. No, she couldn't be. Wrong couple. She was a friend of Bridget's, not JP and Emily.

Although it didn't matter if she was or if she wasn't. She was a friend of Bridget's so she was off-limits. Mat wasn't sure why that mattered but it did. No nameless faceless sex with someone he'd meet again. That was the deal. It didn't matter that he just now made the deal with himself, didn't matter that nobody else would know about it. If he was going to turn over a new leaf and get rid of that stupid, ill-deserved reputation and asinine nickname, then he was going to do it all the way.

With a complete stranger.

Except now the girl was resting her hand on his arm, still grinning up at him. Somebody jostled her from behind, pushing her even closer. Mat didn't think, just brought his arm around her waist to keep her from stumbling and frowned at the guy staggering past him.

"Dude, watch it already, will you?"

The guy kept going, not even bothering to look

their way. Probably for the best. Hell, the guy probably didn't even realize he'd bumped into them, not with it being so crowded. Mat frowned again as the guy disappeared into the pushing throng of people, then looked down at the girl in front of him.

Shit. He still had his arm around her. Her eyes widened when he met her gaze, like she was just as surprised as he was. Or maybe he was just reading too much into her expression. Slightly parted full lips. Head tilted back and to the side. Deep amber eyes that looked a little dazed. From the alcohol? Or something else?

He really should move his arm. But she felt nice against him. Soft curves with a hard body, warm and flush. Yeah, he really should move his arm, let her step back. But she didn't try to move away, just kept looking at him with a hint of smile on her oval face. She tilted her head back a little then reached up with one hand and brushed a few strands of hair out of her face, pushing them to the back where a clip of some kind held most of her hair in place. Her hair was almost the same color as her eyes. A lighter brown, with amber and dark gold mixed in along with a few streaks of bright pink throughout.

Yeah, he was definitely just a bit more than buzzed if he was noticing the different shades of a color in a girl's hair, even if the bright pink was really noticeable. And he really should move his arm.

He leaned down instead, just enough so his mouth was closer to her ear so he wouldn't have to shout. She smelled nice. Light and fresh, not quite flowery. Definitely better than the stronger smells of Bourbon Street that hung over everything, permeating skin and clothes, especially in the June heat.

"What's your name?"

"Nicole."

Even her voice was light and fresh. Yeah, he was definitely a little buzzed. He should just finish the drink and go back to the hotel. Better yet, he should put the rest of the drink down. Just put the tall plastic tube that passed for a glass on the bar and turn around and leave. But Nicole was still looking up at him, those luscious lips curled in a small smile as she watched him, the palm of her hand flat against his chest. And hell, when had she placed her hand there? Just above the point where his shirt opened, so her fingers were resting against his bare skin. Warm. Teasing. Too damn tempting.

Mat swallowed, told himself to step back, to move his arm and put some distance between them. But Nicole leaned even closer, her breath warm against his skin when she spoke.

"Did you want to leave?"

And shit, just like that, all his good intentions flew out the door. His mind was telling him to say no but the rest of his body—from the goofy-ass smile on his face to the raging hard-on that sprung to life in his pants—was cheering at the idea. And why the hell not? Isn't this what he wanted to do? Change his image, have some fun, do what he wanted? Get rid of that damned reputation for once and for all. No, Nicole wasn't exactly a stranger, someone he wouldn't see again. But it's not like he'd be running into her all the time. Hell, he really might not see her again even if she was a friend of Bridget's.

So why the hell not?

Nicole was still looking up at him, her hand still resting up high on his chest, the tips of her fingers lightly caressing his skin, so damn tempting. Mat finally nodded, his heart thumping at the answering smile that crossed Nicole's face. He looked around, his gaze finally dropping to the unfinished drink in his hand. He lifted the tall tube to his mouth and drained the sweet liquid in several long swallows, then took a half-step toward the bar and placed the empty container on the varnished counter. He smiled down at Nicole and grabbed her hand, wrapping his fingers around her slender ones, then pushed his way through the crowd, clearing space for Nicole to follow. They were a few feet away from the door when a hand clamped onto his elbow, stopping him. Mat turned, not exactly surprised to see Derek frowning at him. Derek's gaze slid over to Nicole, down to their clasped hands, then back to Mat.

"Where are you going?"

"Someplace quieter." Mat tugged his arm from Derek's hold and tried to take another step but he wasn't fast enough. Derek grabbed him again and leaned even closer, his voice a harsh whisper when he spoke.

"Mat, I don't think that's a good idea—"

"I didn't ask for your opinion."

"Mat, seriously, I don't think—"

"Don't care." He pulled his arm free again and stepped away, Nicole close behind him. Two more steps and he was outside, leading Nicole through the crowds that lined the crooked and sloping brick sidewalk. Mat felt a tug on his hand, felt himself being pulled off the sidewalk and into the street. He started to pull back then relaxed at the last minute, his hazy brain finally remembering that it was okay to walk in the street, that everyone did it.

"Your name is Mat, right?"

"Hm?" Mat stopped when she did, blinking when she stepped closer and placed her hand high on his chest again. He grinned and nodded. "Yeah. Mat. That's me."

She smiled and stepped even closer, rising up on her toes. And then her arms were around his neck and her mouth was on his. Heat, fire, desire. Instant, consuming. Mat wrapped his arms around her slender waist and pulled her even closer. His mouth opened under hers and their tongues met, thrusting, teasing, tasting.

Yells and whistles echoed around them, louder than the other noises filling the humid air. Mat groaned and pulled away, looking around with dazed eyes as reality seeped into him.

He was standing in the middle of the street, in New Orleans, with his tongue down some stranger's throat. He should be embarrassed. Mortified. He should tell her goodnight and go back to his room and catch the first flight home tomorrow.

That's what he should do. But tonight, he didn't give a fuck.

Instead, he pulled Nicole tighter against him, cupped the side of her face and tilted her head back. Her eyes widened the slightest bit just before his mouth claimed hers. Strong, possessive. Demanding. He swallowed a groan—his, hers, maybe both—and swept his tongue inside. She tasted sweet. Addictive. Sinfully delicious.

He couldn't get enough.

No, his mind corrected. He couldn't get enough *here*. Not in the middle of the street, not with an audience cheering them on. He pulled away with a grin and grabbed Nicole's hand, squeezing her fingers as he tugged. The hotel where they were staying was one block up, right on Bourbon Street, complete with balconies that overlooked the nightly revelry unfolding on the street. The last two nights, Mat had been content with being an onlooker, sitting on the balcony and just watching.

Not tonight. No, tonight was going to be different.

Nicole stumbled, her body falling sideways against him as they stepped back onto the sidewalk. A twinge jerked at Mat's conscience and he paused, looking down at her.

"Are you okay? You're not drunk, are you?"

"Me?" Nicole laughed, the sound almost musical against the backdrop of all the other noise. She shook her head then pointed down at her feet. "No, I'm not drunk. It's the shoes."

The shoes were open-toed sandals with a platform heel at least four inches high. Mat's gaze dropped to the bright green nails peeking out from the open canvas weave of the sandal when Nicole raised one long shapely leg, holding it out in front of her with a balance that surprised him. His gaze drifted from the bright nails up along that lean tanned leg then stopped at the hem of her short skirt. Heat spread across his face and he hoped to hell he wasn't blushing.

"What about you?"

Mat pulled his gaze away from the hem of her skirt, from the tanned flesh of her upper thigh, and tried to stop thinking about tan lines—or the lack of them. He cleared his throat and swallowed, his face burning even more. "Me what?"

"Are you drunk?"

"Not really, no."

Nicole raised one well-shaped eyebrow in his direction, her full mouth tilting up in a small smile. "Not really?"

Mat thought for a second, then grinned and shook his head. "Nope. Just feeling good."

Nicole's smile widened and she tugged on his hand, pulling him toward the steps of the hotel. "Let's see if we can make good feel even better."

Now it was Mat's turn to stumble, thanks to the rock hard erection in his shorts. He reached down and adjusted himself, hoping the movement was inconspicuous. But Nicole's gaze followed the movement of his hand and her smile grew even wider as she led him through the doors and across the courtyard lobby to the elevators.

They finally reached his room, the air humming between them. Electrified, thrumming with anticipation. Mat dug the cardkey from his front pocket and jammed it into the card reader, surprised to notice that his hand was shaking just the slightest bit. He had just enough time to hang the Do Not Disturb sign on the outside door handle before Nicole was in his arms, her body pressed against him, her mouth warm and willing under his.

Holy shit, she was liquid fire in his arms. Hot, supple, coming alive under his touch. He dropped his hands to her ass, cupping the firm flesh as he rocked his hips against hers. She moaned, the sound lost in their harsh breathing.

And holy fuck, was he really going to do this?

Nicole dragged one hand between them, stroking the length of his erection under the thin cotton of his shorts.

Fuck yes, he was really going to do this.

He pulled her more tightly against him, only briefly surprised when she jumped and wrapped her legs around his waist. He adjusted his hold and stepped forward, carrying her through the small sitting room of the suite to the open door of his bedroom.

He paused, wondering about the sign on the doorknob, wondering if he really needed it since he had his own room. Wondering if Kenny would pay attention to it, worrying about where Kenny would sleep.

Fuck Kenny. He could figure it out on his own. It wasn't Mat's job to take care of his teammates. Not now, not anymore. Not ever.

Mat nudged the door closed with his foot and kept walking, not stopping until he reached the bed. Even then he didn't stop, just leaned forward until Nicole's back rested against the mattress. He broke the kiss and pushed up with his hands, kneeling between her legs. Light from the ongoing party on the street drove the shadows from the room, bathing Nicole in a soft rainbow of colors. She smiled then pushed herself to a sitting position before reaching behind her and undoing the clip at the base of her neck. She shook her head and thick strands of soft hair fell around her shoulders, long and luxurious, glowing in the odd light that filled the room. Mat's mouth went dry when she reached down and grabbed the hem of her shirt, pulling it over her head and tossing it to the side in one graceful move. Mat swallowed, his gaze resting on the generous swell of her bare breasts, on the dark nipples that hardened under his stare.

She shook her head again, dislodging the beads that caught in her hair. The colorful strands fell, landing against her chest and curling around one firm breast. Mat blinked, mesmerized at the sight even though he knew he shouldn't be staring. He sensed her smile, knew she was watching him watching her, and he still couldn't look away. Not when she reached up and gently cupped both her breasts, pinching the nipples and making the peaks harden even more.

Whatever blood was left in his head shot straight to his cock, leaving him momentarily lightheaded. He saw Nicole's lips move, knew she was saying something, but he couldn't make out the words through the buzzing in his ears. He shook his head and finally looked up at her, at the playfulness in her warm eyes and the full smile on her luscious mouth.

"Touch me, Mat."

He didn't need to be told twice. He reached out and skimmed the back of his hands over the hard nipples, softly, gently. Nicole's breath caught in her throat and her head fell back.

"Like that?"

"Yes."

Mat did it again, brushing the peaks a little harder this time. He shifted his hands, cupping each breast in his palm, their weight warm and heavy. He brushed each nipple with his thumb, over and over, lightly, teasing. Then he leaned forward and took one nipple in his mouth, grazing it with his teeth before sucking, licking.

Nicole gasped and arched under him, her hand cupping the back of his head and holding him in place. He moved to her other breast, teasing and sucking, licking, until the sound of her harsh breathing echoed around him. He eased her back on the mattress, kissing his way down her body. Using his mouth, his lips, his teeth. Teasing, tasting. He dragged the tips of his fingers along her sides, smiling at the little sounds she made. Short gasps peppered with little moans, the noise both oddly sweet and completely enticing. Enchanting.

He reached the edge of her silky skirt, hesitating only a second before dipping his fingers into the waistband and dragging it past her hips. Mat shifted, just enough to pull the skirt down the long length of her legs before tossing it to the floor. He sat back on his heels, his gaze hungry as he stared at her.

Full firm breasts with dark pointed nipples. Lean waist and flat stomach, the flesh firm and tanned. Flared feminine hips, slightly round, tapering down to long toned legs. The flesh of her body glowed with a warm tan, honey and gold.

He reached down with one hand and dragged his fingers up her leg, slowly, teasing, dipping behind to caress the sensitive flesh at the back of her knee. Her body arched and she gasped, the sound small and breathy. Mat swallowed his own groan and continued dragging his finger up her leg, gently tracing the lines of the tattoo that covered the top of her left thigh. A fairytale castle protected by a dragon, surrounded by flowers, boldly colored.

He didn't waste time looking, not when his focus was elsewhere. Higher up, there at the juncture of her thighs. Completely smooth and bare, the soft skin there as tanned as the rest of her body.

He dragged his hand up, his palm covering her heated skin for just a second before he slid his finger along the delicate folds. Nicole's hips arched up, her legs dropping to the sides, opening her to his gaze, his touch.

Mat traced the soft opening with the tip of his

finger, back and forth, her flesh damp and hot. He reached behind him and grabbed her right ankle with his free hand, bending her leg and moving it further to the side, opening her even more. She moaned, reaching out with one hand before it curled around air and dropped to the mattress beside her. Her eyes were closed, her head turned to the side, her teeth pulling at her lower lip. He stroked her again, sliding the tip of his finger inside until it disappeared into the rosy flesh. Wet. Hot. Welcoming.

In. Out. In once more as her hips tilted higher, searching. He grabbed her, holding her still as he lowered his mouth to her.

Fuck, she was so wet. Sweet. He ran his tongue along her clit, teasing the sensitive flesh until her moans became louder, her breathing harsher. He reached up with one hand, spreading her moist flesh, holding her open, giving him more. His other hand drifted up to one full breast, kneading and squeezing as he feasted on her.

Her hand drifted up from the mattress, her fingers tangling in his hair as her hips thrust against his mouth. Her moans drifted off, becoming whimpers mixed with words that made no sense. Then her breathing stopped and her body tensed under his touch, her back arching as she held herself above the mattress.

And screamed his name with her release.

The noise startled him and he pulled back, but only for a split second before he grinned. A cocky, satisfied grin that he quickly hid by kissing the inside of Nicole's thigh. Her fingers dug into his hair, tugging then releasing as tremors racked her body.

Mat slid off the bed, quickly removing his shirt and tossing it to the floor before pushing his shorts and briefs down and stepping out of them. He leaned over and pulled his wallet out, grabbing the foil packets he had tucked inside earlier, then tossed the wallet on the pile of clothes. Condoms securely in hand, he climbed back on the bed and stretched out beside Nicole, tossing the foil packets next to the pillow as he watched her body slowly relax.

She was beautiful, but not in a calendar or lingerie model kind of way. Her body was lean but full, supple yet firm. Healthy golden skin stretched over muscle and curves, soft and hard all at the same time. Her hair fanned around her, the long lengths tangled on the pillow. Mat reached out, fingering the thick strands. Soft and smooth, vibrant, almost alive as they curled around his finger. Nicole shifted, her head turning toward him as her lids fluttered open. Her gaze was warm, slightly dazed as she looked at him, a small smile teasing the corners of her full mouth.

Her tongue darted out, a soft peek of pink running across her bottom lip. She rolled to her side and propped her head in her hand, still smiling at him. "Wow."

Mat grinned. "Wow, huh?"

"Definitely."

He reached out and ran a finger along her collarbone then down, tracing the bold colorful lines of the partial sleeve tattooed on her left arm. Another dragon, more fairies and flowers. He met her gaze once more, the corners of his mouth curing in a grin. "There's definitely more wow available. If you're interested."

Nicole laughed then moved so quickly that Mat barely had time to blink before finding himself flat on his back, his arms stretched above him as Nicole straddled his waist. She leaned forward, her full breasts pressed against his bare chest, and playfully nipped his bottom lip.

"Oh, I'm definitely interested."

Mat's grin faded with a small groan as she kissed her way down his chest. He gasped when she nipped one flat nipple, moaned when she teased it with her tongue. And then her hand closed around his cock, stroking, and he forgot to think, forgot about everything except her touch.

And then her touch disappeared, was simply gone. Mat swallowed his groan of disappointment, wondering if she changed her mind, if maybe he had pushed too far, too fast. He lifted his head from the pillow and opened his eyes, almost afraid he'd see her getting dressed. Fuck. He wasn't any good at this. He should have wooed her some more, should have—

No, she wasn't getting dressed. She was sitting back on her heels between his legs, a sultry look in her exotic eyes as she watched him. She grabbed several of the tangled strings of beads and pulled them over her head, the purple and gold plastic rubbing together with a whispered clicking as she let them run through her fingers. A teasing grin played at the corners of her mouth when she leaned forward and dragged the beads down his stomach—

And across his cock.

Holy shit, he hadn't been expecting that. Hadn't expected the thrill that shot through him at the sensation. Nicole wrapped the beads around the base of his cock, around his balls, tightening them just a little. Then she leaned forward and—

Mat's breath escaped in a rush when her mouth closed over his cock. Hot, sweet. Christ, her mouth was a wet dream come to life. Not just her mouth. Her hands, gently squeezing his balls, gently stroking the beads up and down his throbbing erection.

And holy shit, the way the beads tightened around his cock, his balls, the way she sucked him, like she was working on a thick milkshake, trying to draw it through a straw and—

What the fuck was wrong with him, thinking about milkshakes when he was getting the best fucking blowjob he'd ever had? And shit, Nicole's mouth really was a wet dream come to life because if she didn't stop, he'd be making his own fucking milkshake right in her mouth.

He reached down, searching, trying to stop her— or hold her in place, he wasn't sure which. But just before he lost it, just before he came right in her mouth, she pulled back, that devilish grin still in place. She stretched forward, one hand still playing with the beads around his balls, and grabbed one of the condoms. Mat held his breath, his jaw clenched as she ripped open the packet and rolled it in place. Fuck, just that much was nearly enough to send him over the edge. It had been too long, too damn long, he wasn't used to—

And then she was straddling him, her hand stroking him as she guided him closer to home. He thought this would be it, that she'd lower herself on his cock but no, not yet. She tilted her hips forward, rubbing her clit along the hard length of his cock, back and forth. He watched, afraid to move, afraid to so much as breathe, as she grabbed the beads and moved them so the strand was between her clit and his cock.

And holy fucking shit, he didn't think he'd ever felt anything quite like that. Rough, hard, soft, wet.

31

And he wasn't even inside her yet. Fuck, if he didn't get inside her, soon—now—he wasn't sure he'd make it.

But then, yes thank God, she lowered herself on him, the beads still wrapped around his cock, tightening around his balls. Mat sucked in his breath with a sharp hiss. Air filled his lungs, threatening to burst as he raised his head, his gaze locked on Nicole.

Her eyes met his, warm and glazed with desire. The corner of her mouth lifted, just briefly, before she caught her lower lip between her teeth. Her head dropped back and she braced her hands behind her, resting them on his thighs. The movement thrust her full breasts forward as she raised and lowered herself, riding him.

Slow, so slow.

Too fucking slow.

He grabbed her hips and thrust up, burying himself deep in her wet heat. She gasped, a low keening cry, and dug her nails into his thighs. Mat bent his knees and pressed his heels into the mattress, bracing himself, and thrust deeper.

Slow, fast. Deep. Steady. Over and over, burying himself. Losing himself.

Nicole's body tensed, her gasps turning into sharp moans. She held herself still, her nails scoring the flesh of his thighs, her legs tightening around his hips. Her internal muscles clenched, gripping, squeezing his cock for one long second before exploding around him in a million tiny tremors. She cried out again and collapsed against him, her teeth nipping at his neck and collarbone. Mat clenched his jaw, holding himself still for the briefest moment, straining. Too much. It was too much.

He groaned and thrust up. Once, twice. Then his

own climax ripped through him. Hard, intense, blinding. Long seconds went by, filled with nothing but sharp sensation and the feel of Nicole's body against his.

His breathing slowed as contentment filled him. Soothing, reassuring. He reached up and cupped one side of Nicole's face, turning her head and claiming her mouth with his. The kiss was slow and languid, over too soon when she pulled back and grinned down at him. Mat groaned when she shifted and rolled to her side, his body already missing hers.

He pushed himself from the bed and moved to the bathroom, untangling the beads and disposing of the condom before washing up. He almost tossed the beads in the trash then stopped. Before he could think too long about what he was doing, about how silly the whole thing was, he rinsed them off and tossed them into his shower kit. He didn't know why, didn't even want to think about why.

Nicole smiled when he returned, rolling to her side and patting the mattress beside her. Mat hesitated, not quite able to hide his own smile, then climbed into bed and stretched out next to her.

"Did you need to leave or anything?" And shit, what a stupid thing to ask. Why would he even say something like that?

"Not unless you want me to."

"No." Mat shook his head, hoping he didn't sound too eager now.

"Good." She smiled, a small tired one, then curled up next to him, draping her arm across his waist and resting her head on his chest.

Mat stiffened, surprised, then relaxed and wrapped his arm around her. He pressed his mouth

33

against her temple, his lips lingering on her skin. "Good."

But his whisper was lost in Nicole's soft breathing. He looked down, noticed her closed eyes and the dark shadow of her lashes against her skin, the relaxed line of her full lips. Something warm and unexpected flowed through him, something he didn't understand.

He brushed it away and closed his eyes, his arm tightening around Nicole and holding her close as he drifted off to sleep.

Chapter Two

Mat stirred, his mind fighting against the pull of wakefulness. No good, not with the sun pouring in through the room's window and heating the air. It shouldn't be this warm, not with the air conditioner on.

He groaned and rolled to his back, his eyes slowly opening. A hazy minute went by as he got his bearings.

Strange bed. Warm room. Combined scents of sex and light perfume.

A slow grin spread across his face and he pushed up on his elbows, looking to the side. Shit. The bed was empty, all except for a few strands of Mardi Gras beads draped across the pillow. His grin turned into a full smile at the memory of other beads, the ones he tossed into his shower kit last night.

Holy hell, he'd never look at beads the same way again.

He pushed himself to a sitting position, throwing the heap of covers off to the side. No wonder he was so hot. Nicole must have tossed all the covers on top of him.

Where was she? Mat cocked his head to the side, listening for the sound of running water. No, she wasn't in the bathroom. A quick look at the open door and the darkened room beyond told him that much. Maybe she was out in the main part of the suite. Yeah, now that he was a little more awake, he could just make out the smell of coffee.

Still grinning, he grabbed a pair of gym shorts from his open suitcase and stepped into them. Maybe he could convince Nicole to take a shower with him. Better yet, maybe he could talk her into using the oversized Jacuzzi tub.

Thoughts of soapy bubbles gliding over her silky skin firmly in mind, he opened the bedroom door and walked into the living area. "Did you sleep as well as I did?"

"Once all the noise from your room finally stopped, I did."

Mat froze, the hard-on in his shorts quickly dying at Kenny's dry words. He looked around, his subconscious registering the fact that Nicole wasn't anywhere in sight a full thirty seconds before his mind actually accepted it.

"What are you doing here?"

Kenny quirked one dark brow at him, the coffee mug paused halfway to his mouth. He shook his head and took a long swallow, then placed the mug on the low table in front of him. "We're sharing the suite, remember? Or did all the sex last night fry what's left of your brain?"

"But I put the Do Not Disturb sign out."

Kenny shrugged and turned back to the paper he'd been reading. "Must've fallen off."

Mat wanted to call bullshit but figured it wasn't

worth it. Figured Kenny would either deny it or just laugh. And it didn't matter anyway, not really. It wasn't like Kenny had walked in on them, or stopped to watch.

Mat finally forced his feet to move and made his way over to the small coffee pot. There was barely enough left for one cup. He tossed a dirty look over his shoulder then poured the remnants into the small mug and took a sip.

It was awful. Too strong, too dark, too bitter. But he drank it anyway, just for the caffeine hit. One more sip, then he leaned against the counter, going for what he hoped was a casual look. "So. Did you, uh, happen to see a woman around anywhere?"

Kenny lowered the paper, one brow quirked in amusement. "Your girl left about an hour ago."

Disappointment, sudden and unexpected, swirled in Mat's gut. He took another swallow of coffee, grimaced at the bitterness, and put the cup down. "Did she, uh, say anything?"

"Nope. I was just coming out of the room when she opened the door. I got a grin and a finger wave and that was it."

"A finger wave?"

"Yeah." Kenny held up one large hand and wiggled his big fingers like a little kid. "Like this."

"Oh." Mat lowered his head, trying to hide his frown. "And she didn't say anything?"

"I already told you no."

"Oh." There were other questions Mat wanted to ask but he didn't, not when he figured they would just make him sound desperate. And he didn't understand the disappointment lodged in his gut. Had he really expected her to stay? She probably had things to do.

Or maybe she wanted to take a shower back in her own room, so she could change clothes.

Yeah, that was probably it. He could understand that. Who wanted to take a shower only to put on the previous day's clothes? Some of the disappointment left at the rationalization. That had to be it. Even he wouldn't want to get dressed in dirty clothes.

But he still wished she would have let him know she was leaving. He could have walked her to her room.

If she was even staying in the same hotel. Maybe she wasn't. Maybe she was staying somewhere else. He hadn't thought to ask her last night.

Disappointment flooded him again, deepening his frown. What if he didn't get a chance to see her again? He hadn't even thought about getting her number, had no idea how to get in touch with her.

So what the hell was he supposed to do now?

"Hey, Casanova. Did you hear a word I just said?"

"What?" Mat looked up, surprised to find Kenny staring at him in amusement. He mentally shook himself and tried not to look completely lost. "Dude, sorry, no. I was thinking."

Kenny tossed the paper on the table with a muttered curse then stood. "Yeah, thinking. You're already planning the wedding."

"Why would I do that? Emily and JP already have everything—"

"Oh for shit's sake. Not their wedding. Yours."

"Mine? What the hell are you talking about?"

"You've got that look on your face, like you're already in love and counting the days to the wedding."

"Dude, fuck off. You have no idea what you're talking about." Mat shook his head and prayed that the heat he felt warming his face wasn't a blush. He liked Kenny better when he didn't talk quite so much—a trait that seemed to have disappeared in the last year since he'd been called up to the team. And Kenny was an idiot for even saying something like that. He had no idea what he was talking about and it was so far from the truth, Mat didn't even know how to respond.

So what if he was already wondering when he'd be able to see Nicole again? That didn't mean anything— even if last night was supposed to be just a one-night thing. He had fun. And he was pretty sure Nicole did, too. There was nothing wrong with wanting to have some more fun.

Kenny nudged Mat to the side and put his mug in the small sink. "You're killing me."

"What? Why?"

Kenny rolled his eyes, the expression almost as exaggerated as his heavy sigh. "Because you are."

"Like that makes sense. You know, this is why I'd rather room with Justin instead of you. You're all—" Mat waved his hands around, searching for the right word. He gave up and blew out a deep breath. "You're just a pain in the ass."

Kenny didn't say anything, just watched him with one raised eyebrow. That was another thing that annoyed Mat. Even though Kenny talked more than he used to when he first joined the team, he was still too quiet at times, always noticing too much. And always doing that one eyebrow thing. How the fuck did he do that? Mat couldn't figure it out, couldn't do it no matter how hard he tried. He just ended up looking like some psychotic owl on crack.

"Whatever you say." He glanced down at his watch then gave Mat a pointed look. "If you're planning on joining us, you better get ready. We need to meet everyone else in forty minutes."

"Meet for what?" The words had barely left his mouth before the answer came to him. Everyone was getting together for a walking tour of the Quarter, at Emily's insistence.

"At that café place for coffee and donuts."

"Beignets. They're called beignets."

"I don't care what fancy word you want to use, they're donuts."

"Dude, donuts have holes. These don't."

"You're really going to argue with me on this?"

"No. I'm just trying to help broaden your horizons."

Kenny rolled his eyes again then pointed to his watch. "You're not going to do anything if you don't get moving. I figured you'd want to get there early to see your girl again."

A broad smile split Mat's face. Of course. Why hadn't he thought of that? He felt like an idiot for not realizing it sooner, for having Kenny point out the obvious. That had to be why Nicole left early: to get ready for the tour. It made perfect sense now.

His grin grew even wider as he pushed past Kenny and hurried to his room, suddenly eager to get ready and leave. He ignored the off-key humming from Kenny, refused to even give him a dirty look when he recognized it as the Wedding March. What the hell did he know, anyway? Just because Mat had one night of fun didn't mean he was looking to get married.

Twenty minutes later, Mat was ready to sucker punch Kenny. If he didn't stop humming that stupid song, he was going to do exactly that. He turned and rammed his elbow into Kenny's side then jumped out of the way when the man's coffee sloshed over the rim of the white cup. Kenny just laughed, but Derek gave him a frown when some of the coffee splashed on Bridget. She narrowed her eyes at the two of them then pushed away from the cramped table, muttering something about little kids as she walked away, probably to get some napkins to clean up the mess.

Guilt swept over Mat and he went to stand, knowing Bridget shouldn't be the one to clean up the mess he made. Derek stopped him with a quick kick in the ankle, his frown even deeper.

"What is your problem, Herron?"

"He thinks he's in love."

"Dude, shut up. I told you before—"

"In love? Who with?"

"Nobody—"

"Some girl he picked up last night."

"Kenny, I said—"

"Last night?" Derek looked away from Kenny, his eyes narrowing on Mat. He shifted under Derek's look, the metal chair suddenly too hard, too uncomfortable, the air around him suddenly too hot and humid. Mat cleared his throat and reached for the plate of beignets. He popped one into his mouth, ignoring the generous dusting of powdered sugar that coated his fingers and drifted onto his shirt. If his mouth was full, he couldn't talk, couldn't answer the questions that filled Derek's eyes as his friend stared at him in disbelief.

"You have got to be kidding me."

Mat looked away, heat filling his face as he tried to chew the fried dough. And shit, now he needed something to drink, something to wash the dough and powdered sugar from his dry mouth.

Then he forgot all about drinking anything

because Derek burst out in laughter. Not a small chuckle, but a full-blown belly laugh that doubled him over. Mat narrowed his eyes, suddenly wishing he could talk, wishing he could tell Derek to shut the hell up. He chewed faster, resisting the urge to swallow the partially-eaten dough so he wouldn't choke. He'd love to choke Derek, though. That thought stayed with him even as Derek's laughter slowly faded.

"What's so funny?"

Mat shook his head, trying to tell Kenny that nothing was funny, wishing to hell they would just change the subject. He looked around, wishing Bridget would hurry back to the table. If Bridget was here, maybe Derek would stop acting like an ass.

But there was no sign of Bridget. And great, here came JP and Ian—without Emily and Kayli. Where the hell were all the women? Mat finally spotted them across the open-air room, walking into the kitchen. No doubt heading to the restrooms tucked back into the corner there.

"The girl from last night? Was she sporting a half-sleeve, all tatted up? That one?"

Mat shook his head at Kenny and tried to kick him under the table, but he couldn't reach him in time.

"I only got a glimpse when she left this morning but yeah, that sounds like her."

"Oh man." Derek laughed again then reached for his iced coffee and took a long swallow. "I told you she wasn't a good idea."

"Who's not a good idea?" JP and Ian reached the table, hovering on either side of Derek. He glanced up at them then looked back at Mat, his eyes dancing with amusement.

"The girl Mat picked up in last night and took back

to his room."

"You? No way." JP shook his head, a small smile playing at the corners of his mouth. Mat finally choked down the last of the beignet and reached for his own coffee, washing the last bit of powdered sugar from his mouth.

"I did not pick her up."

"Yeah, you did. And she is so not your type."

Mat opened his mouth to disagree but Kenny spoke over him. Again.

"I don't know. She was pretty. I admit I was surprised about the tattoos, though." Kenny nodded then glanced over at Mat. "Derek's right. Ink isn't really your style."

"That is so—"

"I'm not talking about the tattoos." Derek shook his head one more time, the smile finally dying as he stared at Mat. "I'm talking about her being married."

Stunned silence swept over the table, made louder because it was so out of place among the conversations and laughter and street noise that surrounded them. Mat blinked, the beignet and powdered sugar turning to concrete in his gut. He opened his mouth but only a strangled sound came out.

"No fucking way. She's married?" Kenny turned in his seat and stared at Mat, his dark eyes narrowed in disbelief. "Holy shit, Mat."

A thousand different words whirled through Mat's mind, all of them some form of denial. A chill filled him, chasing away the heat and humidity that had been threatening to suffocate him moments earlier. His stomach turned, a sickening twisting that threatened to reject what little was in it.

Fuck. Fuck. Fuck. Derek had to be wrong. This

had to be a mistake. Nicole hadn't been wearing a ring, he had looked.

His mind latched onto that, even though he knew it meant absolutely nothing. No. No way. She couldn't be married. Derek had to be wrong.

"Well, I guess that takes care of your reputation as a saint, eh?"

JP's words barely registered. Nothing registered. Not the noise around them, not the oddly mixed scents of sweet dough and strong coffee and New Orleans in the heat. Not the laughing words of Bridget and Emily and Kayli as they approached the small table.

She's married.

The words repeated in his mind, over and over with dizzying speed, threatening to turn his stomach inside out.

Nicole was married.

What the hell did I do?

"Holy shit."

"Mat, breathe—"

"What's wrong with him?"

The voices swirled around him, a word here and there reaching him but nothing making sense.

Fuck. What the hell had he done? This was a nightmare come to life. Regret, guilt, recrimination. Disbelief. How could this have happened? This couldn't be happening.

A part of him—a very small part—wondered if he was overreacting. It had been a mistake, one he hadn't realized he was making. Did that excuse him? Some small, rational part of him was saying yes, it did. He didn't know, had no way of knowing, wasn't responsible for what he didn't know.

No, that wasn't his conscience speaking, it was

Kenny. Leaning over him, his large hand banging him on the back between his shoulder blades, his deep voice lowered into a gravelly whisper.

"You didn't know, man. It's not your fault."

But it was. He should have asked, should have checked. Fuck. She hadn't been wearing a ring. Why the fuck would he have thought to ask?

"Oh my God, he's hyperventilating. Mat, bend over. You need to bend over." A cool hand, small and feminine, clasped the back of his neck and forced him to lean forward. Bridget? Yes, he could see the sun playing in the red of her hair from the corner of his eye. He tensed, wanting to argue with her, then gave in and bent over, wrapping his arms around his waist and trying to catch his breath.

"What did you guys do to him?" Emily's voice, filled with disbelief and accusation, came from his other side. Hands rubbed his back, gentle and cool through the wicking fabric of his polo shirt. Mat squeezed his eyes closed, watched the black spots slowly disappear from the inside of his lids.

"I did nothing, *ma chere*. It was Derek."

"Derek?" Bridget's hand stilled on his back. Mat sensed her stiffen, sensed her turn toward Derek. "What did you do?"

"Nothing, I swear!"

"You must have done something."

Mat groaned and tried to sit up, tried to turn his head and silently tell Derek not to say anything. It was bad enough he was already making an ass out of himself in front of the girls. He didn't want them to know what he'd done, didn't want their opinion of him to change if they found out.

But Derek wasn't paying him any attention, his

focus completely on Bridget. His expression changed, going from humor—no doubt at Mat's theatrics—to conciliation.

"Honest, Bridget, we didn't do anything. Mat just found out that the girl he was with last night—"

"No!"

"—is married." Derek snapped his mouth closed and looked over at Mat but it was too late. The words were already out. Mat groaned again and leaned forward, dropping his head into his hands.

The silence following Derek's admission only lasted for a few seconds. A few, very long seconds. Mat felt three pairs of eyes on him, felt their surprise and disbelief. He held his breath, waiting for their judgement, for their censure. Nobody moved. Or maybe it was just Mat's imagination, his own guilt that was making him sense things that weren't really there.

Bridget was the first to speak, confusion clear in both her voice and her gaze as she looked first at Mat then at Derek. Her brows lowered, her green eyes flashing. "Who are you talking about?"

Mat wanted to tell Derek to just shut up, tell him he had already done enough damage. But Derek didn't even look at him, just squirmed under Bridget's gaze and finally shrugged with a long sigh.

"Your friend. The one with the tattoos."

"Nicole? Nicole Taylor?"

"I guess, yeah."

Mat nodded, still not quite able to look at Bridget. At any of them.

"She's not married."

Mat's head shot up. "What?"

"But you said—"

"Dude, shut up." Mat sliced his hand through the

air, cutting Derek off. He looked up at Bridget, something close to relief filling him. "She's not? Are you sure?"

"Yeah. I mean, I guess maybe technically she still might be but—"

"What do you mean, 'technically'? She either is or she isn't."

"She's been separated for about two years. I don't know if her divorce went through yet or not."

Mat slumped down in his chair and took a deep breath. A clear breath. The weight that had been sitting on his chest was gone. Mostly. He looked back up at Bridget then kicked Kenny. "Dude, go get me an ice coffee, let Bridget sit down so we can talk."

Kenny blushed and immediately pushed away from the table, muttering something as he held the chair out for Bridget. But she shook her head and glanced over at Emily then down at her watch.

"Guys, we need to leave. The tour is getting ready to start and we still have to walk to the meeting point."

Chairs were pushed back from the table, the noise rough to Mat's ears as everyone stood up, suddenly talking. Everyone except him. He looked around, noticed everyone starting to move away from the table. How could they leave? Didn't they know he had questions? So many questions.

He pushed to his feet and hurried to catch up, shortening his strides when he reached Bridget. He reached out and placed a hand on her shoulder, silently asking her to wait as everyone moved ahead of them. She tilted her head and gave him a questioning look, then motioned for Derek to go ahead. He frowned at Mat, his irritation clear, then moved to catch up with everyone else.

Mat jammed his hands into the front pockets of his shorts as they walked, several feet behind everyone else. "So she's really not married?"

Bridget shook her head, reaching up to tuck a strand of wavy hair behind her ear. "Not anymore, no."

Mat blew out a deep breath, relief filling him again. "Good. That's good." They walked a few more feet, Mat stumbling over an uneven brick before catching himself. "So, um, is there anything else I should know about her?"

"Like what?"

"I don't know. You're her friend. I just thought maybe you could tell me more about her. Maybe give me a few pointers or something."

They were almost to the tour office now. Mat stopped in the middle of the sidewalk, his attention drifting to the group gathered at the corner, his eyes searching for Nicole. He didn't want anyone else to overhear their conversation—especially not Nicole. The entire morning was embarrassing enough, he didn't need to add to it. But he missed whatever Bridget had just said and he turned to her, offering her a small grin by way of apology.

"I'm sorry, what was that?"

"I said I can't. I don't really know her that well."

Mat frowned, wondering if he had missed more than he thought. "Don't know who that well?"

"Nicole."

"But—" Mat swallowed and cleared his throat, looked over his shoulder then back at Bridget. "I thought she was your friend."

Bridget shook her head. "Not really, no. I just know her from the hospital."

"Oh. I thought...well, I guess it doesn't matter. I

can just talk to her during the tour."

Bridget frowned, tilting her head to the side as she watched Mat. "She's coming on the tour?"

"Yeah. I mean, isn't she?"

"Why would she?"

"Isn't she here for the wedding party?"

"No. Why would you think that?"

"I don't know. I just thought...I mean, she's here with you so I figured—"

Bridget laughed, the sound soft and gentle. Any other time, her laughter would have lightened his mood. But not now. Instead, the sound filled him with anxiety, like something wasn't quite right and was about to get worse.

"Mat, she's not here with me. I just happened to run into her last night."

"Oh. I thought..." His words drifted off and he glanced over at the crowd, saw their waves as they motioned for him and Bridget to hurry up, to join them. He swallowed back his disappointment and forced a smile to his face. "Well, no worries. I'm sure I'll run into her tonight."

Bridget's hand folded around his arm, her touch gentle. He was sure she meant it to be reassuring but his gut twisted and knotted when he looked down at her, saw the worry in her soft eyes.

"Mat, from what she told me last night, her flight was leaving this morning. She's probably already on the way back home."

Chapter Three

"Nikki! What are you doing?"

The shriek echoed up the stairs and straight to the back of her neck, scraping every nerve along her spine and causing her to jerk back in the chair. Nicole grabbed the edge of the makeshift desk as the old chair tilted sideways, nearly dumping her to the floor. Her elbow hit the cup of water; it teetered, threatening to spill everywhere.

"Dammit." She grabbed the plastic cup just before it fell, holding it out to the side as she tried to regain her balance in the old chair. Her heart hammered in her chest and she took a deep breath, then another, trying to restore the frazzled edges of her nerves. Footsteps, hesitant but still loud, echoed outside the room, getting closer.

Nicole closed her eyes and took one last deep breath, this one to steady her before the confrontation she knew was coming. It was always a confrontation, no matter what she did. Why did that still surprise her? And why, after all this time, did it still have the power to disappoint her?

She reached for the computer mouse, trying to save the images on the screen and back out of the program. But it was too late; the steps were louder now, coming to a stop just inside the doorway to the small room. A hiss of disbelief, followed by a sigh that clearly expressed disappointment.

"Really, Nikki? You're still wasting your time with that nonsense?"

"Could you please stop calling me that? And it's not nonsense, Mom." She didn't bother turning around, already knowing what she'd see: her mother, leaning against the doorway, her thin lips pressed into a pale line of disapproval and censure. Nicole bit back the words that wanted to tumble from her mouth and focused on saving the latest files, on making sure they were properly backed up to three different locations. Paranoid? Overly cautious? To others, maybe. But it had only taken one time—one cruel act of spite—for her to learn her lesson the hard way.

She had learned a lot of lessons during that one very long year, lessons she wouldn't soon forget, no matter how much she wanted to.

Nicole closed her eyes, squeezing them tightly as she pushed the unwanted images from her mind. She had been young and stupid, making a long series of mistakes in a short span of time. But that had been over two years ago. Surely enough time had gone by. Hadn't it? Or would she be paying for those mistakes for the rest of her life?

She shook her head, almost afraid of the answer, then pulled the memory stick from the computer and tossed it into the open backpack resting on the floor. She unplugged the external hard drive and carefully placed it inside the metal security box, making sure to lock it before pocketing the key. Her mother blew out a breath of impatience, the sound a sharp hiss in the stifling air of the small room.

"I don't know why you bother locking everything up. You act like all of that nonsense is so important."

"It is important, Mom. To me." Nicole grabbed her camera and tucked it into the backpack then zipped the bag closed. She held onto the arm of the chair and carefully stood, holding the battered thing steady so it wouldn't tip, then grabbed the bag and tossed it over her shoulder.

Her mom was still leaning against the doorframe, her thin arms crossed tightly in front of her, a frown on her worn face. Nicole caught a whiff of stale cigarette smoke, just above the mixed scents of alcohol and perfume. But she didn't say anything. Why, when it didn't matter? It was her mother's disappointment that came first, always. Nicole could feel it even now, sharp and biting, radiating from the woman in front of her. She shouldn't be surprised, she knew that, but it still stung.

Would it ever get better?

Nicole adjusted the strap and tugged the bag higher on her shoulder, her chin held high as she watched her mother. Tired, worn out. A faded shadow of vibrant beauty battered by years of hard living and careless loving.

Was Nicole looking at a reflection of herself ten years from now? Fifteen? Five?

Please God, no.

Guilt immediately swept through her. Deep down, she loved her mother. She really did. She just didn't want to be her. Was that so wrong? So terrible? To actually want something from life instead of just coasting along? Not even coasting—more like being tossed from minute to minute, day to day, year to year.

No, Nicole didn't want that. But she had come so close to doing that same exact thing, to making the same exact mistakes, in an attempt to avoid becoming what she feared most. She'd learned her lesson. At least, she hoped she had.

Nicole stepped forward, the small room suddenly stifling, unbearable, but her mother didn't move. She swallowed, ignoring the beads of sweat forming along her hairline, and tried to smile. "Mom, I need to get going. I'm going to be late."

Her mother's lips pressed together more tightly, her thin shoulders hunching around her ears. Nicole stiffened, trying to hide her sudden irritation and wondering if she'd be allowed to leave in peace—or if she was in for another lecture.

A minute dragged by, long and silent. Her mother released a long sigh. She raised one shaking hand and dragged it through the tangle of graying brown hair, causing the short strands to stick up even more.

"I don't know why you even bother going. You're just wasting your time. It's not like they pay you."

Nicole bit the inside of her cheek, telling herself not to respond, not to rise to the verbal bait. They'd had this conversation before. Too many times.

No, she didn't get paid for her work at the hospital. But it was still important to her. Important to the kids. It gave her photography a sense of purpose— it gave *her* a sense of purpose. But her mother didn't understand that. She didn't think she'd ever understand.

Nicole pulled the strap higher on her shoulder, her

hand tightening around it, and tried to hide her irritation before stepping around her mother. "Mom, I need to go."

But her mom didn't move. She just stayed there, leaning against the doorframe, her mouth pulled tight in that disapproving line. She finally sighed, the sound too loud and harsh, and shook her head.

"Will you be home for dinner?"

Nicole knew her mom was really asking if she was going to bring dinner home. She swallowed her impatience, tried to keep her voice neutral when she spoke. "No, Mom. I have to work tonight. I won't be home until late."

Her mother's shoulders slumped and Nicole was immediately filled with guilt. She shouldn't be, knew her mother well enough to know it was a calculated act. Everything was with her. But the guilt still came, unwelcome and bitter. Nicole pressed her lips together, knowing she shouldn't do it, she shouldn't give in.

She couldn't afford to give in, in more ways than one.

But even as she told herself that, she reached into the outer pocket of the backpack and pulled out her tattered wallet. She didn't have to look to see how much she had: sixteen dollars. She thumbed through the bills, hesitating, then finally pulled out the biggest bill she had, a ten, and held it out.

"Here, you can have this."

Her mother reached out to grab it, her hand closing over the bill and snatching it away, like she was afraid Nicole would change her mind. She didn't miss the scowl on her mother's face, though, the look of disappointment and accusation as she tucked the bill into the pocket of the robe.

"I need the rest, Mom." And she did. But that didn't stop her from feeling guilty for not giving it all to her mother

"I didn't say anything."

You didn't have to.

But Nicole didn't say that out loud. She couldn't. And it wouldn't have made a difference even if she had because her mother wasn't listening anymore. She had what she wanted and now she was moving down the stairs, her steps slow and hesitant, her hand gripping the railing. Nicole watched her, wondering if the money would be used for food—or something else.

She swallowed back more guilt and disappointment and followed her mother down the stairs, watching as she turned and moved through the door leading to the kitchen. Nicole almost followed, almost gave in to her mother's silent accusation to give her the rest of the money, but she didn't. Past history told her the futility of that. So she kept moving, straight out the door, pulling it shut behind her and checking to make sure it was locked before descending the cracked steps leading to the sidewalk.

She checked her watch then hurried her steps, walking the two blocks to the bus stop, afraid she'd miss it. It was too far to walk all the way to the hospital, and she didn't have enough for a taxi.

She just made it, finding an empty seat as the bus pulled away from the curb. Stale air filled the inside, not even coming close to passing for air conditioning. Nicole adjusted the grip on her pack and leaned against the window, not really seeing the dirty streets and block after block of broken down rowhomes they passed.

Yes, every penny mattered. It had to, if she wanted to get out on her own, make something of herself. She wanted to do more than just survive, and she didn't want to rely on anyone else for that. Her mother had done that—was still doing that—and it hadn't turned out well.

Nicole herself had thought she could do the same thing, and look where that had gotten her. More than a year in hell, and over two more trying to claw her way out. But she was getting there. Slowly, so slowly. She had money saved up now, all cash, in a secret cubby her mother didn't even know about. She couldn't use a bank, not yet, not without risking losing everything. But she was getting there. She'd even had enough for that quick trip to New Orleans. A trip to celebrate her recent freedom.

Her hand patted one of the side pockets of the backpack, her fingers tracing the ridges of the plastic beads tucked inside. She felt herself smile before she realized what she was doing and tried to stop it. A month had gone by, she shouldn't still be smiling.

But she couldn't help it. She'd only been there for two nights, barely long enough to get a quick taste of the city. It was so alive. The architecture, the people, the food...no, she hadn't splurged for any of the finer meals but she'd still been able to get a taste. It was amazing the deals you could find when you were looking. And she'd been able to capture so much with her camera so she had more than just memories.

But it was her last night that stayed with her. Her night with Mat. She shouldn't have gone back to his room, she knew that. But she'd taken one look at him, one look at those unusual deep green eyes, and all common sense had flown from her mind. She knew better, but she did it anyway.

And she didn't regret one second of it.

No, that wasn't quite right. She did have one regret: she hadn't been able to get a picture of him. She'd thought about it, thought about snapping a quick one before she left the next morning, but she couldn't quite bring herself to do that, no matter how much she knew the camera would love him. It seemed too…perverted. Cheap. It didn't matter that it had only been one night, it wasn't a cheap encounter.

Not to her.

She'd seen Bridget at the hospital once since then and had thought about asking her about Mat. But she changed her mind at the last minute. She didn't know Bridget that well, more like a passing acquaintance. And she didn't know if Bridget knew she had gone back to the hotel with Mat. She thought the woman probably did but still, just in case…. No, it was better if Nicole kept the memory to herself, to savor and revisit when she needed.

The bus pulled to a stop, jerking her to the here-and-now. She grabbed her bag and stood, her hands running along the back of each seat as she jostled up the aisle with the handful of other people getting off at this stop. There was still another block left to go but it would be an easy walk, one she would enjoy while savoring the memory of deep green eyes and softly whispered words.

Chapter Four

Mat glanced down at his phone, debating if he should reply to the text or just delete it. He could always say he never got it. He didn't think that excuse would go over well, not since Derek and Kenny both were texting him.

He put the phone on silent and tossed it into the cup holder then shifted in the seat. If he was smart, he'd leave and head over to The Maypole. Grab a bite to eat, maybe a quick drink, then go home. It wasn't like he had anything else to do, not until the golf game tomorrow morning with Ian, JP and Derek.

He was half-tempted to cancel. If Bridget told Derek that he asked about Nicole, asked when she'd be at the hospital, he'd never live it down. Derek would read him the riot act and tell him he was acting like an obsessed fool. And if JP found out, he'd never hear the end of it—especially after he accused JP of being a stalker last year.

What was he doing now, if not stalking?

The reality hit him, making him feel like a fool. He

was sitting in his car outside the hospital, hoping to catch a glimpse of a woman he didn't even know. And he had accused JP of being a stalker?

Mat glanced at his watch then leaned forward and hit the ignition switch. The engine rumbled to life before smoothing out under him. He was leaving, just going straight home. He wasn't in the mood to socialize, didn't want to hang out with his teammates and their wives and girlfriends.

Didn't want to feel the like fifth wheel again.

He put the car in reverse and packed away from the curb, his mind only partially focused on the traffic. It was still rush-hour, still hot and humid with the sun beating down on asphalt and concrete and brick. Mat leaned forward and cranked the AC to high, thankful that he wasn't walking outside in the heat like so many others. The foot traffic was almost as heavy as the vehicle traffic. Not surprising, since this area wasn't exactly a prime location in downtown Baltimore. At least, not from what he could see, not if the vacant, boarded-up rowhomes meant anything.

The car in front of him squealed tires, shooting out into the intersection before making a hasty right. Mat slammed on his own brakes in reaction and muttered under his breath. It was supposed to be a no-turn-on-red light but the idiot in front of him apparently didn't care and had damn near caused an accident.

And wouldn't that just top off his night? It would be no less than what he deserved for stalking. He shook his head and muttered to himself again, his attention still focused on the car that had been in such a hurry to make the turn.

It was stopped off to the side now, not quite at the

curb, gray exhaust pouring from the rusted tailpipe as traffic tried to get around him. Mat watched, wondering what the driver was doing, why he was stopped like that and making traffic either stop or go around him. More horns blared, the sound harsh even through the closed windows. Mat could see the silhouette of the driver leaning across the seat, knew without really hearing that he was shouting something to the group of people walking along the sidewalk. The car pulled ahead another few feet, almost getting hit by a truck that was trying to pass.

Why didn't the idiot just keep going instead of blocking traffic? Or move up ahead where there were no cars parked along the curb?

A horn blared behind him and Mat looked up, saw that the light was now green. He absently waved and pulled out, trying to make the right turn. But the other car was still sitting there, still blocking traffic. Mat inched a little closer, his gaze darting to the side mirror to look for a break in traffic so he could go around. He started to move then hit the brakes as another car zoomed around him.

"Damn. Really dude?" He blew out a deep breath and clenched his jaw. Yeah, this was no more than what he deserved. If he had gone out with Kenny and Derek, he wouldn't be stuck in this mess.

If he had just stayed home, he wouldn't be stuck in this mess.

But no, he had to go acting like some crazed lovesick fool and try tracking down a woman he didn't even know. Idiot. Nicole obviously didn't want to stay in contact—she would have left a phone number or a note or something. It had been a month already since that night in New Orleans. Kenny was right, he just needed to let it go.

And yeah, he really did need to let it go because he could swear that woman standing near the curb looked exactly like Nicole. Mat squeezed his eyes shut then opened them, glancing at the traffic to his left then back at the woman by the curb. It wasn't her, he knew that. But he wanted to look again, just in case.

Just as he thought, it wasn't Nicole.

Except it was.

He slammed on the brakes and leaned forward, squinting to make sure he wasn't seeing things.

No, it was definitely Nicole. She looked different, dressed in skin-hugging ripped denim capris and some kind of flowing shirt. Her hair was pulled back in a loose ponytail and a frayed backpack was slung over her left shoulder. He couldn't see her eyes because they were hidden behind large sunglasses. But he could see her frown. Not just a frown—she looked angry. And maybe even a little frightened as she shook her head and stepped away from the curb.

Mat still had his windows up and couldn't hear, but he was pretty sure the idiot in the car in front of him—the one that was blocking traffic—was shouting something to her. She shook her head and moved away, walking up the sidewalk. The car followed her, moving slow enough to keep up, slow enough to still make a mess of the traffic.

Mat clenched his jaw and moved forward, no longer caring about the other cars. His focus was completely on Nicole and the car following her. Was somebody giving her a hard time? Yeah, from the look on her face—a frown changing to worry—somebody was. Who the hell was it?

Did it matter?

No, it didn't.

Mat glanced to his left then gunned the engine, pulling out into traffic. Horns blared and tires squealed as cars hit their brakes but he didn't care. He pulled forward, darting in front of the car that was following Nicole, and hit the brakes one more time. He opened the door and put one foot on the ground, partially stepping out of the car.

"Nicole!"

She paused, confusion marring what he could see of her face as she looked toward him. She shook her head then kept walking, her steps faster now. The car behind him, the one following her, moved forward again. Mat scowled, wondering if the idiot was going to keep going or if he was going to stop before hitting Mat's car.

The car lurched and the driver leaned on the horn. Mat couldn't really see who was driving, not with the late sun reflecting off the dirty windshield. But he didn't care. He turned back to Nicole and pulled off his sunglasses, hoping she might more easily recognize him if he did.

"Nicole!"

She stopped again, her right hand coming up and grabbing the strap of her bag, like she was trying to secure it before taking off running. And damn, he didn't mean to scare her.

Scare her more, that is. Because she *was* scared. He saw it on her face, in the slight tightening of her features when she glanced over her shoulder at the car behind her then back at him.

He didn't know if their eyes actually met or not. It felt like it, but that could just be his imagination. But he knew when she recognized him, saw her body relax just the smallest bit as something like relief crossed her face.

"It's Mat." And what did it say about him that he felt the need to tell her his name? Yeah, he remembered her, remembered that night…but he couldn't be sure she did.

A horn blared again, the sound ending on a dying squeal. He glanced back at the car behind him then looked over at Nicole. "Did you need a ride or something?"

She didn't even hesitate, just stepped off the curb and made a beeline for his car. Mat hit the button for the power lock at the last minute, just before she pulled on the handle. The car behind them blared the horn one last time then shot out into the traffic, damn near causing another accident. Mat jumped back, wondering if he had come as close to being hit as he thought, or if it was just his imagination.

He climbed back into the car and shut the door, hurriedly buckling his seatbelt as he eased his way into the now-moving traffic. His heart beat a little harder, a little faster, and he wasn't sure why. Because of the car that had been following Nicole? Because he was worried about her? Or because she was finally here, sitting next to him?

He didn't let himself think about the other option—that she had gotten in his car only to get away from whoever was following her. Mat didn't think he possessed an excessive ego, not even on the ice, but the idea that he was the lesser of two evils didn't sit well with him. So no, he would try not to think of it that way.

He glanced over, noticed that Nicole was sitting up straight, maybe a little stiff. She faced forward, her arms wrapped tightly around the backpack, like she was afraid of losing it or something. He cleared his throat, afraid of startling her, then motioned to her lap when she looked over.

"You, uh, forgot your seatbelt."

"Oh. Sure, no problem."

And Christ, he was a fucking idiot. He'd been thinking about the woman next to him for a month and the first words out of his mouth were about her seatbelt? Yeah, maybe the guys were right for calling him Saint Mat.

He cleared his throat and tightened his hands around the steering wheel. "So. Was that guy giving you a hard time or something?"

Nicole didn't answer right away, just gave him a quick glance before turning her attention straight ahead again. Mat knew she heard him, though, because she stiffened just the slightest bit. A full minute went by before she shook her head.

"No. I mean, not really. Um, no, it's all good."

She was lying. Or maybe she just didn't want to tell him. Maybe she thought it really wasn't his business. If that was the case, she was right—it really wasn't. But that didn't mean he didn't want to know, didn't mean that he couldn't help her if she needed it.

"Was he your ex?"

Nicole whipped her head around so fast that Mat was surprised she didn't hurt her neck. He still couldn't see her eyes, not behind those large sunglasses, but he could tell she was definitely surprised. Her mouth dropped open, forming a small O, and he heard the swift intake of her breath in the silence that followed his question.

The silence that filled the car with a heavy weight,

bearing down on him. He probably shouldn't have said anything.

"You, uh, know about him?" Her voice was just above a squeak, hesitant and surprised. Mat looked away, forcing himself to study the traffic in front of him instead of the woman next to him. Maybe if he didn't look at her, she'd be more comfortable. Yeah, he definitely shouldn't have said anything.

"Bridget mentioned something about him. Um, that next morning. In New Orleans." Smooth. Real smooth. He hadn't meant to bring that night up, didn't want her to get the wrong idea. Like maybe he was looking for another night. Not that the thought hadn't crossed his mind once or twice or a hundred times. But that's not why he tried looking for her. And great, now she was shifting in the seat, like she was suddenly uncomfortable. And was her face turning just a little pink? He couldn't tell—

"The light's green."

Mat jerked his attention back to the traffic and muttered to himself before hitting the gas. Maybe a little too hard, because the car shot forward a little too fast. He eased off the gas and readjusted his grip on the steering wheel.

"Yeah, that was my ex. I'm not sure how he—" Nicole's mouth snapped shut and she shook her head, obviously thinking better of saying whatever she had been going to say. She shifted again, tossed a quick glance his way, then looked out the window. "I guess I should have told you. That night, I mean. I didn't think it made a difference, though—"

"No. No, it didn't. Doesn't." Mat shook his head and cleared his throat. No, it didn't make a difference, not anymore. Not when he knew the mystery guy was really her ex and not actually still married to her.

Some of the tension seemed to leave her. Or maybe that was just wishful thinking on his part. But she shifted in the seat once more, turning the smallest bit so she was partially facing him now instead of staring straight out the window. He glanced over and gave her a smile, then looked back at the traffic crawling forward in front of them.

"Thank you, by the way. For the ride."

"Yeah, no problem."

"I guess that was pretty lucky for me. You showing up like that, I mean."

Mat nodded but didn't say anything. Better for her to think it was just luck. He sure as hell didn't want her to find out he'd been stalking her, trying to get a chance to see her again.

"So what are you doing in this neighborhood, anyway?"

"Oh. I, uh—I mean…" Great, now what? He didn't want to lie to her, but how could he tell her the truth? He frowned, trying to come up with a good answer, but she kept talking.

"Did you have a doctor's appointment or something?"

"Um—"

"That was too personal, I'm sorry. It doesn't matter. It was just lucky that you were there."

Mat released the breath he'd been holding, grateful that he hadn't been forced to answer, grateful that Nicole had kept on talking. Although he didn't quite remember Nicole being such a fast talker before. Of course, they hadn't been doing much talking in New Orleans. Not really.

"You can let me out the next block up, if you don't

mind."

Mat heard the words but didn't understand them, not at first. He must have missed something because what she said didn't make any sense. He eased to a stop at the traffic light then looked over at her.

"Let you out?"

"Yes please. The next block up."

"Why would I do that?"

"That's the next bus stop."

"And?"

"That's where I can catch the next bus."

"But—" Mat snapped his mouth closed, not wanting to sound too eager. Too disappointed. He cleared his throat and relaxed in the seat, trying to look casual and nonchalant. "I can take you wherever you need to go."

"No, you've done enough, thank you. You can just let me out the next block up."

"Where do you need to get the bus to?"

Nicole shifted again, turning away from him as she looked out the window. He sensed the slight discomfort and wondered if maybe he had pushed too hard, maybe gotten a little too personal.

"Just to work."

"I can take you."

"I don't want to impose—"

"No, really, it's not a problem. I don't have anything planned. And, well, I thought—" Mat cleared his throat and hoped the heat he felt at the back of his neck wasn't a blush. "I thought maybe we could use the time to talk, get to know each other."

He glanced over at her then muttered when the car behind him blew on the horn. Mat eased his foot off the brake and moved forward, driving as slow as he dared. The bus stop was coming up but he didn't want to reach it, didn't want Nicole to leave just yet. If she did, he had no idea when he might see her again. If he could convince her to let him drive her to work, maybe he could get her number. Maybe he could even get the chance to ask her out.

But she still didn't answer. In fact, she looked uncomfortable, more than she had when he first picked her up. And she wouldn't look at him. That bothered him for some reason.

And maybe he should just drop her off and let it go. He was probably worrying her, probably coming on too strong. Yeah, knowing his luck, she probably thought he was being too pushy, too aggressive.

He blew out a quick breath and pulled his shoulders up to his ears, trying to ease the knots, the tension, that suddenly gripped his neck. "I'm sorry. I didn't mean to push. I'll drop—"

"No." Nicole said the word so fast, louder than he expected, that he almost jumped in surprise. She looked over at him, just a quick glance, her teeth nibbling on her lower lip. Mat tried not to focus on her mouth, tried not to remember what her mouth felt like on him.

All of him.

She turned away and Mat bit back a sigh, wondering if maybe he had been too obvious, if he had stared too hard. Wondering if she could read his mind and knew exactly what he was thinking.

The bus stop was coming up, two car-lengths away, but traffic was still moving slow. He figured he only had a few more minutes left, if that. He glanced over at her but she was still facing front, still chewing on her lower lip.

"Did you, uh, want me to drop you off here? Or take you to work? It's not a problem, really."

Silence. The bus stop was closer now, just in front of them. Mat tried to hide his disappointment as he maneuvered the car closer to the curb, out of the way of the traffic behind him.

Just a few more feet and Nicole would be getting out of the car, disappearing. He should ask for her number, should say something—

"Work." The word came out in a rush, like she was afraid it wouldn't come out at all if she said it any other way. Like she was afraid to accept his offer—which didn't make sense to Mat. It was just a ride to work, not a big deal.

Except it was, because it meant he could spend more time with her.

"You can take me to work." Nicole repeated the words, still looking uncomfortable. "If it's not a problem, I mean."

"No. No problem. I, uh, I'd like that." And why did he have to sound like such a moron around her? It was like every last conversational skill he possessed completely disappeared in her presence.

Mat smiled, trying to reassure her, then eased away from the curb and back into the slow-moving traffic. He stopped at the light then looked back at Nicole, wishing she would at least look over at him. Maybe smile. Or at the least, not look quite so uncomfortable.

"So where do you work?"

There it was again, the slight shifting and the nibbling on her lower lip, like she was already regretting her decision. Mat tightened his grip on the steering wheel, wishing he could say something to put her at ease.

"Um, Pulaski Highway."

Mat frowned. That wasn't exactly an answer, not really. And it was further away than he thought, especially if she had planned on taking a bus. But he didn't say anything, just moved into the left lane so he could change directions to get on the highway.

"Where on Pulaski Highway?" His mind was mentally travelling the long highway, trying to imagine where she might be working. It ran from the city to the county, a long stretch of questionable neighborhoods, industry, trucking companies, and clubs. He wasn't completely familiar with the area, though, so he was having a difficult time trying to figure out where she might be working.

"Um, I'll let you know when we get closer."

Was it his imagination, or was she still uncomfortable? More uncomfortable than before? Which made no sense so maybe it was just his imagination. He leaned back in the seat, hoping he looked relaxed and confident, something he wasn't exactly feeling at the moment. Which was ridiculous. He wasn't normally like this, so hesitant and uncertain. What was it about this woman in particular that made him feel so inadequate? Maybe it wasn't her, maybe it was the comments from all the guys that morning in New Orleans, from the jokes and ribs he'd had to endure the rest of that trip.

The jokes and ribbing he was still enduring.

It didn't matter. At least, it shouldn't matter. And he should really try to find something to talk about, because he didn't want this entire ride to be done in silence. Especially if he wanted to find some way to see her again.

"So how was your flight?"

"My flight?"

"Yeah. Last month. Um, from New Orleans?" And now he just felt like an idiot again for even bringing it up. He hadn't meant it as a reminder of their night together but he got the feeling she was taking it that way because he could see a small flush paint her cheeks a pale pink. Or maybe that was just a reflection of the sinking sun.

"It was fine. I guess. I've never really flown much before so I don't know if all the jumping and bouncing was normal or not."

"Turbulence. Yeah, I'm not a big fan of that myself."

"I guess you fly a lot, huh?"

"Yeah. During the season, especially."

Nicole nodded. Silence settled over the interior once more, still heavy but not as oppressive. Maybe she was feeling a little more comfortable. Or maybe Mat was just being a little too optimistic.

She looked over. Was it his imagination, or was that a hint of smile teasing her mouth? "Did you enjoy the rest of your trip?"

Mat wanted to tell her the truth: no. Because he had been worrying about her, thinking about her, dreaming about her. But he couldn't tell her that, not without sounding like a complete fool, so he nodded and gave her a small smile. "Yeah, it wasn't bad. I was glad to get home though. I can only take so much of New Orleans. It's a great city, don't get me wrong, but sometimes the crowds get to me."

Nicole nodded but he got the impression she didn't exactly agree with him. Great. Nothing like putting more distance between them by pointing out their differences. He cleared his throat and glanced over at her. "How about you? Did you enjoy your stay?"

A bright smile lit her face as she looked over at him. Really looked, not just a quick uncomfortable glance. "I had so much fun. It was my first time there and oh my God. The people, the smells, the tastes. It was so much better than I imagined. I'd love to go back again when I can stay longer, spend more time there and really get to know it."

"That's right, you didn't stay long, did you?"

"No, just two nights. That was all I could aff—I mean, all I could swing. With work, I mean."

He caught the word, mentally finished it even though she didn't. She was going to say 'afford'. Mat suddenly wondered if maybe she was embarrassed by that and he wanted to tell her not to be. But he didn't want to make her uncomfortable again so he just nodded.

"You'll have to let me know when you go back. Maybe I can tell you some different places to go or see."

"Yeah. Maybe."

But she didn't look convinced, like she already knew she wouldn't be going back. And Mat suddenly wanted nothing more than to prove her wrong. To turn the car around and go straight to the airport and take her away, right back to New Orleans so she should could explore it for as long as she wanted. Anything to see her face light up the way it had just a moment ago.

Except some people would probably call that kidnapping.

"Well, I'm glad you had fun." He cleared his throat and offered her a grin, wondering if he sounded as idiotic as he felt. She glanced over at him and smiled but just a small one, not nearly as bright as before.

"I did. And I got some great pictures so it was definitely worth it."

"You like that? Taking pictures, I mean."

Her smile came back, bright and enthusiastic. "Oh yeah, definitely. That's what I do at the hospital: take portraits of the kids and finesse them, show them how cute they are. It gives them hope, you know? To see that they're not just hospital gowns and IVs and machines. I've always loved photography. That's what I really want to do. Not just portraits but everything. I love it."

Mat found himself smiling back, wrapped up in her enthusiasm and excitement. "Maybe you could show me some of your stuff. I mean, if you want."

"Yeah. Maybe." But her smile faded, more forced now than genuine, and Mat didn't understand what he'd said to make it dim. He opened his mouth, thinking maybe he should apologize, but she shook her head and pointed ahead of them. "You can just drop me off up there."

'Up there' was in front of a row of fenced-in storage units, the kind where people could rent them by the month. It looked run down, dilapidated, with an air of desperation surrounding it. He could imagine, for just a second, what it must feel like to be forced to keep all your possessions in one tiny unit, locked away and then abandoned. No, he took that back. He couldn't imagine, didn't want to imagine.

"Is that where you work?"

Nicole shifted in her seat, not looking at him. "Um, no. But I can walk the rest of the way."

"Don't be ridiculous. I can drive you. Just tell me where to go."

"Really, it's not that far—"

"Nicole. I am not dropping you off on the side of Pulaski Highway and making you walk to wherever. It's not safe. Just tell me where to take you."

She didn't answer right away. And when he passed the storage area, she glanced over at him with a look of surprise. And something else. Desperation? Panic? And shit, he didn't want her to panic, even though he couldn't understand what caused it. Unless she thought he was just going to keep going, not drop her off anywhere. Shit. He should have thought of that, should have realized that maybe he was giving her the wrong impression. She was a woman alone in a car with someone who was essentially a stranger. Never mind that they'd met already, that they'd slept together. They were still really nothing more than strangers.

And he'd just driven past where she asked to be dropped off. He could only imagine what thoughts were going through her mind.

Mat cleared his throat again and started pulling the car over to the side of the road. He could turn the car around, take her back to where she asked to be dropped off. "I'm sorry. I shouldn't have—"

"No." She glanced over at him, then looked back out the window, her jaw tense. "No, it's okay. Um, you can drop me off up ahead. That's where I work."

Mat squinted, looking up the highway to see where she meant. There really wasn't anything he could see, at least not any place he could imagine she'd be working. Nothing except a strip club, the neon lights bright and garish in the shadows of the evening sun.

He slowed the car, glancing first at the single story concrete building then at Nicole. He cleared his throat, not sure what to say, and pulled the car into the gravel parking lot.

No, not gravel. The lot was asphalt, but so torn up and rutted that he'd thought it was gravel at first. The car lurched and bounced over a deep pothole and he clenched his jaw at the sound of the undercarriage scraping against asphalt. He pulled into one of the empty spots and sat there, staring at the building in front of him, not quite sure what to say.

He wasn't a prude. Despite that damned nickname Derek had started, he wasn't a prude. And he certainly wasn't an innocent. Hell, he'd been to strip clubs before. Not many, and only because one teammate or the other had dragged him along. He didn't have anything against them, they just weren't really his style.

And the one he was looking at now was on a different scale than the others he'd been to. He didn't want to go so far as saying it was rundown but—yeah, not far from it. But maybe that was just what he could see from the outside, because the lot was half-full and it was still early. So yeah, maybe it wasn't as bad as he thought.

Yeah, sure it wasn't.

He tightened his grip around the steering wheel and tried to relax his jaw, tried to look calm when he was anything but. The thought of Nicole working here, of her prancing around on the stage in next-to-nothing while other men ogled her, touched her, shoved money at her… No, he was anything but calm on the inside. On the inside, he was seething. And that surprised him, because what he was feeling was jealousy.

And how fucking crazy was that? What right did he have to be jealous? The woman seated next to him, looking as uncomfortable as he felt, was essentially a stranger. Yes, they'd had sex. One night. That was pretty much the definition of a one-night stand. He knew before taking her to his room, back in New Orleans, that it was only supposed to be for one night. He'd taken her back to his room for that sole intention. Nothing more. That had been *his* decision. The woman next to him owed him nothing, least of all an explanation for why she was working here. It wasn't his place to judge.

So why the hell was he feeling this irrational jealousy?

He cleared his throat and glanced back at Nicole. "So. This is where you work?"

She turned to face him. And even though he couldn't see her eyes, he could feel her gaze, knew that she was watching him, studying him. Waiting for him to pass judgment? Waiting for him to say something? Mat wasn't sure, but he felt like he was being tested.

A few long minutes went by, weighted with silence. Nicole finally nodded and looked away, her shoulders sagging just a bit.

"Yeah. This is where I work."

Chapter Five

Nicole couldn't believe she'd told him where she worked. No, not told him. Showed him.

She should have never told him. She should have insisted he drop off her up the street instead. No, take that back. She should have never gotten in the car with him. But she had been so rattled, so upset and pissed and angry when Donnie pulled up to the curb, that she hadn't been thinking clearly. All she wanted was to get away, to escape. And when Mat had pulled up, had called her name, she had homed in on him and grasped at the chance to escape, not stopping to think about anything else.

She certainly hadn't expected him to offer to drive her to work.

When they had pulled up to the club, when she had told him this was where she worked, Nicole had expected him to…well, she wasn't sure what she had expected, not really. Maybe make a comment about her virtue, or a snide offer, or something similar. Or to get that look on his face, the one she'd seen on so many others. Like she was cheap or worthless or beneath him. But Mat had done none of that. No, she hadn't missed the way his hands clenched the steering wheel, just for a split-second. And she still wasn't sure what to make of that, what he'd been trying to do.

And he had beautiful hands. Large, muscular and well-defined, with long fingers and neatly trimmed nails. She would love to photograph those hands, in black and white, to capture their strength, their masculinity...their tenderness. Because yeah, despite the strength in his hands—in him—he was tender. Surprisingly tender. And when she remembered how those hands felt against her skin, what he could do with those hands—

"Shit." Nicole jumped back, just missing being soaked with the soda overflowing the glass she was filling. She shook her head and grabbed a rag from the sink, quickly mopping up the spill. She could feel eyes on her, and not just any eyes. *His* eyes. Dark green, deep, seeing too much.

And oh God, why had she agreed to let him pick her up? She should have said no, should have never given in. But Mat had looked genuinely concerned when he asked her how she was going to get home. Genuinely horrified when she told him she sometimes walked if she couldn't get a ride with one of the other girls.

And then he had had offered to pick her up. Not offered—insisted. Like he really cared. Which was ridiculous. He couldn't care. He didn't know her. And even if he did, guys like him didn't care for girls like her. They'd had one night together, a night that she held close to her, thinking she could pull the memory out and savor it whenever she needed. It was only meant to be one night, no matter what kind of silly fantasy she might spin of it.

But here he was.

Nicole rinsed the rag then twisted it, watching the dirty water run out in a small stream before slowing to a drip. She kept twisting it, squeezing even tighter, like she could ring out all her frustrations and worries and doubts at the same time.

Mat had shown up, just like he said he would. She shouldn't be surprised but she was. Part of her wished he was like every other man in her life, full of empty promises and empty words, saying one thing with no intention of ever following through. But he was here, and just his presence was enough to fluster her.

He'd shown up not quite an hour ago and walked straight to the bar, taking a seat away from everyone else. And he had grinned at her, a charming boyish grin that made her stomach twist and twirl like it did before the first big drop of a roller coaster. It was the same grin he'd had on his face when they met in New Orleans. Not a full smile, but more than just a lifting of the corners of his mouth. And it was real, reflecting in the depths of those gorgeous eyes of his, like the green was lit from within.

But what surprised her most, more than the fact that he had actually shown up like he said he would, was that he didn't seem to be paying any attention to the other girls. They'd zeroed in on him as soon as he walked through the door. How could they not? He was wearing nothing more than faded jeans and a polo shirt but he still stood out among the normal patrons. There was something about him besides his athletic build and good looks, his arresting eyes and charming smile. Some kind of presence, an aura or something that set him apart from everyone else. So yeah, a few of the girls had headed right over to him. But he just smiled and shook his head, not quite looking at them even though they were directly in his line of vision. And Nicole swore she saw him blush, just the tiniest bit. Almost like he was embarrassed.

Or maybe it was just a reflection of the neon. Or her imagination. Or wishful thinking.

And oh God, she was in so much trouble. She should have left work early, just so she wouldn't be here when he got here. But how could she do that? Especially when she hadn't expected him to show up. And now he was here, waiting for her shift to end so he could drive her home.

"Nikki!"

She jumped at the sound of her name and turned around, the dishrag still clenched in her fists. Tony Williams, her boss, was standing at the edge of the bar, his lined face puckered even more with a frown as he watched her. His pale gaze lowered to her twisting hands then back to meet her eyes. She tossed the rag into the sink behind her then gripped her hands together, suddenly wishing the stupid short-shorts she was wearing had pockets. No such luck, not with the skin-tight black spandex cut so high that her ass was hanging out.

Tony's eyes darted toward Mat then back at her. He motioned her over with a quick jerk of his head, the scowl never leaving his face. Six months ago, that expression would have scared her, but not now. Tony might look intimidating as hell but he was nothing more than a big teddy bear. And he'd taken a chance on her, hiring her as a barmaid and server when she didn't really have the experience necessary. Nicole tried to convince herself it had nothing to do with the way she looked in the costumes.

She made her way over to him, wondering if she was going to get into any trouble for Mat being there. She couldn't imagine why, not when all he was doing was sitting there, drinking a soda.

Then again, maybe that was reason enough.

"Is he giving you a hard time?"

The question caught her off-guard and she had to stop her mouth from dropping open in shock. A hard time from Mat? The question was almost funny.

"Who, Mat? No, he's harmless. Why?"

Tony kept frowning, not bothering to hide the fact that he was staring at Mat. No, not staring. Glowering. Nicole glanced over her shoulder, expecting to find Mat doing nothing more than sipping on his soda and playing with his phone, which is exactly what he'd been doing for the last thirty minutes. Only he wasn't doing that now. And the look on his face sent a shiver straight through her.

He was looking at Tony with a glower of his own, not showing the least sign of being intimidated. The expression on his face was just as dangerous as Tony's. Intense, watchful, like he was sizing Tony up and warning him all at the same time.

Harmless? Had she really used that word? There was nothing harmless about the way he looked now.

But then his gaze slid to her and his expression softened, that small grin lighting his face as his green eyes studied her. Nicole swallowed and looked away, not understanding the little shiver that went through her, leaving her skin tingling. Was it a shiver of excitement, or something else?

She swallowed again and shook her head. "Uh, no.

He's not bothering me."

Tony finally looked away from Mat, his expression telling her he didn't quite believe her. "You know who he is?"

Was he asking if she actually knew him? Or asking if she realized who he was, that he was a professional hockey player for the Baltimore Banners? This time she nodded, trying to give Tony a convincing smile.

"Yeah. He's, uh, he's a friend of mine." That might be stretching the truth a little. Or a lot. But she wasn't about to tell Tony the truth. "He's giving me a ride home tonight."

"Hm." Tony didn't say anything else, just watched her for a long minute. He finally nodded, nothing more than a short jerk of his head. "Then why don't you change and get out of here, head on home."

"But my shift—"

"Ends in fifteen minutes. It'll be fine. Now go."

Nicole thought about arguing but didn't, just tossed another glance over her shoulder then moved away from the bar, heading to the dressing room. She felt Mat's eyes on her the entire time, watching as she made her way across the room. And for the first time since she started working here, she had the urge to tug her shorts down, wishing they weren't cut quite so short.

Less than ten minutes later she was back at the bar, dressed in her capris and shirt, standing on the other side as Tony handed her an envelope with the night's tips. She shoved it into the backpack without opening it, knowing she'd have to wait until she got home to count it. If she had counted correctly during the course of her shift, there should be close to seventy dollars in the envelope after the tips were divided. Not the best night of tips she'd ever gone home with, but not the worst, either.

Nicole zipped the backpack shut and tossed it over her shoulder, not quite sure what to do now. Should she just turn around and tell Mat it was time to leave? Start walking out and have him follow her? Discomfort made her shuffle her feet. Why was she being like this? Why was she letting him have this effect on her?

Discomfort gave way to irritation—with herself for letting Mat get to her like this. It was silly and irrational. And dangerous, because she could see herself easily falling for him. Sharing one night with him in New Orleans was one thing because that was all it was supposed to be: one night of memories, a celebration of what she hoped was a new beginning, a way to prove to herself she still knew how to live, how to feel.

She hadn't thought she'd see him again, had never planned on seeing him again, and now she wasn't sure how to act or what to do or even what to think. And falling for the attractive hockey player was the last thing she needed, not when she had been down that road once already, with dire consequences she was still suffering.

She clenched her jaw and turned around, ready to just walk out. Maybe tell Mat she didn't need a ride after all, that she'd just catch a cab. Not that she could really spare the money but he didn't have to know that. Except when she turned around, he was standing right there, so close her nose almost brushed against his chest, high up near the base of his throat. She caught a whiff of his cologne, or maybe it was his soap. Something faintly spicy, a little woodsy, totally masculine and completely him.

She stepped back in surprise and almost stumbled because of her stupid shoes but his hand shot out and cupped her elbow, steadying her. Awareness ripped through her at his touch, pebbling her skin and causing tingles to spread over her, inside her, until the sharp sensations came together and pooled low in her stomach. And oh God, this was not good. Not good at all. It was just his hand on her elbow, for frick's sake. How could something that small, that simple, create such an intense reaction in her?

Because it wasn't just his touch. It was the look in his smoldering green eyes as he watched her, the scent of his warm body so close to hers, the memory of their one shared night and how his body felt pressed against hers. How he felt buried deep inside her.

And oh God, she was in so much trouble.

"Are you ready?"

No, she wasn't ready. She'd never be ready. But Nicole just nodded, trying to step around him to lead the way. Even that didn't work because he slid his hand from her elbow to the small of her back and walked with her. Not behind her, not in front of her, but with her. Right by her side. That shouldn't matter. She shouldn't let it matter. But it did.

And then they were outside and he was opening the car door for her, helping her into the low-slung sports car that cost more than she could ever hope to make in her lifetime. It wasn't until he closed the door after her that she realized she had another problem.

Mat was taking her home. And in order to do that, she had to tell him where she lived. Embarrassment and shame, deep and upsetting, burned through her and she wished she could jump from the car and just run. Run away and never look back.

But that had never worked before. It wouldn't work now.

She looked straight ahead through the windshield as Mat started the car. The engine hummed to life, purring beneath her as he asked for her address.

Nicole rattled off the address, afraid to look at him. "It's my mom's place. I'm staying with her for a little bit. Just for a little while."

If Mat recognized the street name, if he knew what part of the city it was in, he didn't say anything. And he didn't really talk, either. It was almost like he knew she didn't want to talk, wasn't up for conversation. But the silence wasn't oppressive or uncomfortable. In fact, Nicole felt so at ease that she felt herself drifting off, her head falling back against the buttery soft leather of the seat. She wrapped her arms around the backpack, holding it loosely in her lap, and stopped fighting the drifting of her lids.

"Nicole." Her name came through a dark haze, the sound soft, sweet, and enticing. A gentle touch along her cheek, against her hair. The sound of her name again, a little louder this time, laced with something that made her dream of smiles and light. "Nicole. Sweetheart. We're here."

"Hm?" Her eyes fluttered open, closed, opened again. She blinked against the harsh light shining through the windshield, blinked again to bring everything into focus.

A dark street, lit by the single light at the corner. A handful of cars lining each side, rusty and old, some missing wheels and propped up by cinder blocks. Brick rowhomes, a few with boarded windows, their marble stoops cracked and worn.

Home.

Nicole turned her head to look out the window, her eyes automatically finding the rowhome where she lived. No, where her mother lived. Nicole was only staying there. She couldn't think of herself as living there, not without feeling like she was giving up.

She blinked again and turned her head to the other side. Mat's hand was still resting against her shoulder, large and warm and too comforting. Their eyes met and held and Nicole's breath caught in her throat. It would be so easy to lean forward, just a few inches, and brush her lips against his. To feel the warmth of his mouth, to taste him and see if she had only imagined the spicy sweetness of his kisses that one night.

Mat smiled and dropped his hand, moving away and reaching for the door handle before she could do anything. Then he was out of the car, coming around to her side. Nicole muttered under her breath, calling herself every kind of fool. At least she hadn't tried to kiss him, hadn't embarrassed herself even more.

She reached for the door handle but she wasn't quick enough because Mat was already opening the door for her. He held his hand out, reaching for hers. She ignored it, grabbing her backpack instead and getting out of the car on her own.

"Thanks, I appreciate—"

"I'll walk you to the door." He placed his hand against the small of her back, waiting. Nicole blinked, thinking maybe she was still dreaming after all, maybe she hadn't really embarrassed herself.

Then she shook her head and told herself to stop being a fool. He was just being a gentleman, being nice. Nothing more. She moved toward her mother's rowhome, pulling the key from the side pocket of her backpack as she stepped over the raised slab of one of the cracks in the sidewalk. Mat must not have seen it because he tripped, stumbled, then quickly righted himself. Nicole paused, fighting the sudden insane urge to apologize. But before she could say anything, Mat offered her a small grin and shrugged, like he was saying tripping was his fault.

Nicole snapped her mouth shut and kept walking, closing the short distance to the door. She stepped away, dislodging the hand at the small of her back. "Uh, this is it. My mom's place. Thanks again."

Nicole moved, wanting to race up the three cracked steps and disappear inside, but Mat caught her hand, stopping her. Not just stopping her, but turning her toward him. He was so close, she could feel the heat of his body, warmer than the muggy air that surrounded them. He didn't say anything, though, just watched her with those intense eyes that made her heart beat too fast and heavy in her chest.

"I'd like to take you out. I mean, if that's—if you'd like to, I mean."

The words stunned Nicole and for a few long seconds, she didn't say anything, certain she was hearing things. Was Mat actually asking her out? She wanted to say yes, more than she wanted to admit, but she couldn't—not when she knew how easy it would be to fall for him.

"I—I'd like that." Her mouth snapped shut, her mind not completely understanding how those words had come out. But Mat grinned, a bright smile that lit his eyes and sent a shiver through her. He reached out and cupped her chin, his hand warm and gentle. And then he leaned forward and brushed his mouth against hers.

Nicole held her breath as a hundred-thousand different sensations shot through her, sending her body—her mind—into a dizzying tailspin. Her hands tightened around the backpack and she leaned forward, her body automatically seeking the warmth of his even as her mind screamed to run away.

Then the kiss was over and Mat pulled away, leaving her breathless and dizzy. She blinked, trying to focus on his sculpted face, his soft lips and shining eyes and the shadow of stubble that darkened his square jaw. He stepped back and Nicole had to bite her lower lip to keep from moaning in disappointment.

"Good. I'll, uh, I'll call you later."

Nicole nodded, still not sure what to say. Mat took another step back and nodded toward her door. "You should probably get inside."

She looked behind her, saw a shadow cross the window and knew her mother was watching. Waiting. Even that wasn't enough to stop the turmoil, the excitement and surprise and doubt and worry, that pulsed through her. But he was right, she needed to get inside, she couldn't stand out here all night. Nicole took a step back, then another, until she reached the stoop. Then she turned and went up the steps, her hand shaking as she jammed the key in the lock. She glanced over her shoulder, not surprised to see Mat standing by his car, waiting, watching to make sure she got inside okay.

Nicole pushed the door open and hurried through, still watching him over her shoulder. He waved and she slammed the door, not understanding the emotions running through her, not understanding how just the sight of his smile could twist her insides and turn her mind to mush.

Thirty minutes later, her insides were twisting for another reason. She sat cross-legged on her bed with the tips envelope opened in front of her, frowning as she counted the money. Then recounted again and again.

There was close to three hundred dollars spread out on the faded quilt. A pile of crumpled ones and fives—and two crisp hundred-dollar bills. And she knew, without a doubt, that the large bills had come from Mat.

She stared at them, frowning, fighting the flood of anger that was pushing all the other emotions that had been swimming through her away.

And tried to figure out what she was going to do about the extra money.

Chapter Six

"No fucking way."

"Seriously? This is where you're bringing us?"

"Quick, inside before he changes his mind."

Something hit Mat on the shoulder, hard enough to cause him to stumble forward. He grunted then shot a dirty look at Harland Day. He shouldn't have bothered because Harland, along with Kenny and Dillon Frayser, were already moving across the parking lot. Not for the first time—or even the hundredth—Mat questioned what he'd been thinking when he came up with this idea.

It hadn't seemed quite so bad earlier, when he called a few of the other single guys from the team and asked them to join him. A few of them, like Brad Goodrich and Jens Ulfsson and Ethan Kincaid, were out of town, back home visiting with friends and family during the off-season until JP's wedding next month.

But not everyone had gone home. Some of them, like Kenny and Harland, spent most of their time here in Baltimore. Dillon had already gone home, staying just long enough to visit his parents before they left on a month-long cruise he had treated them to.

Mat wouldn't be making the trip to Michigan this summer, since he was in JP's wedding and supposedly helping out with things. With what, he had no idea, since the only thing he'd had to do so far was get fitted for his tux.

And go on that trip to New Orleans.

So yeah, calling up some of the guys and inviting them out had seemed like a good idea at the time, because Mat would have felt uncomfortable coming by himself. At least, until the trio walking in front of him had started acting like a bunch of under-sexed, hormonal teenagers as soon as they got here.

Mat glanced back at his car, wondering if maybe he should just leave. It wasn't like the boys would be stranded, not since Kenny had driven as well. Except if he left, the three of them would be in the club by themselves.

With a bunch of strippers.

With Nicole.

"Fuck." Mat ran a hand through his hair, his jaw clenched in frustration. What the fuck had he been thinking? He hadn't, that was the problem. If he had, he would have known right away that asking any of the guys to come with him was the stupidest of ideas. But he'd been so distracted, so wrapped up in just being with her, that he'd forgotten to get Nicole's phone number when he dropped her off last night. And how the hell was he supposed to call her if he didn't have her number? So he'd come up with the idea of stopping in here while she was working.

Definitely not his brightest idea.

"Mathias! Are you coming or what?" Kenny stood

just outside the blacked-out door, holding it open as their teammates hurried in, pushing against each other. Mat cursed beneath his breath then closed the distance, mentally counting all the ways this could backfire on him.

But Kenny grabbed him at the last minute, stopping him. He looked around then lowered his voice. "Do you want to tell me why we're really here?"

Mat could lie but why? Kenny would figure it out as soon as he saw Nicole behind the bar. So he just shrugged, not quite able to meet the other man's eyes. "I just wanted to stop in and see someone."

Kenny did that single eyebrow-raise thing again but didn't say anything. Mat was thankful for that, at least. Until they walked deeper into the darkened club and approached the bar. Kenny stopped beside him, his body stiffening in surprise.

"Hey. Isn't that the girl—"

Mat elbowed him in the side, hard. "Yeah. And not a word."

Kenny just stood there, studying the bar through the dim lights and flashing neon. A minute went by before he looked back at Mat, the expression on his face unreadable.

"I hope to hell you know what you're doing." Then he walked off, heading toward the main stage where Dillon and Harland were already waving bills at the dancers.

Know what he was doing? Not a chance in hell. But he was here now so he had to follow-through. Follow-through with what, though?

"Fuck." He muttered the word under his breath then jammed his hands in the back pockets of his jeans and stood there. Yeah, this really wasn't a good idea.

Not just bringing the guys here—showing up, period. What would Nicole think? Was he coming on too strong? Being too pushy? Or maybe this whole thing just reeked of obsession. Of desperation.

He was still standing there, arguing with himself, when Nicole turned around, a bottle in one hand and glass in the other. She was gorgeous. Breathtaking. Her hair floated loose around her bare shoulders, the neon lights playing with the pink streaks. His eyes drifted down, skimming over the colorful tattoos covering her upper left arm before settling on the curves of her breasts. She was wearing a shiny black strapless top with crisscross laces down the front, something that looked like it could pass for a corset. Something that made it look like her breasts were ready to spill out.

Mat bit back a groan as his cock hardened at the sight, his mind immediately flashing back to that night in New Orleans, remembering how those breasts felt in his hands, remembering the sweet taste of her skin.

He groaned again, telling himself this wasn't the time or the place. Never mind that he was in a strip club, never mind that there were at least a dozen mostly-naked women walking around or dancing up on the stage. He only had eyes for Nicole, only wanted Nicole.

But he didn't want her to think he was here just for that. He wasn't. So yeah, he should probably leave because she might get the wrong idea, especially if she saw him standing here, damn near drooling at the sight of her.

He started to turn, ready to do just that, when she looked up. Something must have caught her attention. Or hell, maybe she just felt him staring at her. It didn't matter because she turned her head, just the slightest bit. Their eyes met and held each other, long enough that he could see her surprise, see the faint blush that colored her cheeks.

Shit. He couldn't leave now, not without her getting an entirely different wrong idea. So Mat bit back his worry and doubt and walked forward, heading to the bar. There were several open seats and he chose one away from the few patrons already there. He didn't want to be close to anyone, didn't want to be close enough to see them ogling Nicole. There was no telling what he might do if he saw that.

He climbed onto the stool and hooked his leg around the rung, sliding it closer to the bar with a quick hop and shift. Nicole was still watching him, nibbling on her lower lip as she shot glances at him from the corner of her eye. And shit, didn't she know what watching her do that did to him? He doubted it, not if the uncertainty in her eyes meant anything.

She turned away, handing drinks over to one of the waiting servers. Mat's eyes drifted down her body, settling on the delicious roundness of her ass. The shorts, if you could call them that, were cut in a high V, giving him a generous view of the curves of her cheeks. He blinked and looked away just before she turned around, wondering if he had been caught staring. Again.

Nicole worked her way over to him, hesitation clear in every move. She placed a warped cardboard coaster on the bar in front of him then just stood there, chewing on her full lower lip again.

"What would you like to drink?" Her voice was a little stiff, a little too formal. Mat smiled, hoping to set her at ease.

"Just a soda. Please."

Nicole's eyes narrowed for a fraction of a second before she turned away to fix his drink. He kept watching her as she filled the glass with ice, as she grabbed some kind of small hose from under the bar and filled the glass.

She placed it in front of him without saying a word. Mat was afraid she was going to turn around, that she was going to leave. But she didn't. She just stood there, watching him with a frown, like she was trying to figure him out.

He took a quick sip, trying to steady his thoughts, trying to figure out what the hell he should do now. He shifted on the stool, looked over to where his teammates were hanging out, then looked back at her. He opened his mouth, hoping something at least halfway intelligent would come out, when Nicole spoke.

"I have something that's yours." Her voice was a little clipped, maybe a little impatient or irritated or something, he couldn't tell. And he had no idea how to respond, no idea what she could be talking it.

"Uh, you do?"

She nodded, her lips pursed. And yeah, that was definitely a flash of irritation in her eyes. "Yes. Your money. From last night."

"I don't understand—"

"Yes you do. Tony told me you gave it to him, to include it in my tips."

Mat ducked his head and stared into the soda, not sure how to respond. He still wasn't sure what had possessed him to do that. He'd been watching as her boss counted out the tips, dividing them up into several piles. It had seemed like such a small amount. And he hadn't thought, just reached for his wallet and pulled out a couple of bills and handed them over with the lame excuse that he'd forgotten to tip Nicole.

He didn't think she'd notice, not really. It wasn't like she'd been there, watching him hand the money over. And he sure as hell didn't expect her boss to tell her where it had come from.

"I'm sorry. I didn't mean—"

"I don't need your money."

"I know, I just thought—"

"I don't want your money."

"But I—"

"You need to take it back." She moved away, saying something to one of the other girls behind the bar before ducking around the side and disappearing.

Great. He hadn't expected that, had no idea what to do next. Where had Nicole gone? Did it really matter? Probably not. All he knew was that he had probably just blown whatever small chance he may have had with her. He'd come here tonight, just wanting to see her. To get her number and ask for that date again, to remind her she had said yes.

And he blew it. There was no doubt in his mind that whatever date he had hoped to have would never happen now. All because he hadn't been thinking, had reacted on instinct and some idiotic idea that he was helping.

Yeah. A lot of help he'd been.

Mat drained the soda then slid off the stool. He glanced over at the main stage, his eyes searching out his friends, thinking he should find them and at least tell them he was leaving. But Harland and Dillon were both preoccupied, each of them with a girl in their laps, their faces filled with bare breasts. He had no idea where Kenny was and figured he was better off not knowing. They'd eventually realize he wasn't here. At least, when they saw his car was gone they would. Maybe.

He was pushing through the door, anxious to leave, when he heard his name called. The voice didn't belong to any of the guys so he kept going. But Nicole called him again, then once more as he neared his car. He finally stopped, calling himself every kind of fool imaginable, and leaned against the side of his car, waiting.

With no idea what to expect, no idea what he was really waiting for.

Nicole hurried across the parking lot, her steps steady despite the fact that she was wearing ankle boots with a pointy heel at least five inches high. And she was still in her costume, or outfit, or whatever it was called. It didn't matter what she called it, she shouldn't be dressed like that. Not outside, not in the middle of a parking lot chasing him down because he was too big of an ass to wait for her.

She finally reached him, her chest rising and falling, her breasts threatening to fall out with each heavy breath. She reached up and brushed at her hair, pushing it off her face. Then she thrust her arm toward him, her hand curled into a fist just under his chin. Mat stepped back, wondering for just a second if she planned on hitting him.

"Here. Take it." She uncurled her fingers, showing him two crumpled hundred dollar bills. He shook his head.

"No. The money's yours. I don't want—"

"I said take it."

"Nicole, I don't want it. Okay? Just…give it to one of the other girls if you don't want it." He tried to step back, to move away, but he was already leaning against the side of his car with nowhere else to go. Unless Nicole stepped back, he was stuck just where he was.

And she didn't look like she was ready to step back. She looked angry, fire flashing in her bright eyes, a flush staining her cheeks. Her breathing was too heavy, too deep, like she had to force each breath into her lungs. Was she really this angry because he'd left a tip for her?

She took one last deep breath, her eyes dimming as some sort of calm seemed to settle over her. She glanced over each shoulder, looking for who knew what. Then she stepped forward, erasing the distance between them, and settled one hand in the middle of his chest.

"Fine. Then what do you want?"

"Want? I—"

"A blowjob?" Her hand slid down, across his stomach, lower. He jerked back in surprise when her hand cupped his erection.

"No, I—"

"Really? Because your cock is so hard." Her voice had changed, becoming a little lower, sultry. But it sounded forced, not natural like it had been in New Orleans. Mat tried to swallow, tried to breathe as she stroked him through his jeans.

"Nicole, you—"

"Maybe something a little more? Not just regular sex, not for that kind of money."

"What? I—"

"A threesome? I'm sure one of the other girls would love to join us. Your pick."

"Stop!" He grabbed her hands, holding them between his as he turned, desperate to put space between them. What the hell was she doing? Is that what she thought? He wanted to say more but the words jumbled together in his brain, stalling before he could get anything out.

Then it didn't matter because she ripped her hands from his grasp, anger flashing in her eyes. She crumpled the bills together and threw them at him. They hit him in the face and fell to the ground.

"I'm not a whore so take your money and get away from me." She turned, her back rigid and head held high, her steps slow and steady as she walked away.

A whore? Fuck, is that what she thought? That he wanted to pay her for sex? That he wanted to buy her? Could he have screwed up any worse than he already had? He wanted to say no, that wasn't possible. That what he'd done, without even realizing it, was bad enough. He should let her walk away.

But he couldn't. The knowledge of what she was thinking—of her, of him—was too bitter. He didn't think of her like that. Not even close.

"Nicole, wait." He followed her, hurrying his steps until he caught up to her. Then he stepped in front of her, walking backward so she'd have to face him. He slowed his steps, praying she would stop. "Nicole, please—"

"I need to get inside."

"Please. Stop. That's not—I didn't mean it that way. I didn't think—fuck." She stepped around him, not even listening. "Nicole, please. Would you please just stop and listen to me? Please?"

Maybe it was the pleading in his voice. Maybe it was something else. He didn't know and didn't care, not when she finally stopped and turned to face him. She folded her arms in front of her and looked at something just beyond his shoulder. He had hoped that maybe she would look at him, meet his eyes so she could see his guilt and torment, but he'd take what he could get.

He ran a hand through his hair, his mind searching for the right words, not knowing if they even existed. "I'm sorry. I didn't mean for you to take it that way. I wasn't thinking. I just...I thought—"

"You thought what?"

"I—sometimes I don't think, that's the problem. It was just a tip. That's all. I swear."

"So you just go around leaving two hundred dollar tips everywhere you go?"

"Uh, no. Not exactly—"

"Then why me?"

"Because I...because..." Fuck, now what? He took a deep breath, wondering what to tell her that wouldn't make him look like a complete ass.

"I'm not a whore."

"I know that! God, I would never think that. Never. And I didn't think you'd think that I thought that." And Christ, could he make this any worse if he tried?

"In a place like this, a tip like that usually means something else."

"No. Nicole, please, you can't really think that. I didn't know, didn't even think—"

"Then why?"

"Because I...because—" Mat took a deep breath and shook his head, no longer able to look at Nicole. He focused his gaze on the neon sign above the door, the bright letters blurring as he stared at them. "Because I thought you could put it toward your next trip to New Orleans. You said you wanted to go back and I thought…"

Fuck, it didn't matter what he thought. He'd blown it, about a hundred different ways. Blown it in ways he hadn't even imagined. He jammed his hands into his back pockets and finally pulled his gaze away from the sign. He couldn't look at Nicole, not yet, so he stared at the cracked asphalt at his feet.

"I'm sorry. I don't think you're a…that you're—" Christ, he couldn't even say it. "I don't think of you that way. I never did. I'm sorry."

He turned, figuring the best thing he could do now was just leave. He reached his car and looked down, his gaze resting on the two crumpled bills. He paused for a second. No, let them stay there. If Nicole didn't want them, someone else could take them.

His hand curled around the door handle, ready to pull it open, when he heard footsteps behind him. Hesitant, unsteady.

"Why did you come here tonight?"

The question surprised him enough that he turned around, that he actually looked at Nicole. Her arms were still crossed in front of her but the angry defiance was gone from her face, from her eyes. She watched him, her head tilted to the side, simple curiosity on her face. Should he lie? No, let her know the truth. Maybe it would take the sting out of what she thought before. Not for himself, for her. No woman should ever think that way about herself, ever. And if him feeling like an ass made her feel better, then that was a small price to pay.

"I forgot to get your number last night for our date. I thought that maybe I could get it tonight. And, well, I just wanted to see you again."

Her eyes widened as she watched him. Mat told

himself to leave, that leaving would be better for both of them, but he couldn't seem to make his feet move. Nicole uncrossed her arms, crossed them again, uncrossed them once more.

"My number? You wanted my phone number?"

"Yeah. For our date."

"That was it?"

Mat shifted, not quite sure what else to say. Hadn't he already said that? "Well, and to see you again."

Nicole stepped closer, still studying him with curiosity and something that looked like surprise. The corners of her mouth twitched and she cleared her throat. They twitched again and her mouth curled into a smile, a bright smile that Mat felt deep in his gut. And then she laughed, the sound clear and musical.

Mat wanted to smile in return, fought his answering laughter. Because fuck, what if he laughed and it turned out he was laughing about the wrong thing? He didn't want to do anything else wrong, whether he meant to or not.

Nicole stepped closer, reaching for his hand. Her touch was soft, warm, reassuring. But Mat didn't move, not until she tugged on his hand and pulled him away from the car. She paused, bending down to scoop up the bills, then led him back toward the club.

"My number. Only I could screw something up that bad."

Mat thought he heard her but he couldn't be sure, not when she was turned away from him. And he certainly wasn't going to ask her to repeat herself. But he did pull on her hand, not stopping until she turned to face him.

"Uh. Where are we going?"

"Back inside. I'm going to treat you to a few drinks

while we talk." Then she leaned forward and pressed a soft kiss to the corner of his mouth, that bright smile lighting her eyes.

She pulled away, leading him back inside. And Mat suddenly couldn't think of a better thing to do.

Chapter Seven

Pain shot through his elbow, sending a shooting tingle that was anything but funny up his arm. Mat bit back a gasp. Of pain, of pleasure. Fuck, he didn't know. He could barely think, barely breathe. Not when Nicole was touching him that way, not when her mouth was searing a hot trail of wet kisses down his chest, his stomach.

And fuck, they shouldn't be doing this. Not here, not like this. Not when he had a house with a fucking king size bed and all the privacy they'd ever need.

He wasn't a lanky teenager anymore, looking for a secluded area to make out and maybe get lucky. And his sports car was a far cry from the old Chevy pickup he'd used for dates back home, even with his seat reclined back as far as it would go.

But it didn't matter, not now, not with Nicole's body stretched across the console, leaning over him with her short skirt pushed up to her waist. Not with her mouth and hands all over him. He hadn't planned this, hadn't thought things would go this far when she asked him to take one turn then another and another, ending at a dark secluded lot filled with overgrown weeds. But here they were, their clothes astray, getting as close to each other as they could in the small confines of his car, the windshield steaming in spite of the open windows.

Mat gasped again as she swirled her tongue around his navel. He fisted one hand along the doorframe, the other anchored to her sweet bare ass, caressing, squeezing, clenching. She moaned and thrust her hips, reached back for his hand and dragged it lower, down past the cleft of her ass, down to the hot opening of soft sensitive flesh.

He ran his finger along her clit, back and forth as she worked the zipper of his jeans. God, she was so wet, his fingers, his palm, slick with her moisture. He slid one finger inside, then another, in and out as she twirled her hips, her breath teasing his skin with each soft little moan.

She arched her back, driving that sweet ass up higher. Mat pumped his fingers inside her, once, twice, then slid them up, grazing the cleft of her ass before spreading his hand along one firm cheek, squeezing. Back down, teasing the delicate folds, sliding two fingers back inside.

She moaned, shifting, then dragged the zipper of his jeans down. Mat lifted his hips, helped her ease the jeans down to his thighs. Helped as much as he could, with only one hand and a mind on the verge of disintegration.

Her hand closed around his cock, stroking, squeezing. Her hair brushed against the tops of his thighs, his balls, the soft strands teasing the hypersensitive flesh. He tossed his head back, a low groan escaping from between his clenched jaw.

"Nicole, baby, we shouldn't—"

"Shh. I want to do this." Her breath was hot, her voice sinfully seductive against his chest as she kissed her way up to his neck.

"You don't have—"

She cut him off, her mouth closing over his, her tongue thrusting against his, teasing. And God, she tasted so good. Sweet, spicy. Temptation and redemption all rolled into one. But then she pulled away, her eyes dark with passion, with need. He moaned—or maybe it was a whimper—when her hands left his cock, his chest. She sat up, thrust her hips forward, up and down, riding his fingers, her gaze locked on his the entire time.

"You are so fucking wet."

"You like that?"

"Fuck yeah." And fuck, was that really him talking, saying those things? Yes, it was.

And he meant it. God, she was so beautiful, with her hair tangled around her, her full breasts bared to his gaze. With her skirt shoved high around her waist, her bare tanned pussy satiny slick, riding his fingers, his hand. She reached up and grabbed her hair, pulling it behind her and twisting it. Then she reached down and grabbed his wrist, sliding it away with a sigh.

"Nicole—" Her name was a soft growl, the sound surprising him.

But she didn't say anything, just smiled a sweet seductive smile as she guided his wet hand up, brushing it across her nipples, up along her throat, to her mouth. Her gaze steady on his, she flicked her tongue out and slid it along his middle finger, up around his index finger. Licking. Tasting herself. Then she took both fingers into her mouth, sucking, teasing, nipping.

Holy fuck. Shit. Mat reached down and closed his hand around his cock, stroking his hard length as he watched her. Her eyes glistened in the faint light, her pupils dilating until all he could see was black. She twirled her tongue around his fingers again then slowly, so slowly, eased them from her mouth. But she held onto his hand, stopping him from touching her again. Instead, she guided his hand to her hair, wrapping the long strands around his fingers, closing each one until his hand was fisted in her hair.

Her gaze slid down to his lap, her mouth parted as she watched him fisting his cock. Fuck, what the hell was he doing? He started to pull his hand away but she shook her head.

"Don't stop. I like watching you."

And holy shit. Much more of this and he was coming to cum, right here. But he didn't stop, just stroked his cock, long strokes, back and forth. He tilted his head back and swallowed a groan.

What the fuck was he doing? They couldn't keep doing this. Not here. He took a deep breath, forced himself to slow down, to think.

"Nicole. I—I don't have any condoms with me. They're back at my house. We should—"

"We don't need them."

He blinked, trying to understand the words. Why didn't they need them? He blinked again, his gaze following Nicole's hand as it trailed across her body. She pinched her nipples, her gasp sharp in the heavy air. Down, down across her stomach, lower until her fingers reached her clit. He watched, hungry, enthralled, as she rubbed her clit. Her hips thrust against her hand and her head fell back, soft moans escaping her parted lips.

Mat's hand tightened in her hair, pulling as he watched, as he stroked his cock harder, faster. Nicole gasped again, the sound different, a little sharp as she moved her head. He immediately loosened his grip. "I'm sorry, I didn't mean—"

"Do it again."

Holy fuck, was she serious? The breath hitched in his chest, short shallow breaths that barely filled his lungs. He hesitated, then gently tightened his fist and tugged, just a little.

She gasped again, then moaned, a deep throaty sound that ignited something primitive inside him. He tightened his hand even more around his cock, each stroke harder, faster, bringing him dangerously close to the edge. He dropped his gaze, watching as Nicole's fingers slid along her clit, faster, faster. Her hips thrust, searching, over and over.

"Again. Please." A soft whimper, filled with desperate need. Mat clenched his jaw and tightened his fist once more, tugging her hair, a little harder this time. Her hips bucked, once, twice, reaching. Then she screamed his name, a throaty rasp as she rode her fingers, her hips dropping down, over and over in time to each breathy moan.

And fuck, he wasn't going to last much longer. He held his breath, stroking his cock faster, harder. He couldn't—he wanted—

He threw his head back, his jaw clenched, searching for control. Fuck. He didn't want control. He wanted to let go. Here. Now. With Nicole watching. "Nicole, I'm going to cum."

Her hand was suddenly on his, her slick fingers wrapping around his and pulling them away. Mat groaned, a sound that was almost a growl. And then her mouth was on him, her hot mouth, sucking. And shit, he hadn't meant for her—

"Fuck!" His orgasm ripped through him, tearing a howling groan from his lips. His hand was still fisted in Nicole's hair as her head bobbed in his lap. He held her in place, thrusting his hips up. Harder, faster, deeper, her sweet little moans and moist sucking sounds drawing his climax out.

He fell back against the seat, his lungs bursting with each breath he struggled to pull in. His body and his mind were both limp, completely spent. Time slowed, stilled. Seconds, minutes, he had no idea. He only knew he couldn't move even if he wanted to.

He felt Nicole stir, felt her shift as she eased her hair from his fist. Reality slammed into him, freezing the air in his lungs and the blood in his veins. Holy hell, what had he just done?

Mat bolted upright, his hands reaching for Nicole, an apology on his lips as he helped her sit up. But she shook her hair out and fixed him with a shy smile.

"Nicole, I'm sorry, I didn't mean—"

"I'm not." She leaned forward and pressed a shy kiss against his mouth. He moaned and reached for her, pulling her closer as he deepened the kiss, sweeping his tongue inside. He took his time, teasing, tasting, enjoying each touch of their tongues, each little whimper.

He gentled the kiss, slowly ending it. Then he eased Nicole away from him, watching her for any signs that he'd crossed some line, that he'd accidentally hurt her. But she just sat there, stretched across the console as she curled against him, that same shy smile on her face.

"I—I didn't hurt you, did I?"

"No." Her smile broadened, just a tiny bit. "I didn't hurt you, did I?"

Mat laughed, he couldn't help it. He shook his head, turning serious once more. "No, you didn't hurt me. Are you sure you're okay? I've never—I mean, I haven't—" He cleared his throat and forced himself to meet her eyes. "I've never done anything like this before so this, uh, was a first for me."

The shy smile on her face changed, growing, becoming brighter. She pressed a kiss to the hollow of his throat then looked up at him, her eyes sparkling in the faint light.

"Good. This was a first for me, too."

Chapter Eight

Nicole read the email for the third time, hoping the words would somehow miraculously change. But the message was the same, no matter how many times she blinked or squinted or tilted her head.

The message was always the same.

Thank you for your interest, blah blah blah.

Admire your work, blah blah blah.

Not interested at this time, blah blah blah.

She closed the email then backed out of the program before disconnecting from the internet. Disappointment surged through her. The short email hadn't been worth the hassle of trying to get connected, of waiting for the ancient dial-up to actually work. She should have waited and used the wi-fi at the hospital, or taken the bus to the coffee shop or even to the library. Any of those things would have saved her time instead of fighting with the old system. But it was all she had, and that just barely since it was always a crapshoot whether or not or her mother remembered to pay the phone bill with the money Nicole gave her.

Just another lesson learned.

Had she really expected to hear anything different? No, not really. Not when the answers had been the same for entirely too long. Everyone liked her work. Her photography had promise. She had talent, a unique eye. But everyone seemed to be looking for someone with more experience, more published credits, and that was the one thing she didn't have. Not even freelance experience.

Well how was she supposed to get experience when everyone wanted her to have experience before giving her a chance? One break, one shot. That was all she needed. Just one tiny little break, one tiny little chance.

Volunteering at the hospital, taking the pictures, broadening her expertise with the different computer programs out there...all of that had helped. But she couldn't use those pictures—wouldn't use those pictures. They were private, meant for the kids and their families. So none of that counted. Which didn't matter, because that wasn't why she was doing it.

But everything else had come at an expense. The expensive laptop, the different programs and add-ons, all of it. And even though they were expenses she couldn't really afford, they had all been worth it.

At least, that's what she kept telling herself. But she couldn't afford anymore expenses, not when she was trying to save enough to move out, get her own place. The divorce had cost more than she thought it would. And the trip to New Orleans had been a splurge she probably shouldn't have taken. But she wanted to celebrate her new freedom, wanted to visit someplace exotic and different and exciting. So she didn't regret it—couldn't regret it. Any of it.

But God, how she wished it was easier to save. She wanted her own place. Some place nice, that didn't have holes in the walls and floor or rust stains in the toilet and tub. Some place that didn't smell of stale cigarettes, cheap perfume and even cheaper booze.

Guilt weighed down on her as soon as she had the thought. Her mother was trying, in her own way. Nicole knew that. Just like she knew her mother didn't have to let her move in here. It was an adjustment, for both of them.

No, her room wasn't much, barely large enough for her single bed and makeshift desk. But she didn't have much, and it was a hundred times better than living on the street. A thousand times better than where she'd been before.

That didn't mean she was willing to give up, to resign herself to the same life her mother had accepted. And maybe Nicole hated her job, hated working at the club and fending off unwanted advances and knowing that the men who came in thought she could be bought. But the money was decent, cash tips at the end of each night, some nights better than others.

Nicole propped her elbow on the plywood then rested her head in the palm of her hand. Yeah, some nights were definitely better than others—when she didn't overreact and throw money back in someone's face. But how could she have known Mat's intentions had been innocent? Not just innocent, but actually honorable. At least, she'd thought they could be called that. He was so different from other men in her experience. Real, genuine. And he'd been so shocked, appalled even, at her accusation, at learning what she'd first thought when she'd seen the large tip.

So what did she do? Throw it at him and accuse

him of thinking she was a whore, someone who could be bought. And if that wasn't bad enough, she turned around and acted the part later that night when he'd done nothing more than offer her a ride home.

Heat spread throughout her at the memory, tingling along her nerves and settling into a damp pool between her legs. What was wrong with her? She'd never acted that way before, never done even half of what she'd done the other night. Never even thought about doing things like that before. Sex had never been about her pleasure; it had been about being controlled.

She wasn't sure what surprised her the most: the fact that she'd done the things she'd done, or the fact that she wanted to do them—and so much more—again. With Mat. But why? What was it about him that brought out this side of her, a side she'd never even expected she had?

Maybe because he seemed as genuinely surprised as she had been. And maybe he was lying to her, trying to make her feel better or something, but she actually believed him when he told her the things they'd done had been new to him as well. Not that what they'd done had been all that extreme, not really, not compared to some of the other things she heard the girls talk about at work. So yeah, maybe he was just trying to make her feel better.

Or maybe she was just trying to prove to herself that she could enjoy sex. That it was something pleasurable for both parties. Not something to be demanded. Not an act where she was at another person's mercy, forced to relinquish control, forced to endure or suffer even worse. Was that what she was doing? Taking control, choosing her own experiences? Or was she just fooling herself into thinking that? She thought it was the former—hoped that was the case.

Or maybe she was still that gullible naïve girl she'd been all those years ago, willing to fall for any line that made her feel better.

Her hand closed around the crystal hanging at her throat, the familiar warmth of the stone and coolness of the metal soothing against her palm. Calming, reassuring. No, that girl was gone, any remnants long since washed away by the cold pummeling of reality. So maybe that meant she was nothing more than a fool for believing him, for convincing herself she was finally in control.

For some reason, she couldn't find it in her to be get upset about that. Not after New Orleans. Not after the other night.

"Nikki! Is that all you can do now, sit in front of that silly computer?"

Her mother's harsh voice startled her. She jumped back, her hand dislodging from the pendant as she tried to keep her balance. How had she not heard her mom coming up the stairs? Had she been that lost in her thoughts and memories?

She swallowed back the words that wanted to tumble from her mouth. It didn't matter how many times she tried explaining, her mother would never understand. To her, Nicole's photography was a nuisance. A worthless hobby that cost precious money and meant nothing. She didn't understand Nicole's hopes and dreams, her desire to one-day start making money with it. Not much, just a little. Just enough so she could prove to herself that she could do it. To prove that hopes and dreams really mattered.

No, her mother would never understand, no matter how many times Nicole tried to explain. So she said nothing, just reached out and powered the laptop down.

Footsteps shuffled behind her, the scrape of worn slippers scratching against the cracked linoleum floor. A sigh, long and heavy, followed by the sagging creak of aging bedsprings. Nicole closed her eyes, fingering her pendant once more as she searched for patience. Her mom never came into her room, never sat down on her bed—which meant something must be on her mind, that she wanted to talk about something. Whatever it was, Nicole didn't think she wanted to hear it.

"You came home late the other night."

"Uh, yeah. I saw you had company, didn't want to intrude." That was putting it mildly. Nicole had noticed right away when Mat pulled in front of the house. It was hard to miss the two shadows so clearly outlined in the living room window. That was why she'd asked Mat to keep driving. And she wasn't going to complain, not after what that drive had led to.

"Oh." A shaky sigh, ending in a cough. She heard her mom rustle in the pockets of her frayed robe, heard the click and spark of a lighter. Nicole turned in the chair, frowning.

"Mom, can you not smoke in here please?"

Her mother took a long drag from the cigarette, watching her with impatience as she exhaled a stream of smoke. "It is my house." But she looked around, her eyes settling on the glass of water Nicole always kept next to her bed. She reached over and tossed the cigarette in it with a small hiss.

Nicole closed her eyes, her hand tightening around the pendant again as she made a mental note to throw the glass out. Completely out. If she didn't, her mother would just leave it sitting there.

"Why do you do that?"

"Do what?"

"Always grab that necklace like you do. You'd think you were a Catholic with a string of rosary beads or something the way you're always playing with it."

Nicole took a deep breath, trying not choke on the lingering smoke that hung in the still air. There was no way she could explain to her mother the sense of calm she got from fingering the crystal. How just looking at the small dragon filled her with an odd peace. It was a whimsical design, the dragon carved from pewter or silver or some other metal, his majestic head held high, his wings folded around his body and his intricate tail wrapped around the oddly shaped milky crystal. She bought it when she was still in a high school at a mall kiosk that sold cheap jewelry and dragon sculptures and an assortment of other trinkets. It had been pure impulse that she still, to this day, didn't understand. And if she didn't understand, how could she possibly even try to explain to her mother?

She couldn't, so she just shrugged. "I don't know. Just a habit, I guess."

"Well I don't understand it."

"Mom—" Nicole stopped herself, knowing it would just lead to an argument. She took another deep breath and forced a smile. "Did you need something?"

"No. I was just worried about you. Where did you go?"

Nicole hoped her shock didn't show on her face. Her mother, worried? "Out with some friends."

"Oh. That's good." She ran a hand through her hair, nodding. "That's good."

"Yeah. Mom, I need to get going—"

"Are you seeing anyone?"

Nicole's mouth dropped open in surprise. Yeah, there was no way she could keep the shock from showing on her face. Since when did her mom ask personal questions? Since when did she care?

And she wasn't sure how to answer. Maybe, technically, she was seeing Mat. Maybe, if you stretched it. They'd seen each other a grand total of three times and two of those times had turned into a sex marathon. Okay, maybe that was a slight exaggeration, but Nicole didn't know what else to call it. Did that mean they were seeing each other? The sex aside, she had enjoyed spending time with him. He was different, so different, from any other man she'd ever met. There was something about him, something besides his rugged good looks, something that pulled her. Yes, she could definitely see herself falling for him. But was that something she wanted to do? Or something that would just lead to more trouble down the road? And what if her instincts about him were wrong?

Nicole reached for her backpack, digging through it so she wouldn't have to look at her mom. "Uh, maybe. I've gone out with him a few times." And she was going out with him again this weekend.

"Is it anything serious?"

"No. I don't know. Maybe. Probably not." Nicole put the pack aside and turned to face her mom, wondering at the sudden questions, wondering why her mom was suddenly so curious. "What's up with all the questions, Mom? You never worried before."

Her mom wouldn't look at her, her attention focused on the ragged cuticle of her thumb. She picked at it, a frown deepening the lines on her face. Long minutes went by before she shrugged and glanced at

Nicole from the side. "I just think you need a man in your life. Someone to take care of you."

Not again. Please, not again. How many times had they had this conversation? Too many. Nicole shook her head and grabbed the backpack again. "No, I don't, Mom. I don't need anyone to take care of me, not when I'm more than capable of taking care of myself."

"Nicole Lynn Taylor, every woman needs a man."

God, she couldn't do this again. If she had to sit here and listen to this, she'd end up saying something she'd regret. She shook her head and stood up. "Mom—"

"What about Donnie? Have you thought of getting back with him?"

"What?" Her brain was going to explode. That had to be the only explanation for the sudden terrible pounding in her head. How could her mom even say such a thing? "No! No, Mom. Never. I should have never gotten with him in the first place."

"But he's a nice man—"

"Nice? Nice?" The words were barely audible, lost in the shriek of her voice. "No, Mom, he's not nice. He was never nice. Or don't you remember all the times he smacked me around? All the bruises and marks he left?"

"Not all the time. Only when you—"

"No!" Nicole screamed the word, anger spilling through her, causing her hands to shake, her whole body to shake. How many times had she said the same thing? Tried to convince herself that things would get better if she did this or if she did that? Too many. She'd fought, long and hard, to escape the relationship. Fought long and hard to believe in herself, to understand that none of it was her fault, had never been her fault.

"No," she repeated, as much for her mother as a reminder to herself. "I'm not discussing this again, Mom. Okay? So just drop it."

"He's changed, Nikki. And I know he still cares about you, wants to see you again."

The words froze Nicole mid-step. Ice filled her, the dread and fear weighing her down until she thought she'd collapse. She couldn't have heard right, must have misunderstood. She closed her eyes, her hand wrapping around the pendant once more, and took deep breaths. Long, deep, cleansing breaths.

Please, let her have heard wrong.

"Mom, why do you think that?"

"He told me. He stopped by the other day—"

"No. No, no, no. Mom, why did you talk to him? Please, Mom, don't ever talk to him again. Don't even open the door. Please. If you love me at all, please—"

"You're overreacting, Nikki. As usual. Donnie just wanted to see you. He misses you."

Nicole faced her mother, not even bothering to hide the sheen of tears she couldn't blink away. How could her mother do that? How, when she knew what Donnie had done to her? When she had seen the marks and heard the screams? How?

Betrayal slice through her, as acidic and sour as the bile building in her stomach. Nicole shook her head. In denial or disbelief, she didn't know. She didn't know anything except that she needed to leave, needed to get out of the house. Now. Before she went crazy, before the pieces of her that she had struggled for so long to put back together shattered because of her mother's interference. Because of her mother's betrayal.

She shook her head again and brushed at her eyes,

not understanding why her mother would do that, would say that. Not understanding the look of confusion on her mother's tired and worn face, like Nicole was the one to blame.

She didn't understand any of it.

Nicole tossed the backpack over her shoulder and fled from the room, her hand barely skimming the railing as she took the steps two at a time. She needed to get out of here, needed to escape.

Needed to settle the disjointed thoughts tearing through her mind long enough to figure out what she should do now.

She threw open the door, barely hearing the creak of wood as she slammed it behind her. Bright sun greeted her, bouncing off the cracked concrete to blind her. She reached for her sunglasses then realized they were still upstairs, in her dim lifeless room.

They could stay there. She couldn't go back inside, not now. She turned left and headed to the next block, squinting against the bright light. She didn't know where she was going, didn't care. She just needed to go, to get away, to escape.

Needed to figure out what to do next.

Chapter Nine

If Mat could breathe, he'd kill Derek. That wasn't an option right now, not with his muscles stretching, not with his lungs burning. He tightened his jaw, his breath hissing between clenched teeth as he raised the bar, groaning as he lifted the weight from his chest. Derek stood above him, a scowl on his face as he spotted Mat.

"I just don't understand what you see in her. She's not your type."

Mat grunted and lowered the bar, raised it once more and blinked against the sweat dripping into his eyes and down the sides of his face. His arms shook, burning even more as he pushed himself. Two more reps. Down, up. Slow, deliberate.

"And why are you even asking her out? I mean, you already slept with her—"

The noise that came from Mat was louder than a grunt, ferocious and impatient, startling them both. He dropped the weights into the rack with a slam then sat up and swung his legs over the side of the bench.

Derek jumped back, his hands held up in either surrender—or protection.

"You're really going to say shit like that? After what happened with you and Bridget?"

"Keep your voice down." Derek glanced over his shoulder, eyeing the growing crowd coming in for their lunch time workout. Or maybe was checking to see where Kenny and Harland were, making sure they weren't within earshot. It wouldn't matter even if they were, not with the classic rock music that constantly blared from the speakers, not with the noise of clattering weights and loud conversation that surrounded them.

Derek shook his head and turned back to Mat. "That's not the same—"

"Bullshit." Mat grabbed the towel and swiped it across his face then fisted it in his hands. He kept his gaze on Derek, frowning. Maybe a little too hard, a little too dangerous, because Derek actually took another step back. "It's exactly the same and you know it."

"No, Mat, it's not. Bridget isn't a damn stripper!"

"Neither is Nicole. She works the bar."

Derek laughed, the sound short and sarcastic. "Yeah, okay. She works in a fucking strip joint. Are you really so naïve that you don't think she's dancing?"

Mat tightened his fist around the towel and shook his head. He'd thought the same thing at first, had been completely surprised when he realized where she worked. But the guy who paid her at the end of the night, her boss, had made the comment that Nicole could make so much more money if she decided to dance, but she wouldn't do it. Mat still didn't know why the guy told him that. Making conversation? Or for some other unknown reason? He had no idea. Mat hadn't said anything but he got the impression—just from the guy's one-sided conversation—that Nicole needed the money.

He moved from the weight bench, turning his back to Derek. "She's not a dancer. She serves drinks."

"Yeah, you keep on believing that." Derek moved closer, stepping around Mat until they were facing each other. "I don't get it, Mat. Why are you so hung up on this girl? You've been obsessing about her for more than a month. You already slept with her. And from what I understand, she left without saying goodbye. That doesn't sound like she's interested if you ask me. So why are you wasting your time?"

Mat stared at Derek for a long minute, his jaw clenched against the words that wanted to rush from him, words he knew better than to say. Because he'd had the same exact thoughts Derek was voicing, at least at first. If Nicole had been interested, at all, wouldn't she have at least left a note the morning she left in New Orleans? Her number? Something? It had been nothing more than sheer chance that he found her last week, and even he had to admit that she'd seemed surprised—hesitant and uncertain—the entire time he'd been with her. But she'd said yes when he asked her out. She wouldn't have said yes if she wasn't interested, right?

And then the other night happened. Holy fuck, had it ever happened.

He wasn't sure what he'd been expecting at first. Maybe just a chance to talk, to get her number, just like he'd told her. And then she blew up at him, throwing the money back in his face—along with accusations that still made him feel sick to his stomach. But then he explained, in a bumbling and embarrassing way, and she seemed happy with that. Well, maybe not happy, but she seemed to accept it. But she still wouldn't take the money he'd left the other night, giving it instead to one of the dancers when he refused to take it back.

He offered to take her home, not really expecting her to accept. Except when he pulled up in front of her place, she'd gotten this odd look on her face. Part horror, part resignation, part defeat. And when she asked him to keep driving, he had.

And then she'd blown his mind. Completely and utterly. He hadn't expected things to go that far. Would have never dreamed, not in his wildest fantasies, of things going that far. Okay, maybe in a few of his fantasies, but that was it. Seeing her touch herself, watching her lick his fingers, tasting herself…watching her go down on him while he fisted his hand in her hair, pumping his hips until his cock brushed against the back of her throat. Hearing her little moans as she sucked and swallowed while he came—

Fuck. He had to stop thinking about it, stop remembering it. Not here, of all places, not when it would it be so easy for anyone passing by to notice the way his cock was standing at attention, rock hard and ready to go. He fisted the towel in front of him and moved to the leg press, Derek following him.

"I like her, okay? What is so fucking wrong with that?"

"Because 'fucking' is the keyword with this whole thing. You're just hung up on the sex. And no, don't even give me that look. You're not one to sleep around, you never have been. And now some bad girl has caught your attention and you don't know which side is up."

"Nicole is not a 'bad girl' so shut the fuck up."

"Oh man, really? Dude, look at her, all tatted up and shit, working at a strip joint."

"Judgmental much? Just because she has tattoos—"

"Okay, so there's nothing wrong with her tats. I like tats, lots of people do. My point is that *you* don't do ink. How many times have you said you're not into tattoos? That you don't find them attractive?"

"I like Nicole's tattoos."

"Holy shit. Are you not even listening? She picked you up in a fucking bar!"

"Doesn't matter. I like her and I want to see her again. And I am. Tomorrow. I asked if you guys wanted to join us because I figured she might be more relaxed if the four of us went together, since she knows Bridget. Stupid idea, so just forget I asked."

"Why are you getting so pissed?"

"You really have to ask me that? After everything you just said?"

"I just want to make sure you know what you're doing, that you're not making more out of this than it is."

"I'm not making anything out of it, you are. All I'm looking for is tomorrow. One date, that's it. You don't want to go, fine."

"I didn't say that. You want us to go, we'll go."

"With that attitude? Yeah, that'll definitely make her feel comfortable. No thanks." Mat turned his back on Derek, adding more weights for this round. This was supposed to be a light work-out, just something to keep them in rhythm during the off-season, until training camp started in six weeks. But Mat no longer wanted a light workout. He wanted to sweat, to burn, to push himself.

No, what he really wanted was to go ten rounds in a ring—preferably using Derek's face as a punching bag. Too bad he wasn't a boxer.

Mat adjusted his position on the bench, ready to start. But he didn't move, didn't tear into the reps. His mind was elsewhere, replaying Derek's words, replaying each tiny bit of conversation he'd had with Nicole—which really wasn't much. In fact, the only time she'd really talked at all, the only time she had initiated the conversation, had been when she talked about her photography. She had come alive then, her face lighting up, her expressions animated. It had been easy to see—no, to feel—her excitement.

The rest of the conversations, if he could even call them that, had been short. Maybe a little tense and uncomfortable, like she wasn't sure what to say. Like she wasn't sure how to act around him. Did it have something to do with their night in New Orleans? Maybe she was embarrassed. Or maybe she thought he was just looking for a repeat and nothing else. But if that was the case, what about the other night? Maybe he was reading too much into things, or listening too much to Derek.

And maybe he should just let it go. He could sit here all day and play the 'what-if' game, trying to read her mind after the fact. It wouldn't do him any good, though, not when each of his thoughts focused on something negative. Yeah, definitely not productive.

He lifted his legs and placed his feet against the plate, gripping the handles by his side and pushing out with a grunt. And fuck, maybe he overdid it with the weights because he had to push harder than he expected. Then he looked over and noticed Derek leaning against the weight plates, holding them down. A large shit-eating grin spread across his face before he started laughing.

"Man, Kenny was right. You really do have it bad for her."

"Shut the fuck up."

Derek stepped away from the weights, still chuckling as Mat started his reps. One. Two. Three. He groaned and pressed down, holding then releasing. Holding then releasing. The weights slammed together with a crash but Mat barely noticed, not with Derek standing next to him, laughing loud enough to drown out everything else around them.

"What the fuck is so funny?"

Derek drew a deep breath and wiped his hand across his eyes, shaking his head. "You. If you could see the look on your face—" He took another deep breath that turned into a snort. "You look like you're ready to bash someone's face in."

"Yeah. Yours, if you don't knock it off."

"Fine, I'll stop." He stepped back, his hands held up in surrender, a smile deepening his dimples. "I still say you're making a mistake."

"Dude, I swear—"

"Okay, okay. I'm done. I won't say anything else about it." Derek leaned against the machine next to Mat's, crossing his arms in front of him. "So what are we supposed to be doing on this big date tomorrow?"

Mat lowered his legs and reached for the towel, swiping it across his face before draping it around his neck. He glanced at Derek then looked away, shrugging. "I was thinking of going up to Oregon Ridge. They have those summer concerts with fireworks and everything. We could do a picnic dinner and—"

But Derek wasn't listening. Of course not. How could he be, when he was laughing again? Mat clenched his jaw so hard his back teeth ground together and stood up. "Why the fuck do I even bother? Just forget I said anything."

Derek grabbed his arm, his grip strong enough to keep Mat from flinging his hand away, which is what he wanted to do. Instead he just stood there, tense and stiff, giving Derek the dirtiest look he could—his dangerous game face. The scowl generally worked, at least on the ice, but Derek just ignored him.

"I'm sorry, really. And I'm not laughing at you. It's just—" Derek released his arm, that big grin still on his face. "Your girl just doesn't look like the type who would enjoy a picnic and fireworks in the country air, you know?"

Mat ignored the 'your girl' part, knowing Derek couldn't be further from the truth. No, he wouldn't mind calling Nicole his girl—despite the sexist sound of it—but wasn't sure she'd agree. It was too soon. And right now, he wasn't entirely sure she was even interested. At least, as interested as he was. So no, he couldn't get excited over that possibility, not yet. That didn't stop him from scowling at Derek.

"Why don't you think she'd be interested?"

"Seriously? Mat, she looks like she'd more comfortable at some kind of head-banging club or something."

"You just don't learn, do you?"

"What's that supposed to mean?"

"Judging people so quick. I really thought you would have learned better after being with Bridget but I guess not." Mat started to walk away. Derek grabbed his arm again and quickly stepped in front of him, his smile gone now.

"That's not fair—"

"Isn't it? That's exactly what you're doing, you know. You're just assuming shit when you don't know anything about Nicole."

"And neither do you, Mat. That's the point I've been trying to make ever since this conversation started. Think about it. This girl picked you up in a bar. In New Orleans. You had sex. She left, never to be seen again. I mean, really, what the hell do you know about her? Not a damn thing. I just want to make sure you know what the hell you're getting into before you jump in with both feet and start making wedding plans."

"Why the hell is everyone so fucking convinced I'm planning a wedding? You. Kenny. I'm tired of hearing it. A few dates. That's all I'm looking for. Hell, I don't even know her last name!"

Silence descended between them, oddly accusing in the midst of the noise and racket surrounding them. Derek stared at him, his brows raised in either shock or confirmation, Mat couldn't tell. He shook his head and looked away, running the palm of one hand down his face. "Fuck."

"Yeah. That's the point we're trying to make. You don't even know her last name. You don't know anything about her except that she works in a strip club. You can't build a relationship on that."

Mat shook his head, in denial at Derek's words, in denial of everything. He looked around, not really seeing the other people getting in their own workouts, the noise surrounding them just that: background noise. Empty, hollow. Devoid of all meaning or consequence. Just…there.

"I know that." He let out a deep breath then ran a hand over his face again. "I know. I'm not."

"You sure about that?"

"Yeah. I'm sure." He nodded, wishing he felt the conviction of his words. Was Derek right? Had Kenny been right? Was he already making more out of it than he should? Maybe Nicole really wasn't interested in anything but the sex. Maybe that was the only reason she'd said yes. Yet here he was, making these grand plans for a fun and relaxing date. Reading into things, making something out of nothing.

And Christ, wouldn't that just suck? The idea soured his stomach and left him feeling winded. Maybe he should call his sister and ask her opinion. Michele would be honest with him, give him a woman's perspective. But how humiliating would that be? Calling his younger sister and asking for relationship advice. Yeah, maybe he really had reached a new low point if he was considering doing that.

He looked back at Derek, wishing his friend would stop looking at him that way. Like he was a lost cause that needed saving. Derek finally smiled again, giving him the wide charming grin that showed off his dimples, and clapped him on the shoulder.

"Fine. We'll go with you. But just know that if I see something, I'm going to say something."

"Funny. Real funny." Mat tried to smile at his friend's attempt at humor but his smile fell flat. It didn't matter, he wasn't trying to impress Derek. And maybe it would help to have someone watching out for him.

Just in case Mat wasn't as objective as he liked to think he was.

Chapter Ten

"You are such a ham!" Nicole laughed then looked through the viewfinder of the camera. Click, click, click. Laughter, clear and innocent and infectious, filled the small room and she hoped the camera would capture it. No, not the camera. Her. She hoped *she* would capture it and do the little girl justice.

Mia jumped up and down, the thin mattress bouncing against the frame of the hospital bed. The tattered feather boa floated in the air around her pale face and Nicole aimed the camera again. Click. Click. Click. Hoping to capture the smile, the innocence, the undying hope.

"You two certainly are making a racket in here."

Nicole lowered the camera and glanced over her shoulder, then offered the nurse a small smile of apology. "Sorry. I guess we got carried away."

Mary waved her hand in dismissal. "No, don't worry. It's good to hear." She turned what Nicole was supposed to be a stern look at Mia. "But I think that's enough for now. Time for your medicine and a nap."

Mia dropped back to the mattress with a theatrical sigh and tugged at the boa. The silk scarf wrapped around her head slid to the side and she pushed it back in place with an impatient swipe of her small hand.

"That's no fun." But Nicole could see the pinched look to her eyes, the even paler color of her skin. Guilt swept through her at the sight. Had they overdone it? Had she made things worse for Mia?

"She'll be fine." Mary put a reassuring hand on Nicole's shoulder then moved to the bed, helping the little girl get settled more comfortably before handing her a small paper cup with two pills.

Nicole looked away, busying herself with capping the camera and stowing her gear in the backpack. A small choke followed by a cough whispered through the room and Nicole flinched. Swallowing medicine was so hard for Mia, so difficult. And Nicole hated watching her, seeing her struggle and trying to be so brave when it was so easy to see—to feel—her pain and discomfort.

Nicole squeezed her eyes shut for a moment, then mentally shook herself. What right did she have to be uncomfortable, when Mia fought so hard to be so brave? She could learn so much from the little girl in front of her. From all the kids on this floor.

"Are you coming back tomorrow? I want to see my pictures."

Nicole moved closer to the bed, the backpack held in one hand as she sat on the edge of the bed. She adjusted the covers, moving them higher so they fell around the girl's thin shoulders.

"No, sweetie. Not tomorrow. But the next day, I promise." She leaned closer and lowered her voice to a whisper, like she was ready to share a secret. "I have a date."

Maybe. Nicole still wasn't sure if she wanted to go. No, that was a lie. She did want to go—more than she wanted to admit. And that scared her.

But Mia's eyes lit up, the glassy surfaces suddenly filled with excitement instead of exhaustion. She pulled her arm from underneath the covers and reached out, her fingers tracing the colorful tattoos on Nicole's arm.

"Does he have pretty pictures on his arm, too?"

The question, asked with innocent awe, caught Nicole off guard and she laughed. A real laugh that made her feel warm and light inside. "No, sweetie. No pretty pictures." No, not a single tattoo in sight. Or out of sight. She had looked, that first night in New Orleans, expecting to find at least one. But Mat's skin was bare except for the few scars that she had seen. Scars that made him even more attractive in her eyes, a reaction she still didn't understand.

Mia dropped her arm to the side and sighed, but Nicole couldn't tell if it was because she was tired—or disappointed. A small grin teased the corners of the girl's mouth as she met Nicole's gaze.

"Is he your dragon?"

Nicole laughed again. It was her fault Mia suddenly had an obsession about dragons. Between the tattoos on her arm and the pendant hanging from her neck, Mia was convinced that dragons were the ultimate superheroes, able to conquer all before swooping in and carrying the princess away to freedom. Her smile faded, becoming just a little forced when she realized she had once thought the same thing. Wished for the same thing.

"No, Mat's not my dragon, sweetie." There were no such things as dragons, not in real life.

"Oh. Well, will you at least take pictures so I can see your boyfriend?"

Nicole opened her mouth, ready to tell the girl that Mat wasn't her boyfriend. But she snapped it closed at the last second. There was a longing expression of excitement and anticipation on Mia's young face and Nicole didn't want to be responsible for making it disappear. So she nodded, trying to smile at the same time, to let Mia think she was looking forward to the date with her 'boyfriend', instead of calling him and cancelling the entire thing.

"If he lets me, sweetie. No promises. How about some pictures of fireworks, though? Will that work?"

"Hm-hm." But Mia's eyes were drifting shut, her words nothing more than an affirmative hum. Nicole tucked the blanket more tightly around her shoulders then sat there, watching as sleep claimed the little girl, finally relaxing the pinched lines around her eyes and mouth.

Nicole sat there for another minute, just watching, wondering if the tightness in her chest would ease up before she left. It never did so she didn't know why she thought it would now. She swallowed against the sudden thickness in her throat then leaned forward and placed a gentle kiss against Mia's forehead.

She was surprised when she turned around and saw Mary still standing there. Surprised—and guilty, like she had been caught doing something she shouldn't have. She tossed the backpack over her shoulder and shifted her weight from one foot to the other, not quite able to meet the nurse's eyes.

"I'm sorry. I shouldn't have stayed so long—"

"Don't apologize. You're good for her. For all the kids."

Nicole didn't say anything, not sure if there was anything to say. But she couldn't help but wonder if Mary would be saying the same thing if she knew where else Nicole worked now, if she knew what kind of past Nicole had. She had seen the raised eyebrows and pointed glances at her tattoos and piercings when she first started coming here. She'd caught some of the whispers, hastily cut-off as she walked by. She knew she didn't look the part when she first started volunteering, not with her clothes and jet black hair and make-up and colorful tattoos on her arm.

The piercings were gone now—at least, not being used. She was back to her natural hair color—kind of, maybe—and her make-up was toned down now, but her tattoos would always remain. And maybe they were more acceptable now—she certainly wasn't the only person in the building with ink—but she still wondered if people were whispering about her, still wondered if people were judging her, even more than a year later.

Nicole readjusted the pack on her shoulder, her hand automatically tightening around the strap. She glanced over her shoulder for one last look at Mia then turned back to Mary. "I should be going."

Mary nodded then stepped to the side so Nicole could pass. "I'll be looking forward to those pictures as much as Mia on Sunday."

"Oh. Uh, yeah, sure." Nicole moved past her and stepped into the hall, not sure why Mary had said that. Was she just being nice? Making conversation? Certainly she wasn't really interested. Why would she be?

And why couldn't Nicole just accept the words at face value? Why did she have to read into everything? Question everything and look for some hidden meaning or ulterior motive.

Dammit. Would she ever break that habit? Ever get over the distrust and wariness she had been conditioned to accept as normal? It had been more than two years, she should be over it by now.

She thought she had been until yesterday, when her mother had come into her room and shifted everything out of balance. Shifted? No, it was more like ripped the rug right out from underneath her, shattering her new existence and threatening to send her back into a hellish nightmare.

Nicole pushed through the open doors and blinked against the bright sun reflecting back at her from the sidewalk, pausing long enough to dig her sunglasses from the front pocket of her backpack. Head down, she focused on moving, her steps brisk and certain as she headed toward the bus stop. Even if the buses were running late—which they usually were—she would still be at work early today. Maybe Tony would let her start her shift early. And if not, she could go into the back and look through the pictures on her camera, start thinking about how she'd arrange and enhance and play with them. It didn't matter that she'd probably do something completely different once she loaded them into the computer program. Just the act of thinking about what to do with them soothed her, like some kind of meditation or therapy.

And it would keep her from thinking about tomorrow, keep her from worrying and wondering what to do. Part of her thought it would be better if she cancelled, or if she just didn't show up.

Except Mat was picking her up at her mother's and the last thing Nicole wanted was for her mom to meet him. Not after yesterday, not after all the things her mother had said, not when her betrayal still stung. The idea of her mom cornering Mat, of interrogating him and maybe saying the wrong thing—saying too much—filled her with dread. And she knew that was exactly what would happen, especially after yesterday, after her mom had brought up Donnie, had told her she needed a man to take care of her.

"No, Mom. I don't need a man to take care of me." She muttered the words between clenched teeth, anger and shame filling her at the memory of the conversation. Isn't that what caused Nicole's problems in the first place? Isn't that what caused all of her mom's problems, even now? Always relying on someone else. Trusting and depending on someone else. Falling into the trap of thinking she couldn't do it on her own, that she was defined by the man she was with.

No. Never again. Maybe her mother would always think that way, would never find a way out of that trap, but not Nicole. She'd learned her lesson—the hard way. Never again.

"Never. Never. Never." Nicole kicked at a piece of discarded brick in the middle of the sidewalk then winced when it hit her toe. It was exactly what she deserved for not paying attention, for acting before thinking. She needed to stop that, needed—

"I guess you're finally losing it."

The voice stopped her cold and she took a step back. Her heart pounded in her chest and she forced herself to take a deep breath, to breathe normally and not react. But that wasn't possible, not when her eyes met those of the man standing so close to the curb, leaning against the beat-up car parked there. How had she not seen him? Not noticed him standing there, waiting?

His pale eyes drifted down her body then back up. Slow, appreciative, meaningful. Menacing. Nicole fisted her hands around the strap of her backpack, wishing it was an iron shield instead of nothing more than a bag made of worn nylon. She took another step back then cursed herself, her fear, her reaction.

Donnie laughed, the sound harsh and cold. He straightened and stepped away from the old car, coming closer. Nicole took another step back, her body on high alert, ready to turn and run. But Donnie stopped, a flat smile splitting his narrow face, his eyes never leaving her. Like he was waiting for her to do something, anticipating her running away. Would he chase her? Or would he just taunt her? Play with her like a predator played with its prey?

Would anyone notice? Would anyone try to help her? She looked around, quickly studying the few people moving along the sidewalk. Nobody paid attention to them, nobody looked their way. Would they keep walking if she screamed? Or would someone stop and help?

No, they wouldn't. Not here, not now. In an hour or so, when traffic got heavier, when there were more people around—maybe then. Maybe. But not now.

Nicole swallowed back her apprehension, hoping her fear and worry didn't show on her face. No weakness. If Donnie saw weakness, he'd be all over it. She lifted her chin and stared at him, her eyes narrowed behind her dark glasses. Could he see them? Did it matter?

He laughed again and stepped onto the curb, coming one step closer. He ran one hand through his shaggy blond hair, pushing it off his forehead. She could see the grease stains on his hands, the dirt and grime under his sharp, ragged nails. A few years ago she had convinced herself that was a good sign, that a man who worked with his hands would be strong, caring. That a man who worked with his hands would never shy away from work.

She had been so naïve to think that, at least when it came to Donnie. The last few years had been educational, but an education that came with a high price. And she knew now that there was a difference between men who worked with their hands—hardworking men—and men who simply pretended. Men who used their hands for something besides work.

Men like Donnie, who only pretended to work, who did just enough to get by and sometimes not even that much. Men whose hands were more comfortable folded around a cold can of cheap beer instead of a wrench or tool. Men whose hands were quick to lash out, to punish simply because there was nothing else to do.

Maybe Nicole hadn't exactly been innocent and naïve all those years ago, when she first thought herself in love with the tough rebellious young man. But she'd grown up since then, had learned so much—at a cost to herself that could never be repaid.

She stood a little straighter, her eyes still narrowed on the man in front of her. It hadn't taken him long to lose the appeal she had first noticed, to lose the charm that had reeled her in so quickly and completely. For her to learn that he wasn't a way out of the trap that still held her mother firmly in its grip. Looking at him now, she didn't understand what she had ever seen in him.

He wasn't tall, maybe only an inch or two taller than she was, and his clothes still hung on his lean frame. Too loose, too worn and baggy. The stained jeans fell below his hips, the frayed waistband low enough that she could see the worn elastic waistband of his washed-out boxers. The sleeves of his dark blue t-shirt were rolled up, exposing the blurred lines of a cheap tattoo that ran across the pale skin of his upper arm. That same tattoo continued up the side of his neck, disappearing into the shaggy length of blonde hair that fell around his face. The shirt was ripped near the hem, like it had been caught in something, and a yellowish stain smeared the front of the shirt, just in the middle of his chest.

If she was seeing him now for the first time, her instincts would warn her to move away from him, to hurry her steps and not look at him, not call attention to herself. But she did know him, knew what lurked behind those dark eyes, and her instincts were screaming even louder for her to move away.

She tightened her hand around the strap once more and glanced to the right. The bus stop was just up the street, less than fifty feet away. But there was no sign of the bus. Not yet. Nicole clenched her jaw and turned back to Donnie.

"What do you want?"

"I want to talk to you."

"There's nothing to say, you know that."

"No, Nikki, I don't." He took a step closer and reached out with his hand. Nicole stepped back, so quickly she nearly twisted her ankle in the heeled sandals. Donnie dropped his hand and shoved it into his front pocket, but not before she saw it curl into a fist.

"I changed my mind. I don't want the divorce."

No! Her mind screamed the denial as an icy cold blast of fear and anxiety shot through her, paralyzing her lungs. No, he couldn't be saying that. Why? Why would he say that?

Agonizing seconds dragged by as she tried to remember to breathe. She sucked in a deep breath, a hissing sound that echoed in her ears. Another second, then another, as the world righted and reality finally sunk in.

It didn't matter what he wanted. It was too late. It had been too late months ago.

"It doesn't matter, Donnie. You signed the papers. The divorce was finalized two months ago."

"I don't care. I changed my mind." He moved again, one foot slightly raised like he was going to step closer. Nicole stiffened but didn't step back. Not now, not anymore. She lifted her chin higher and shook her head.

"No, Donnie. It's over. Leave me alone." She turned, wanting nothing more than to leave, to never see him again. Seeing him last week, seeing him just now, was more than she wanted—more than she had expected. It was over. It had been over before it even started.

The rumble of a diesel engine echoed behind her and she glanced over her shoulder, expecting to see the bus, thankful that it was actually on time today. Movement caught her eye just as Donnie's hand wrapped around her left arm. His grip was tight, biting into the soft flesh of her upper arm, squeezing. She gasped and tried to step away but he pulled her closer, causing her to stumble. Anger colored his face a blotchy red and his mouth curled in a snarl.

"Don't walk away from me, bitch."

"Let me go!" And God, how she hated her voice, hated the quivering pleading, the weak demand that caused him to laugh. His fingers tightened even more when she tried to pull her arm from his grasp and she winced.

"It's not over, Nikki. It'll never be over. You're mine. You hear me?"

"No, Donnie. I'm not." She gritted her teeth against the pain, tasted iron as she bit her tongue when he shook her. No, not again. This couldn't be happening again. He didn't have power over her, didn't control her anymore. She'd earned her freedom, thought she'd never have to go through this again.

"Hey! What are you doing?"

The shout was too far away but still enough of a distraction. Donnie's painful grip loosened and Nicole ripped her arm from his hand. Her flesh burned, a new pain different from the bruising grip but she didn't care. Too late, she brought her knee up and jammed it into his groin. The breath left him in a pained groan and he doubled over but Nicole didn't trust him to stay that way for long. She ran toward the bus, her steps unsteady in the heeled sandals.

An older man, his dark weathered face creased with concern, stood next to the bus, his hand outstretched. Nicole grabbed it and stepped past him, her gaze focused only on the steps in front of her as she climbed onto the bus.

"Are you okay?"

"Uh, yeah. Yeah, I'm fine." She released his hand then looked behind her, expecting to see Donnie chasing after her. But there was only the old man, his dark rheumy eyes full of concern as he watched her.

"I'm fine," she repeated. She took a deep breath and tried to smile, tried to act like she wasn't shaking, like she wasn't terrified. "Thank you."

The man muttered something, his voice lost in the rumbling of the engine. He looked toward the back of the bus once more and said something else, then shook his head and climbed onto the bus. Nicole turned away, her eyes lowered, and found a seat away from the handful of other people onboard. She dropped into it then leaned her head against the window, heedless of the smeared fingerprints and grime that coated the glass.

Deep breaths. Over and over. Again. But oh God, they weren't working. She was still shaking, adrenaline and fear whirling together in her stomach until she thought she might be sick. But she couldn't be sick. Not here, not now.

A few more deep breaths. In and out. Slow, steady.

Oh God, why was Donnie suddenly back? It didn't make sense. She hadn't seen him in over a year, why now? Money. He must need money. That had to be it. Had to be why he'd shown up at her mother's place with his story and lying charm. Why else would he suddenly track her down?

Nicole opened her eyes and stared out the window without seeing anything. She was still shaking, even with her hands clasped tightly together. The sudden urge to laugh seized her, an insane urge she had to fight off. It wasn't a laugh of amusement but one of desperation. And recrimination.

She was a hypocrite. She didn't need a man? Yeah. She could tell herself that all she wanted, but it was nothing but a lie.

Because when Donnie had grabbed her, when his fingers were digging into her flesh and the man called out, she had thought, hoped—for one fleeting second—that it had been Mat. That Mat had shown up again, that Mat would save her, just like he had the other day without knowing it.

The realization scared her, almost as much as the encounter with Donnie. If she was so convinced she didn't need a man to take care of her, why had she been hoping it had been Mat who was there, offering to help her?

And why was she suddenly afraid that made her more like her mom than she wanted to admit?

Chapter Eleven

Mat led the way through the growing crowd, his hand resting lightly in the middle of Nicole's back. Tension rolled from her, in the way she held herself so stiffly, in the way she quickened her steps. It was almost as if she wanted to get away from him, as if she didn't want him to touch her. Maybe she didn't, maybe she just didn't know how to tell him. Which was just wrong. No woman should be afraid to tell a man to leave her alone, to not touch her.

Mat swallowed back a sigh and dropped his hand then readjusted the pile in his arms. An oversized duffle bag holding two thick blankets and sunscreen and some towels, a small cooler bag with drinks and snacks, Nicole's backpack, two sweatshirts for later in case it got chilly. Although as hot it was already, with the humidity settling around them like a heavy weight, he didn't think that would happen.

Nicole stopped and glanced over her shoulder, her eyes hidden behind those large sunglasses she always wore. Her shoulders were still stiff, her jaw clenched just the tiniest bit.

"You should let me help carry something."

"No, I got it." He flashed her a smile, hoping it would put her at ease. She pulled on her lower lip, the action sending a wave of heated awareness straight through him. What the fuck was wrong with him? Nicole was tense and worried about something, it didn't take a genius to figure that out, but his dick apparently didn't care. Well, his dick would just have to wait.

Nicole stopped chewing on her lower lip then turned away, her steps slowing until he caught up. She'd been this way ever since he picked her up an hour ago: tense, a little nervous, not very talkative. At first he thought it was nothing more than normal first-date nerves. Hell, he had his own share of them himself, because this really was their first date. Never mind that they'd already slept together, already had sex, that didn't count. Not as a date, anyway. Not to him.

So yeah, he'd chalked it up to nerves. At least at first. But it didn't take long to realize there was something else going on, something else worrying her.

"Have you ever been to one of these summer concerts?"

Nicole shook her head then reached up and tucked a loose strand of hair behind her ear. "No. I've never really been out this far."

This far? She made it sound like they had been driving forever, to a different state or even country. But Oregon Ridge Park wasn't even quite an hour from where she lived in the city, just off I-83. It was situated in northern Baltimore County, a nature park of rolling hills and scenic woodsy landscape. The park hosted concerts during the summer, complete with a symphony orchestra and fireworks. It was a great place to come and just hang out, relax with friends or family, enjoy the outdoors and music and fireworks.

It was the last weekend of July, a bright gorgeous day filled with sunshine, which meant that the crowds would probably be a little bigger and get here even earlier—which is why Mat had picked Nicole up so early. He wanted to find a decent parking space and a good place to drop their things. Some place close enough without being in the middle of everything. Looking around at all the cars and people, he wasn't sure that was going to happen.

"Well, hopefully you have fun." And God, what a stupid thing to say. He should just keep his mouth shut until his mind actually caught up. From the look Nicole gave him, just a quick expressionless glance over her shoulder, she probably thought the same thing. Yeah, he was certainly impressing her.

He didn't say anything else, just caught up to her then took the lead as they climbed the steps to the lodge. Mat waited for her at the top of the steps, wondering how her feet weren't killing her in those heeled platform sandals. They had some kind of leather strapping that wound up her calf, bringing to mind ancient women warriors. And shit, he really needed to stop thinking like that or else he'd never survive this date.

He gave her a small smile when she reached his side then led the way through the building and out the back. Just as he thought: the hillside was already getting crowded. He reached behind him and grabbed Nicole's hand without thinking, wanting to keep her close as they walked through the throng of people milling around. Her hand was ice cold, a little clammy, and he didn't miss the sudden tensing of her fingers. He dropped her hand and turned to look at her.

"Are you okay?"

"Yeah, fine."

"Are you sure? Your hand is ice cold." And she was wearing a light jacket, made out of some kind of thin material with a high waistline. Mat wasn't sure how useful it would be if it was really cold but it had long sleeves, which struck him as odd. Was she getting sick?

Nicole shrugged, not quite facing him, then finally nodded. "I'm fine. Really."

Mat wasn't sure he believed her but he wasn't going to push. He hesitated, then reached for her hand again. And again her fingers tensed in his hold, but only for a few seconds. She looked up at him, studying him from behind those large sunglasses, and finally relaxed, at least a little bit.

He offered her a smile then headed into the crowd, weaving through the groups of people. There was a prime spot—or what he thought was prime, anyway—about a hundred feet to their right, just a little way up the hill. It was close enough so they wouldn't have to hike too far to reach the restrooms or to grab food and drinks from the different vending trucks if they wanted. And it was far enough away and off to the side so they wouldn't be crowded in later. At least, he hoped not.

Mat dropped the load in his arms then bent over and opened the duffel, pulling the blankets out. He unfolded the first one and shook it out, mumbling when it flew back in his face. Laughter floated to his ears, the sound light and musical and over too quickly.

"Here, let me." Nicole tugged the blanket from his hands and spread it out with one efficient toss. She

149

leaned over to straighten a corner. Mat's eyes automatically drifted down, taking in the firm curve of her shapely bottom and tanned length of her toned legs. The hem of her gauzy black skirt drifted up, dangerously high against the back of her thighs, and he nearly groaned.

Then he looked away, his face heating at the thought of being caught staring. That was the last thing he wanted, because he didn't want Nicole to think he was ogling her. Okay, so he was ogling her. How could he not, with the way she looked?

It wasn't just the black gauzy skirt that drifted high on her thighs and swung and bounced just a little when she walked. Or the high-cut fitted jacket she wore over the snug patterned shirt. The shirt was cut just low enough to give him an enticing peak at the swell of her breasts, at the crystal pendant hanging just above the expanse of her cleavage.

And it wasn't even the matching warrior sandals, although he really, really liked those. It was all of her. The entire package, from her clothes to the careless way she pinned her hair back, those colorful pink streaks peeking out. Even her oversized sunglasses, which actually annoyed him because they hid her eyes and he couldn't tell what she was thinking.

It was so much more than the way she looked and he didn't quite understand it. All he knew was that she had somehow gotten under his skin, beginning with that night in New Orleans. He wanted to get to know her better. He wanted to get to know her, period.

So no, he couldn't get caught ogling, no matter how much he enjoyed watching her.

"You should laugh more often."

Nicole whipped her head around, her mouth

slightly opened in surprise. And damn, why did he have to go and put his foot in his mouth again? He'd meant it as a compliment but it probably came out the wrong way, if the expression on her face meant anything. He shrugged and gave her a small grin, hoping that would help. "I just meant you have a pretty laugh. That was all."

"Oh. Uh, thanks." But she turned away, like she wasn't sure what else to say. Or maybe the compliment just made her uncomfortable. And when would he learn to just keep his mouth shut?

Mat leaned over and pulled the second blanket out, wondering if he'd make an ass of himself again trying to spread this one out.

"We need two blankets?"

"Yeah. One for us, and one for Derek and Bridget. In case they don't think to bring one." He shook the blanket out and managed to spread it on the ground. Well, mostly. Nicole reached out with her foot and straightened the edge.

"I didn't know anyone else was joining us."

And shit. Had he screwed up again? Mat couldn't quite meet her eyes when he nodded. "Yeah. I'm sorry. I should have told you. Is that okay? I could call Derek and—"

"No, that's fine."

But she didn't look like it was fine. Yeah, he screwed up again. Mat glanced at his watch, wondering if it would be too late to call Derek, to tell him not to show up. He reached for his phone, pulling it from the back pocket of his shorts. Nicole stepped closer and placed her hand on his arm, stopping him.

"Really, it's okay. I don't mind."

"Are you sure?"

She nodded and gave him a smile, but it didn't look like a real one, like the ones that had lit her face the last two times they had been together. Mat hesitated then jammed the phone back into his pocket, suddenly at a loss and wondering what he should do.

He moved over to the blanket and lowered himself onto it, stretching out and leaning back on his hands. He tilted his head, motioning for Nicole to join him. She didn't hesitate, which he took as a good sign. But she also didn't stretch out next to him, like he'd been hoping. There was too much space between them, space he wished wasn't there. He inched over the tiniest bit, watching as she pulled a camera from her bag. Not a small handheld one, not one of those cheaper digital models. This one looked like a professional camera, with a zoom lens and everything. At least, as far as he could tell.

"Taking pictures later?"

Nicole looked up from doing something to the settings and nodded, a small smile lifting the corners of her mouth. "Yeah. I told Mia I'd bring her in pictures of the fireworks so she could see them."

"Cool. Is Mia your sister or something?"

A shadow passed across his face, there and gone as she shook her head. "Nope. I'm an only child. Mia is one of the kids at the hospital. I couldn't bring her pictures in today because I was coming here so to make up for it, I told her I'd bring in some of the fireworks, too."

Mat shifted on the blanket, trying to swallow back the guilt building in his gut. "I'm sorry. I didn't know you had something else you were supposed to do. You could have told me—"

Nicole leaned forward, placing her hand against

his arm again. "No, I didn't mean it that way. Honest."

"Are you sure?"

"I'm sure. Really. Mia's just a little spitfire and not very patient. Here, I'll show you." She scooted closer to him, her leg brushing his as she brought the camera up between them so he could see the view screen. Mat tilted his head to get a better look without the glare and almost hit Nicole on the cheek. Heat filled his face and he turned his head to apologize, but she just shook her head and laughed. The sound was soft, only audible because he was so close. He froze, watching her, wondering if she knew what just her laugh was doing to him.

But she wasn't even looking at him. Her eyes were focused on the small screen as she hit the button to scroll through the pictures. Mat wanted to lean forward, wanted to graze her cheek with his lips, with the lightest of kisses—

"Here she is."

He bit back his groan and moved his gaze to the small viewing screen. The pictures were of a young girl, maybe nine or ten years old, frozen for a split-second in time. A large smile lit her thin pale face and shone in her eyes. A feather boa floated around her face, the bright pink even brighter against the dark purple of the scarf tied around her head. One picture caught her mid-air, the boa drifting down around her as she flung her arms out to the side. Mat could see the smile in her eyes, could almost hear the laughter as she hung there, weightless, her small frame hovering above the harsh metal frame of a hospital bed. The pictures shouldn't be anything more than candid shots, but they were. So much more. He wasn't sure how she did it but Nicole had captured the life, the inner essence, of the young girl. No, they were definitely more than just candid shots.

His chest tightened, became heavy as Nicole flipped through the pictures one by one. He blinked, blinked again as his throat thickened with unnamed emotion. "You—" He cleared his throat and tried again. "These are really good. I can almost hear her laughing."

Nicole shrugged then turned the camera off and placed it beside her. "They're okay. They'll look better once I enhance them, do some photo shopping. Different backgrounds, things like that."

Why would she want to change them? As far as Mat could tell, they were perfect. The way she framed the little girl, the way she captured that inner spark and flash of determination inside her. "But they're good now, just the way they are. Really. I mean, I don't know anything about photography but they're really good."

Nicole turned to him, her mouth parted in surprise. Her face softened and before he realized what she was going to do, she leaned forward and brushed her lips against his. The kiss was soft, tender—and she pulled away before he could even think about reacting. "Thank you. That means a lot."

"Oh. Yeah, no problem." He shifted on the blanket and cleared his throat, feeling like an eager teenager. "I meant it, though. Really."

The corners of her mouth tilted up as she watched him. "I believe you. But Mia wants to be a princess, so I'm going to make her a princess."

"That's what you do? I mean, besides taking the pictures."

"Yeah. It's not much, but it makes the kids happy. And it's something I enjoy doing so..." Her voice drifted off and she shrugged, like what she was doing was no big deal.

"So you're going to make Mia a princess and give her fireworks at the same time. That's pretty cool."

Nicole laughed and ducked her head. Was it his imagination, or was the lightest blush fanning across her cheeks? She looked over at him and he felt her eyes on him. A few seconds went by then she reached up and pushed her sunglasses up, anchoring them in her hair. Light sparkled in her eyes, something more than just the reflection of the sun.

"She also wanted pictures of you but I told her no."

"Me?" Mat sat back, surprised. "Why would she want pictures of me?"

Nicole looked away. And this time, there was no doubt she was blushing. "Oh. Uh, nothing. It was silly. She, uh, just thought you were my boyfriend and wanted pictures. I, uh, I told her you weren't—"

"I could be." And Christ, now he sounded like he was fucking twelve years old. He looked away, cringing at the words, and ran a hand over his heated face. Was there no end to the sheer stupidity that would fall from his mouth?

It didn't help that Nicole wasn't saying anything. Yeah, she probably thought he was a moron. Should he apologize? It would probably be better if he just pretended he never said it. Even better if he changed the subject.

"You can take it if you want."

"What?"

Mat glanced over at Nicole then looked back at his hands, studying them, wondering what to do with them. Wondering if he should just shut the hell up again. "My picture. You can take it if you want, I don't mind."

"Oh. That..." Her voice drifted off again, like she wasn't sure what to say. Of course she wasn't. Hell, even he didn't know what to say, not anymore.

"Maybe you could make me a prince, since Mia's the princess." And maybe, just once, he'd learn to keep his big mouth shut. For not knowing what to say, his mouth was certainly having a field day with the verbal diarrhea. He shook his head, thinking he should apologize—again—when Nicole shook her head, her brows lowering in a frown.

"No. A dragon is much better than a prince."

Mat thought about sticking his finger in his ear and cleaning it out, knowing there was no way he could have heard her right. A dragon? But now it was Nicole who was looking away, her face turning a cute shade of pink. "A dragon?"

"Uh, yeah." She bit down on her lower lip then faced him, still frowning. Her expression finally cleared and a small smile teased her mouth. "Sorry. It's your eyes. A dragon was the first thing that came to mind when I first saw you. I mean, your eyes. They're such a gorgeous shade of deep green."

She'd said something very similar to him, back in New Orleans. In fact, those were the first words she had said to him. Did she remember? Maybe, if the look in her eyes meant anything.

"A dragon, hm? Don't they usually get killed by the knights or princes or whatever?"

"Oh, only the bad ones. You're a good dragon." Nicole's eyes widened and she lowered her head, bringing both hands up to cover her face. "Oh my God, I did not just say that."

Mat laughed. A real one this time, one that lifted some of the doubt and tension he'd been feeling. "I'm glad I'm not the only one who does that."

Nicole lowered her hands, just enough so she was peaking at him through her fingers. Her amber eyes glowed in the sun, warming him from the inside out. "Does what?"

"Say things that don't always come out the right way."

"Oh." She lowered her hands to her lap, her left one brushing the skin of his thigh. "No, I guess not. Um, for what it's worth, that was a good thing."

"What was?"

"The, uh, good dragon part. Good dragons are better than superheroes." She ducked her head, no longer watching him. Mat smiled then leaned forward, capturing her chin with his hand to tilt her head back. Her eyes flared then darkened, filling with awareness as he lowered his mouth to hers. He caught her small gasp, felt her lean toward him as he swept his tongue inside. God, she tasted so sweet. Sweet and spicy, like hot cinnamon mixed with honey. He could get drunk on her kisses.

She leaned even closer and wrapped one hand around his neck, her touch warm, her body soft. Mat deepened the kiss, losing himself in her taste, her touch. He shifted, just the tiniest bit, to get even closer. He brought his hand up, dragging it along her arm, thinking to pull her even closer, maybe shift to the side and pull her down on top of him. But she flinched and pulled away, a hiss of pain escaping her. Mat sat back, his brows lowered in concern.

"I'm sorry. I didn't mean—did I hurt you?" He wasn't sure how he could have but maybe he grabbed her too hard without meaning to, without realizing it. Maybe he—

"No. No, I'm fine. It wasn't you." But she wouldn't look at him as she rubbed the side of her arm where he'd grabbed her.

"Nicole, are you sure? Let me look—"

"No, I'm fine. Really." She slid away, putting some distance between them. Mat frowned, not sure if he should push the issue or not.

"I'm sorry. I didn't mean—"

"Really, it wasn't you. I, uh, I just hurt my arm. At work. That's all." But she was looking away from him, not meeting his eyes, and he wondered if she was telling the truth—wondered why she would lie.

He shifted, leaning a little closer, and placed his hand on her shoulder. If he could get her to look at him, if he could see her eyes, maybe he'd be able to tell what was going on. "Nicole—"

She stiffened, her body language speaking volumes. And maybe he wasn't that great at talking, at saying the right things, but he could certainly hear— both what she was saying, and what she wasn't. He dropped his hand and inched away, just enough so he wasn't encroaching on her personal space.

"So I take it you have a thing for dragons?" She turned her head, her eyes widening in surprise. He motioned toward her left arm. "Your tattoos. The dragons and fairies and everything. The one on your, uh, thigh, has dragons and a castle. I just figured you might have a thing for dragons."

Her hand came up and closed around the pendant hanging from her neck. Another dragon, this one wrapped around a milky-colored piece of glass. She must have noticed him watching because she let go of the pendant and folded her hand in her lap.

"Yeah, I guess." She smiled and laughed a little. "Okay, I do. Ever since I was a kid. I don't even remember how it started. I've just always liked them."

"Even if they're supposed to be bad?" He meant it as a joke, as a reference to her earlier comment. But a shadow crossed in front of her eyes, her expression turning sad for just a fleeting second as she looked away. And he felt it, a blast of despair that made him want to fold her in his arms and hold her, protect her, chase away the bad things until the sadness left her.

"No, it's not the dragons who are bad." Her voice was soft, barely above a whisper, and Mat somehow knew that she was lost in a memory or hope or dream. She shook herself and whatever had been there, whatever it was he thought he'd seen and felt, floated away on the small breeze that lifted the hair from her neck. She looked back at him, her eyes clear now, and laughed. "Dragons are just misunderstood, that's all."

"Misunderstood, huh?"

"Absolutely." She laughed again then shifted, moving closer. Mat hesitated then wrapped his arm around her waist, tugging her against him. Then he leaned down and pressed his lips against hers, soft and gentle, coaxing, afraid of pushing. She sighed, opening her mouth under his, her hand coming up to rest in the center of his chest, just above his heart.

Could she feel it? The steady pounding, beating faster with each passing second. Did she know that it was because of her? That she had the power to do this to him? To make him want, need, burn—

"Is this the best spot you could grab?"

Mat jumped back as something heavy landed beside him. He looked up, squinting as two shadows moved in front of him, finally coming into focus.

Leave it to Derek to interrupt at the worst possible time.

He pushed to his feet and leaned forward, pulling Bridget into a quick hug. Then he turned and frowned at Derek. "I thought you guys were coming later."

"We changed our minds." He pushed his sunglasses up to his forehead and glanced over Mat's shoulder, squinting. "Hey. Nicole, right? Nice seeing you again."

Mat was going to kill him. Did Derek have to be so forward and abrupt? Did he have to say 'again'? Mat wanted to believe it hadn't been a deliberate reminder of New Orleans but knowing Derek, anything was possible. He glanced over at Nicole, worrying that she might take it the wrong way, or take Derek the wrong way. Or both. She was looking up at them, a small smile on her face. Mat couldn't see her eyes because she had pulled her sunglasses back down but he got the feeling that the smile was forced. And he wondered if Nicole would relax again for the rest of the night or if those few moments were gone for good.

Yeah, he was really going to kill Derek.

Chapter Twelve

Magical.

That was the one word that kept going through Nicole's mind as she felt herself falling, spiraling. Down and down in a dizzying whirlwind that left her heart racing, that left her breathless.

Mat was magical. His whispered words. His soft touch. His kisses, sometimes gentle, sometimes demanding, always seeking, searching, reassuring.

How could she have been so wrong? Mat wasn't a dragon. He was a wizard. A sorcerer. Weaving his magic until she fell completely under his spell.

Nicole didn't want him to stop. She didn't want the night to end.

Mat pulled away, his breathing shallow and harsh as he rested his forehead against hers. Even this close, in the dark interior of his car, she could see light flaring in his eyes. Passion. Desire. Need. She wanted it all. She wanted to give him it all.

Her hand curled around his neck, her fingers teasing the dark strands of hair that brushed his collar.

Lisa B. Kamps

So soft, softer than she remembered. She wanted to rip his shirt off, to run her hands along his sculpted chest, to feel the springy curl of the hair on his chest under her palm. To follow that thin line of hair down his hard abs, lower to where it disappeared below the waistband of his shorts.

She wanted all of that and more. So much more. And she was pretty sure Mat wanted the same.

Just like she was pretty sure that he wouldn't ask, wouldn't push her. If she wanted it, she'd have to initiate it. At least, initiate it more. Because there was no doubt in her mind that the next move would have to be hers, that Mat was somehow waiting for her to decide how much further to go.

But he was leaving the decision up to her. All she had to do was tell him what she wanted, that she wanted more than just making out in the front seat of his sports car after one of the best days—the best nights—she'd ever had.

She had been hesitant at first, not sure what to expect on their date. Uncertain of herself, especially when she learned they wouldn't be alone. Tension had vibrated through her, leftover tension from her encounter with Donnie, tension from being so hesitant and unsure. But Mat had put her at ease. So had Derek and Bridget after they arrived. It didn't take her long to relax, to loosen up, to finally enjoy herself.

To experience something new and wonderful with people who were truly happy. With people who knew how to laugh and have fun, whether it was tossing a Frisbee back and forth or just sitting there, talking.

Just sitting there with Mat's arms wrapped around her from behind as she leaned against him, listening to music from a real symphony orchestra as fireworks danced overhead. She'd never experienced anything like that before.

And she didn't want it to end.

Mat reached up and gently cupped her face, the heat from his callused palm warming her. So gentle. Reassuring. He traced her bottom lip with his thumb and a thousand different sensations ripped through her, leaving her tingling and aching and hungry and feverish. Then he leaned forward and captured her mouth with his once more, sweeping his tongue inside. Slow, so slow. Nicole moaned, the tiny sound lost in their breathing, and she tried to get closer, to press her body against his, to lose herself in his touch.

But he pulled away again, much too soon, and exhaled. One corner of his mouth lifted in a small grin and he shifted in the leather seat. "I should probably get you inside."

She should say yes. She should let him walk her to the door and say goodnight. But that wasn't what she wanted. Not even close. She wanted him. Wanted another night like they had in New Orleans. Wanted to feel his body pressed against her, inside her, filling her.

God, she wanted that more than anything. To fall asleep in his arms, safe and secure. Protected. But she couldn't invite him in. Not to her mother's house—and not just because it was her mother's, not just because of what her mother had said, of what she might say.

She didn't want him to see where she lived. How she lived. The peeling paint and dented walls of aging plaster, the worn and tattered furnishings with their underlying odor of stale cigarette smoke. Her small room, hot and stifling, barely large enough for the single bed and make-shift desk.

No, she couldn't invite him in. *Wouldn't* invite him.

But maybe, just maybe, she could suggest he take her home—to his place.

"I—" All her doubts and insecurities bubbled to the surface and she snapped her mouth shut before anything else could come out. Maybe he didn't want to take her home. Maybe he just wanted the night to end. Maybe he—

"You what?"

"I—" She took a deep breath, willing the words to come. "I had fun tonight."

No, that wasn't what she wanted to say. Why couldn't she get the words out? Why couldn't she tell him what she wanted, like she had the other night? This wasn't like her, not really. Hesitant, uncertain, doubting herself. Questioning herself. She thought she'd gotten over that, had finally gotten rid of that last influence from her disastrous marriage, her disastrous past. Hadn't that been part of the reason for the trip to New Orleans? Not just to celebrate her new life, but to prove to herself that she had moved on. That her old self—her strong, self-assured self—was finally coming back.

But it wasn't. Not if she couldn't even get the words she wanted to speak to come out.

Mat was watching her, the corners of his eyes crinkling just the tiniest bit as he smiled. He leaned forward and kissed her forehead, the tip of her nose. "I had fun, too. But I should probably get you inside now."

He kissed her once more then shifted in the seat, his hand grabbing the door handle. It would only be another second, maybe two, before he opened the door. Before he got out and walked around to open hers.

Before their night would truly end.

"No!" The word came out so loud, so rushed, that even she jumped. Mat stopped, startled, then turned back to her. His brows were lowered in confusion, the same confusion that was reflected in his deep green eyes. Nicole took a deep breath to steady her nerves, searching for courage. She reached out and placed her hand on his arm, wishing her fingers weren't trembling quite so much.

"I—I don't want to go inside. Not yet." She licked her lips, saw Mat's gaze follow the swipe of her tongue. The muscles of his arm tightened, flexed for just a second, and that gave her hope.

She glanced over her shoulder, at the dark shadows of the buildings lining the street. Even at night, without the harsh glare of the sun, the buildings looked tired, worn. Like they had given up on life, the same way their occupants had given up.

Nicole didn't want that. She'd never wanted that. But that's what she was doing. If she couldn't find the courage to fight, couldn't find the courage to go for what she wanted, she'd be no different than everyone else.

No different than her mother.

She'd thought it had been enough, getting away from Donnie, breaking free from the toxic hold he had on her, but she'd only been fooling herself. The only thing she was doing was coasting along, waiting for life to happen to her, watching it unfold from a distance as life happened for everyone else. She could try to convince herself she was doing something about it but that would be nothing but a lie. Tonight had taught her that. Just a few hours in the sunshine, in the open air surrounded by sprawling countryside. A few hours surrounded by people who were genuinely nice. Who laughed and smiled and actually listened when someone spoke. People who enjoyed each other's company with no strings attached. People who talked to her, smiled at her, and expected nothing in return.

She turned back to Mat, not quite able to meet his eyes. What if she was making a mistake? What if he was only being nice and didn't really want her?

How would she ever know if she kept making excuses instead of taking chances?

"I want to invite you in but I can't. But I don't—" She swallowed, the sound a small gulp that seemed too loud to her own ears. "I don't want the night to end, though."

Mat stilled, his arm tensing under her hand again. Was it her imagination or did something flare in his eyes? He settled back in the seat and rested his hand on the steering wheel, like he wasn't sure what he should do with it. But he wasn't reaching for the door handle. Nicole hoped that was a good sign.

He looked away, his jaw clenching for a brief second, then looked back at her. His chest rose on a deep breath then fell, slowly, like he was forcing himself not to breathe too fast. When he spoke, the words were quiet, almost a whisper in a husky voice that sent shivers racing across her skin, pebbling it.

"Was there somewhere else you wanted to go?"

This was it, now or never. Nicole took a deep breath of her own and forced herself to meet his penetrating gaze. "We could go back to your place. If you want to."

Chapter Thirteen

If you want to.

The shy words still rang in Mat's head. Yeah, he wanted to. Christ, he wanted to more than he wanted to admit. He'd waited a few long minutes, just to be sure Nicole meant what he thought she meant, that she wouldn't change her mind. The searing kiss she'd given him removed any doubt he might have had left. As soon as she pulled away, he turned the engine on and sped away from the curb, breaking the speed limit in his rush to get her home.

Now he was standing in front of his door, trying to get the damn key in the lock. Nicole was right behind him, the scorching heat from her body bathing him, driving him crazy.

And shit. Was the place clean? Yeah. The cleaning service had just been in two days ago and it wasn't like he was a slob to begin with. Good, that meant he wouldn't have to worry—not about the condition of his house, anyway.

The key finally turned and Mat pushed the door

open, palming the light switch for the entranceway then standing aside so Nicole could enter. She offered him a small smile, almost shy, then looked around. Her eyes widened and she blinked but he didn't understand why. Maybe the light was too bright?

He closed the door and locked it, his gaze sliding around as he tried to see the house from her eyes. It wasn't sprawling, not like JP's cedar house on the water, but it was comfortable. Four bedrooms and two bathrooms up the stairs to their left, another full bathroom on the first level, just off the formal sitting room. And okay, maybe that was a bit overboard because he sure as hell didn't need a formal anything, but that's what the realtor had called it.

The living room opened up on their right, decorated in blues and greens and creams. Past that was the kitchen and dining room, an open air concept that ran along the entire back length of the house. French doors opened off the dining room onto the large deck leading to the pool and hot tub.

He glanced around again, making sure nothing was out of place, that everything was presentable. Yeah, just as he left it. So now what? They couldn't stand in the entranceway all night but Mat didn't want to go all caveman on her and carry her upstairs, either. He didn't think she'd appreciate that, not with the way her hands were tightening around the strap of the backpack held by her side.

"You live here by yourself?"

He tossed his keys onto the small table next to the door. "Uh, yeah. Would you like the grand tour? It'll only take about two minutes."

He'd meant the words as a joke but saw something flare in Nicole's eyes. A shadow of...something. He couldn't tell, only knew that whatever it was struck him as something sad. He thought to ask, wondered if maybe she was having second thoughts, but before he could say anything, Nicole was in his arms. Her body pressed tight against his, her mouth seeking his as her arms wound around his neck. The backpack was still in her hand and it hit him in the side but he didn't care. She could hit him with the thing all night as long as she didn't stop kissing him.

But it was more than a kiss. So much more. Mat tightened his arms around her, the palm of one hand curving around the firm flesh of her ass. He pulled her closer, pressed the hard length of his erection against her, and groaned.

Christ, he wanted her. He hadn't stopped wanting her, not since that night in New Orleans. He wanted her with a hunger that was ferocious, frightening, intense. He wanted her like he'd never wanted another woman before.

And fuck, if he didn't stop, if he didn't get control of himself, he'd take her right here. Just pull the hem of her skirt up, back her against the wall, and bury himself in her sweet heat.

Mat broke the kiss, his breathing coming in harsh gasps as he pulled away. Disappointment flashed in her amber eyes, only to be replaced by surprise when he bent down and wrapped one arm behind her legs. Her hands dug into his shoulders, the backpack hitting him in the side again when he lifted her.

"What are you doing?" Her voice was just above a whisper, all husky and smoky, spilling over him like a smooth whiskey. He grinned down at her, glad to see that their kisses had the same effect on her as they did on him.

"I'm carrying you upstairs."

Her hands tightened their grip on his shoulders and her mouth opened into a small O of surprise. She shouldn't be surprised, though, not when he was already halfway up the stairs, not when it should be obvious what he was doing.

His eyes never left hers as he carried her into the bedroom, over to the large bed. Gently, carefully, he lowered her to the mattress, his fingers sliding along the backs of her legs, caressing.

Then he kneeled next to her on the bed and leaned forward, pressed his lips against hers, hesitant and slow. He wanted to devour her in every way imaginable. But not yet. No, he wanted to seduce her first. Tease her, taste her. Make her weak with desire, mindless with need. Except she deepened the kiss, her hands drifting down along his chest to the hem of his shirt. His skin burned everywhere she touched, causing the breath to hitch in his chest, causing his lungs to burn.

She eased his shirt up, breaking the hungry kiss long enough to pull it over his head and toss it on the floor. She pushed to her knees, facing him, her chest pressed against his, her hips searching. She moaned and pressed herself more tightly against him, against the rock hard length of his cock. It took every ounce of self-control he had not to throw her on her back and drive into her, to lose himself in her warm body.

He dragged his hands along her back, down to her ass, lower, until he touched bare skin. Christ, her skin was so soft, like silk. Mat ached to touch every inch of her, taste every inch of her.

His hands drifted up, under her skirt to skim her ass, bare except for a tiny wisp of lace that barely covered her. He groaned, the sound loss in the melding of their mouths, their tongues.

He wanted her. Needed her. Now.

No, not yet. He wanted this to be more than just a hurried romp, more than a stolen moment. He broke the kiss and dragged his lips across her cheek, to her ear, nibbling. Along the graceful lines of her neck, to that spot where it met her shoulder. Nicole gasped and her head fell back, her hair coming undone and falling across his arm, the soft strands teasing his skin.

"Mat—"

He silenced her plea with a kiss, swallowing her soft cry as he tilted his hips, letting her know exactly how much he wanted her. She rested her hands on his bare shoulders, her fingers digging into his flesh as he kissed and licked. Too many clothes, too many boundaries.

He moved his hand up her side, up and around so he could ease her jacket off, careful to not hit her arm where she hurt it. The shirt came next as he slowly eased it up, his thumbs grazing her skin, teasing her nipples through the lacy material of her bra before pulling the shirt over her head.

Mat leaned back, his eyes studying her, drinking her in. From the fall of hair around her shoulders to the graceful lines and curves of her beautiful breasts. From the shadows of the tattoos on her arm, barely visible in the light coming from the hall, to the indentation of her waist and the flare of her hips. He wanted it all. He wanted *her*.

He licked his lips and met her gaze, saw the passion glazing them and knew his own eyes would look the same. "You're so beautiful."

She shook her head, opened her mouth to say

something, but Mat pressed a finger against her lips, silencing her. "Yes, you are. You're beautiful."

Then he kissed her. Not a gentle, hesitant kiss meant to reassure but a deep kiss, meant to seduce. Possessing, claiming. Showing her without words what he wanted, what he thought. He eased back on the bed, pulling her down on top of him, his hand splayed along her back. His elbow knocked into something and there was a sudden bounce followed by a thud. He ignored it, not caring what it was, caring only about the woman in his arms.

But Nicole stiffened and pulled away, scrambled over him to lean over the edge of the bed. And Christ, she was straddling him, her hips pressed against his rock hard cock. If he had been fully naked, if he didn't still have his shorts on, all he'd have to do—

Nicole straightened, the backpack in her hands and a frown on her face as she unzipped it and dug through it. Fuck. The thud had been her backpack hitting the floor. He wanted to tell her to leave it, wanted to tell her that it wasn't important. But the expression on her face—worry, anxiety—told him that it *was* important. To her.

He propped himself on his elbows and watched as she dug through the bag. "Everything okay?"

"My camera." She pulled the camera out then placed the bag on the bed next to them. Mat could feel her anxiety now, pulsing through her as she held it up to her face, trying to examine it in the near-darkness.

He shifted, one hand on her hip, holding her in place as he leaned over and hit the switch on the bedside lamp. Soft light fell over them, not enough to illuminate the entire room but enough that she would be able to see.

Nicole sat back, her firm and mostly bare ass now pressed tight against his erection. But she didn't seem to notice, not when she was studying the camera, turning it this way and that. She turned it on and looked through the view finder then made some adjustments. He heard her sigh, felt some of the tension leave her body.

"Everything okay?"

She finally looked at him, a relieved smile on her face. "Yeah, I think so."

He sat up and wrapped his hands around her hips, holding her in place. He tried to tell himself it was so she wouldn't tumble off the bed when he moved. "Are you sure? Did you need to take a few pictures to check?"

A playful glint lit her eyes and tugged at the corners of her full mouth. Before Mat realized what she was doing, she lifted the camera and snapped a series of pictures. His mouth dropped open and he leaned back.

"Uh, what are you doing?"

"Taking a few pictures like you said." She lowered the camera, her gaze fixed on whatever was showing on the small review screen.

"I didn't mean of me."

"The camera loves you, though. Look." She turned the camera around to show him but damn if he saw what she meant. The only thing he could see was a close-up of his face, his eyes widened in surprise, a stunned expression on his face.

Nicole moved the camera, bringing it up to her face. She smiled then snapped a few more. "I've been wanting to do this since that first night we met." A shy grin spread over her face as she lowered her gaze.

"Since New Orleans."

It was the first time she'd ever specifically mentioned their time together in New Orleans. Yeah, she'd said how much she enjoyed it, but she'd never mentioned their actual time together. Mat thought maybe she was embarrassed or something, though he couldn't imagine why. And yeah, the fact that she was mentioning it now—with a smile on her face—did something to him. A warmth spread through him that had nothing to do with the way her hips pressed against him. At least, not much to do with it. He wanted to see her smile like that again, shy yet somehow uninhibited. He wanted to see the playful gleam in her eyes grow brighter.

Mat grinned, wanting to give her more, willing to do whatever she wanted if it would keep that smile on her face and that light in her eyes. He ran one hand along her back, up to her neck, then gently pulled her down until their mouths met in a long delicious kiss. He pulled away, breathless, knowing that too much more of that would make him forget what he was about to do.

"Then snap away."

Nicole blinked, like she hadn't heard him right. And maybe she hadn't, not if the kiss had the same effect on her that it had on him. Yeah, he was definitely hoping it did.

She blinked again then leaned back, the camera held loosely in her hands. "Seriously? You mean it?"

"Sure, why not?"

Mat had expected her to just stay where she was and snap a few more pictures and that would be it. But no, Nicole apparently had other ideas. She pressed a quick kiss against his mouth then slid off him. He swallowed back a groan of disappointment. What the hell had he been thinking? If he'd known she was going to move, he would have never said anything.

He rolled to his side and propped his head on his hand, watching as she moved around his room, his eyes focused on her mostly-bare ass. So okay, maybe he could enjoy this if it meant watching Nicole prance around in nothing but a lacy bra and skimpy lace thong.

She paused in the middle of the room, looking around, then moved over to the small sitting area. Mat smiled in appreciation when she bent over, then squeezed his eyes shut against the sudden glare when she turned on the floor light.

"Nicole?"

She turned, her hair falling over her shoulder and brushing against the slope of one breast. Mat swallowed and pulled his gaze away, forced himself to look at her face instead.

"Yeah?"

"What are you doing?"

"Just getting more light." She turned around again and his gaze immediately dropped back to her ass. Except he didn't want to just see her ass. He wanted to touch it, feel it. He wanted to cup the warm flesh of her ass in his palms as he held her body against his.

Yeah, maybe this wasn't such a good idea. If he'd known she was going to go to all this trouble for a few candid shots, he wouldn't have said anything. But then she was walking over to him with that beautiful, stunning, mesmerizing smile on her face and he forgot all about his objections.

She raised the camera and snapped several pictures before coming closer. She leaned over and kissed him, running her tongue along the seam of his mouth. He reached for her but she pulled away with a shake of her head.

"Unbutton your shorts."

"Excuse me?"

She tugged on his hand, pulling him off the bed, then took a step back, the camera ready. "Unbutton your shorts."

"Nicole—"

"Not all the way. I just want to get your hands."

"My hands?"

There was that shy smile again, that playful gleam in her eyes when she looked at him. "You have amazing hands."

Mat laughed, the sound odd in his ears. Not really forced; more like...surprised. Or maybe stunned would be a better word. "You're not going to call me Rose, are you?"

Her brows lowered and she shook her head, her confusion obvious.

"Rose? And Jack? He had a thing for drawing hands." But she still looked confused and Mat suddenly felt like an idiot. "Uh, it's from a movie, that's all. We'll have to rent it one night."

Or they could just watch the copy he had in his library but he wasn't about to tell her that. Christ, he'd never hear the end of it if the guys ever found out he watched that movie, let alone owned it.

Nicole still didn't say anything, although this funny little look crossed her face when he suggested renting it. Or maybe he was just imagining it. Then she smiled again and held up the camera, silently letting him know she was waiting.

"Okay, unbutton my shorts. Got it." He dropped his hands to his shorts and quickly unbuttoned them, the sound of the camera clicking loud in the background. "There."

"One more time, but slower."

He would have refused—he already felt like an ass—except Nicole's voice had changed, becoming a little huskier. He looked over at her, saw her gaze focused on his waist, her pupils a little darker. The swell of her breasts rose and fell with each short breath. Holy fuck, she was enjoying this.

His semi-hard cock went to full alert, pressing against the zipper. He swallowed and quickly closed the button of the shorts, his hands hesitating at the waistline for a few seconds, not sure what to do next. Nicole moved in closer, bending over slightly and aiming the camera, waiting. Her breasts pushed forward with the movement, nearly falling out of the lace with each quickening breath she took.

Mat watched her, heat racing through him, turning his blood into something like lava. Slow, hot. He finally moved his hands, the motion slow and deliberate, his fingers hovering just above the button.

Click. Click.

Pause.

Click.

His fingers worked the button free, the rasp of plastic against the material loud in the background. He held his hands in place, his own breathing suddenly a little faster as Nicole moved even closer, doing something with the camera lens.

Click. Click. Click.

And holy fuck, he didn't think his cock had ever been so hard. Didn't realize that he could get so turned on just by having his picture taken.

No, it was more than that. So much more. It was

177

the way Nicole was watching him, the way her skin flushed and her breaths came in shallow gasps. The way she came closer, aiming the camera, capturing each small movement.

Click. Click. Click.

Mat reached for the zipper, eased it down. Slow, so slow. Teasing her. Tormenting himself.

Click. Click.

Pause.

Another inch, down even further. He tugged at the waistband, spreading the material open as he pulled the zipper lower.

Click. Pause. *Click.*

Nicole moved even closer then dropped to her knees, the camera held in front of her. Ready. Waiting.

Another inch. One more until it was down all the way, no longer pressing against his rigid erection. He slid his hands up his hips, hooked his thumbs into the waistband and edged his shorts down. Just a little, just to tease her.

Click. Click. Click.

His cock sprung free and he stood there, his hands wrapped loosely around the waistband of the shorts. He held his breath, wondering if she was going to take another picture, torn between telling her to stop.

Or encouraging her to keep going.

And fuck, this was probably a bad idea. Definitely a bad idea. He knew better, knew what could happen. But it was such a fucking turn-on. Something he never expected, something he didn't think he'd ever do.

And he didn't want to stop.

Nicole lowered the camera and looked up at him. Her eyes were dark, glazed with the same passion and desire that throbbed in his veins. In his cock. She was just as turned on as he was, maybe more. Had she done something like this before? Or was this as new to her as it was to him?

"Do you want me to stop?" Christ, even her voice had changed. Deep and husky. Smoky. So fucking hot, so fucking sexy.

Mat held her gaze, common sense warring with curiosity, warring with desire—for less than two seconds. He pushed the shorts down past his hips, wrapped one hand around his cock, and stroked. Long. Slow. Hard. He clenched his jaw against a hiss of breath and dropped his head back.

Click. Click. Click.

A small hand closed over his, following his touch, drifting down and cupping his balls. Squeezing. Teasing. Christ, he didn't think he'd ever been this turned on, this ready to lose his shit.

"Mat." Nicole called his name, her voice barely above a ragged whisper, harsh and needy. He groaned, slowed the long strokes of his hand around his cock, and forced his eyes open.

She was kneeling in front of him, her mouth parted, hunger blazing in her eyes. Her tongue darted out and licked her lips, the sight of just that enough to make his balls tighten.

She held the camera up for him. He reached for it, thinking she wanted him to place it on the bed, place it somewhere so it wouldn't get damaged. Then she smiled and wrapped her hand around his once more, sliding it off his cock.

"Your turn." She pushed the camera into his hands, her eyes still holding his as she leaned forward and took him into her mouth.

Fuck. Holy fuck. He closed his eyes and clenched

his jaw, said a brief prayer that his self-control wouldn't explode. That *he* wouldn't explode. Then the image, the memory, of her taking him all in, sucking, swallowing his cum, came to mind. Sharp and vivid. And holy shit, he damn near exploded right then.

But she pulled away, her hands still stroking him, caressing him. "Your turn, Mat."

His turn? What was she talking about? He forced his eyes opened, looked down at her. She held his gaze for a second then glanced at the camera in his hands. Another smile lit her face, shy and playful at the same time.

"Your turn."

Oh holy fuck. Did she mean what he thought she meant? Yeah, she did. Mat swallowed and raised the camera, hesitating, not believing he was actually doing this. Then he aimed the lens down just as she closed her mouth over him once more.

Click.

Holy fuck. It was surreal. Like he was watching from a distance but feeling it at the same time. And Christ, her mouth was so hot. So wet. Sweet. Torturing him.

He swallowed again and looked through the viewfinder, adjusting the lens, zooming closer.

Click. Click.

Christ, he'd never experienced anything like this. Desire, hot and searing, ripped through him. Too many sensations, tearing at him from too many directions.

Click.

Her lips, full and moist, sliding around his cock, back and forth.

Click.

Her hands, so feminine and gentle, cupping his

balls, squeezing.

Click.

The heat of her breath against his thigh, the nip of her teeth against his flesh.

Click. Click.

Her eyes focused on his, the pupils so dilated with passion they were nearly black.

Click.

The swell of her breasts, pushed together by her arms, the creamy flesh of her skin nearly spilling over her bra.

Click.

Fuck, it was too much. He was going to explode if she didn't stop.

If he didn't stop.

"Nicole—"

Her head tilted to the side, that shy smile tilting the corners of her mouth as she watched him. "Come for me Mat."

Fuck. Did she want—?

She closed her mouth around him again, taking him in. All of him, down to the base of his cock. Sucking, teasing. Harder. Faster.

Click. Click.

And fuck. No more. He couldn't take it anymore. He grabbed her head with his free hand, his hand twisting in her hair, holding her in place as his hips pumped.

Once. Twice.

Click.

She wrapped her arms around him, her fingers digging into his ass as his hips thrust forward. Harder. Faster. Again and again.

Click.

Click. Click. Click.

Mat dropped the camera behind him and reached for the bed post, his hand clenched around it as he exploded. A hoarse shout filled the room, harsh, breathless. The orgasm ripped through him, tearing him in half as Nicole kept sucking. Her own breathing was shallow, short little gasps punctuated by small feminine moans as he held her head in place.

Lights exploded behind his eyes, everything around him going gray as sensation washed over him. He groaned again, dragged a deep breath into his lungs, tried to open his eyes.

He eased his grip on the bedpost and forced his eyes open then looked down. Nicole was still on her knees in front of him, a dazed look in her eyes as she rested her cheek against his thigh. He still had his hand tangled in her hair and he cringed, wondering if he had been too rough, worried he may have hurt her. He relaxed his fingers, let his hand drop and reached down with one finger to stroke the soft skin of her flushed cheek.

"Did I—" He paused, not quite able to say the words, not sure he could bear the answer if she said yes. He dragged another deep breath into his lungs and let it out in a rush. "Are you okay?"

"I've never been better." God, her voice was like sweet sin and silk, all rolled into one. Mat grinned and grabbed her hand, helping her stand. He kicked off his shorts then guided her to the bed, arranging the pillows behind her so she was propped up.

Her mouth curved into a smile as she tilted her head to the side and looked at him. "What are you doing?"

But Mat didn't answer, just gave her a smile in

return. He reached into the nightstand and grabbed some condoms, tossing them on the bed next to her, like he had done their very first night together. Then he climbed into bed, straddling her legs and leaning forward to kiss her. Slow, deep, possessing.

She raised her arms, tried to wrap them around his neck and pull him closer, but he shook his head and sat back. He didn't miss her small groan of disappointment or the slightly confused expression on her face.

"Mat—"

He shook his head, interrupting her. Then he reached behind him and grabbed the camera from the foot of the bed, holding it out to her.

"Now it's your turn."

"What?"

Mat grabbed one of her hands and forced the camera into it. Awareness flashed in her eyes and she started to shake her head.

"No. I couldn't—"

"Your turn." Mat slid down her legs, his thumbs snagging the tiny waistband of her thong. He eased the scrap of lace down her legs, trailing kisses along each inch of her silky skin. He moved, readjusted her legs so he was kneeling between them, and propped her right foot on his shoulder. Then he bent his head, teasing her with the lightest of kisses along the inside of her thigh. Higher. Higher still, not stopping until he dropped his mouth against the warm sweetness of her smooth, bare flesh.

She gasped, the sound nothing more than a sharp whisper of breath in the still air. Mat lifted his head, a grin on his face as he looked into the lens of the camera.

Click. Click.

Chapter Fourteen

Music filled the sunny kitchen, the volume down low enough that only Mat could hear it. He caught himself humming, stopped, smiled—and resumed the humming. And why the hell shouldn't he? It was a gorgeous morning, with a bright sun and clear blue sky and, best of all, no sign of oppressive humidity. At least, not yet.

Best of all, a beautiful woman was upstairs in his bed, sound asleep. He had thought about waking her up—with gentle kisses and even gentler caresses. But Nicole had looked too content, too sweet and flushed and warm, that he couldn't bring himself to wake her. Not after last night.

A wide smile spread across his face as memories raced through him. Just that was enough to send all the blood rushing to his cock. He groaned and readjusted himself through the loose gym shorts, wondering how in the hell he could be ready again, after last night.

After everything they'd done.

No, he couldn't wake Nicole, not just yet. She

needed her rest. So he'd done the next best thing and came downstairs to fix her breakfast.

He moved away from the stove and reached for his coffee cup, taking a long swallow as he stirred the eggs with the spatula. A few more minutes and they'd be ready. He placed the spatula on the spoon holder then leaned down to pull the bacon from the warm oven.

He snagged a piece and bit into it, chewing as he grabbed plates and silverware and napkins and arranged everything on a large tray. His hand hovered over the coffee pot, hesitating. Did Nicole drink coffee? If so, how did she take it? A brief surge of disappointment sparked inside him. Shouldn't he know the answer to such a simple question? He pushed the disappointment aside. He'd learn the answer soon enough.

He just hoped she didn't use artificial sweetener, because he didn't have any in the house.

He moved to the refrigerator and grabbed the half-and-half, pouring some into a small pitcher. Mugs, cane sugar, creamer. And the coffee pot. There, everything was set.

He grabbed the tray, cursing under his breath when the entire thing tilted to the side. He placed it back on the counter, moved things around to better balance the weight, and tried again. There, much better.

Mat breathed a sigh of relief when he reached the top of the stairs without spilling anything. He stopped in front of the door, nudging it open with his hip. "Hey, Sleeping Beauty."

The room was still dark, filled with an odd gray light filtering through the closed curtains. He moved to the side of the room and placed the laden tray on the small coffee table. "Nicole. I fixed breakfast."

She didn't answer. Mat grinned, thinking she must be more tired than he realized. And what better way to wake her than with those gentle kisses he'd been thinking about?

Nicole shifted on the bed, turning on her side with a small moan as she kicked off the covers. Her head moved, shifting from side to side, her hair tangling in her face. Mat sat on the edge of the bed and reached out, brushing her hair to the side. Heat seared his palm and he pulled his hand back, frowning. Nicole's eyes blinked open, slow and sluggish, her gaze unfocused, her eyes glazed.

He brushed the back of his hand against her cheek, surprised at the heat radiating from her, at the dry parchment quality of her skin. "Hey. You okay?"

Nicole blinked again, nothing more than a few flutters of her eyelids before they closed once more. She murmured something and turned again, wincing. A hiss of pain escaped her, causing her eyes to pop open. Her brows were lowered in a frown, small lines of tension bracketing her mouth. She looked around, her gaze finally resting on him, slowly focusing. She tried to push up, putting the weight on her left arm. Another hiss of pain escaped her and she fell back against the mattress with a small whimper.

What the hell? Mat's concern morphed into something stronger and he leaned forward, sliding his arm under her and easing her to a sitting position. Her head dropped to his shoulder, the heat coming from her body alarming him.

"Nicole, talk to me. What's wrong?" Christ, had he done something to her last night? Even as the thought came to him, he was pushing it away. No, there was nothing they'd done that could have caused this. She was burning up with fever, her skin too dry, too hot.

She mumbled something, her words muffled against his neck.

"What was that, baby? Talk to me."

"Thirsty."

He brushed his lips across her forehead then eased her back against the mattress, adjusting one of the many pillows behind her head. Then he hurried across to the master bathroom, flipping on the light and making a beeline to the medicine cabinet.

Ibuprofen. Acetaminophen. Aspirin. Christ, he had all of them plus some. Which one should he grab? What if she was allergic to one of them? Fuck it. He grabbed all three bottles and filled the glass from the faucet before hurrying back to Nicole.

What could be wrong with her? Was it the flu? Would it have come on this fast, faster than overnight? She had been fine yesterday, fine last night. If it was the flu, wouldn't she have had some symptoms? A scratchy throat? Something?

He placed the glass of water and bottles of medicine on the nightstand then sat on the edge of the bed. Nicole hadn't moved, a frown still etched on her face.

"Nicole? I have your water. And some medicine. Can you sit up?"

Her eyes fluttered open, drifted shut, fluttered open again. She shook her head even as she struggled to push herself up. He reached over, slid his hand under her arm to help her sit up again.

A small scream escaped her lips and she pulled away, reaching for her arm as she rolled to her side.

What the hell? Mat jerked back, afraid he'd hurt

her, afraid he'd done something to her. But that couldn't be. She was holding her arm, her hand wrapped loosely around the back of her bicep. It was the same arm she'd said she hurt at work. He looked down at his hand, saw a smear of something wet on his fingers and palm. What the fuck?

He leaned over and turned on the light. "Nicole, what's wrong?"

She shook her head, her lids fluttering open once more. Her eyes were still glazed, bright with fever as she looked at him. "Nothing. I'm just..." Her voice drifted off and her tongue dashed out, running across her dry lips. "I think I'm coming down with something."

"It's more than that." Definitely more than that, with the way she was holding her arm, with whatever was on his hand. But why would she lie to him? He reached over and gently moved her hand. "Here, let me look—"

She tried to pull her arm away but didn't have the strength. The muscles beneath his hands tensed, then went limp as he gently moved it, lifting her arm up so he could get a better look.

And immediately wished he hadn't.

Mat swallowed, a dozen different emotions tearing through him. Confusion. Concern. Sympathy. And rage. Rage like he'd never felt before. Burning, blinding.

Deep gouges ran across the back of her upper arm, along the sensitive fleshy part. Three of them, each about the width of a finger—or a fingernail. The gouges were deep, each an angry red. The skin around each was swollen, the flesh too hot, the marks themselves oozing pus and blood.

Mat clenched his jaw, biting back each curse that wanted to tumble from his mouth. Nicole hadn't hurt herself at work. No, someone had done this to her. Deliberately.

He eased her arm down then walked over to the curtains, pulling them open to let in even more light. Nicole's breath came out in a sharp gasp when light flooded the room but that couldn't be helped. Mat needed more light, needed to get a better look at her arm.

He sat down next to her and took her arm again, ignoring her weak protests when he raised it for a better look.

The bottom of his stomach dropped open, letting in an icy blast that momentarily froze him. It wasn't just gouges that marred her skin. In the bright morning light, he could now make out the bruising that accompanied the wounds, mottling the flesh and darkening the bright colors of her tattoos. The bruises circled her upper arm, dark shadows that mirrored the image of fingers and thumb.

Bile rose in his stomach, hot and acidic, at the sight; at the realization that someone had done this to her. Deliberately. Mat had been playing hockey long enough, had enough experience with bumps and bruises, cuts and broken bones, to know the difference.

How in the fuck had he not seen this last night? Not noticed it? Because he'd been so focused on sex, so intent on driving himself into Nicole, on losing himself in her body, that he hadn't been paying attention to anything else. He'd been so fucking selfish, so intent on himself, that he'd completely missed it.

So what the hell kind of man did that make him?

Mat swallowed, forced himself to take a deep

breath. He would have to deal with that later. Right now, it was only Nicole who mattered.

"Nicole. Who did this?" His voice was too clipped, his anger clear. He took another deep breath and repeated the question, but Nicole only shook her head.

Had it been someone at work? One of the patrons at the club? Or someone else? Why the fuck would someone hurt a woman this way? Who the fuck would hurt a woman this way?

"Nicole, your arm is infected. Now tell me, who did this to you?"

She turned her head away, her breathing ragged and shallow. For a long minute, she said nothing and Mat was convinced she wouldn't answer him at all. But she took a deep breath as he held his own, waiting.

"It was an accident. It was my fault."

"Bullshit." He growled the word, unable to help himself, unable to hide the anger, the rage, tearing him apart. She turned her head, not quite looking at him, her feverish eyes staring past him.

They sat that way for a few quiet minutes, the air around them thick and heavy. Mat slowly lowered her arm then moved from the bed, his heart thundering in his chest as he crossed the room to his dresser, each step short and clipped as he fought the anger roiling through his body.

He pulled open drawers, rummaging through each, not really seeing anything clearly. None of the clothes he pulled out would work for her, not really, but he didn't know what else to do.

He moved back to the bed, surprised that Nicole had moved, surprised to see her struggling to sit up, reaching for the water. He wrapped an arm around her shoulders, supporting her, holding the glass as she drank. He placed the empty glass on the nightstand then held out the t-shirt he'd grabbed.

"Let's get this on you—"

"Where's my shirt?"

"Nicole, you can't wear your shirt, not with your arm. Come on, put this on then we'll get you to the hospital." He eased the shirt over her head, then her good arm. She blinked, frowned, shook her head.

"I need to go home. I...I have to work." Her voice was just above a whisper, weak and almost desperate as she leaned against him. Mat didn't even think she realized she was doing it.

"Not tonight you don't. You need to get that arm checked out before it gets worse." He finished getting the shirt on her, pausing to roll the left sleeve up so it wouldn't rub against the wounds.

Then he eased her back on the bed and worked the sweatpants up her legs, over her hips to her waist, tying them so they wouldn't fall off. Nicole barely moved, her eyes closed, her breathing shallow. Her skin was still too hot, too flushed.

How long had the fever been burning? And how high was too high? He knew there was a dangerous point, but what the fuck was it? He didn't know, only knew that a sense of urgency suddenly seized him. What if he'd already wasted too much time?

Stop. Mat closed his eyes and took a deep breath, filling his lungs, holding it in for a count of ten. One more. He needed to push away the rage and the worry, because neither one would help Nicole. Not right now. Once he got her to the hospital, got her checked out, then he could lose his shit. But for now, he had to keep his head on straight.

He took another deep breath then moved from

the bed, quickly changing from the loose gym shorts into a pair of jeans and a t-shirt. His foot brushed against something and he nearly tripped, catching himself at the last minute.

Nicole's backpack sat on the floor, partially pushed under the bed. He started to step around it then stopped. She'd need her id for the hospital, and who knew what else.

Mat grabbed the backpack and hooked the straps around his shoulder. Then he leaned over and scooped Nicole into his arms, careful not to move her arm more than necessary.

Her head dropped against his shoulder and she muttered something, her breath warm against his neck. But he couldn't make out the words. It wasn't until he had her safely buckled in the front seat of his car, her backpack resting on the floor between her legs, that he finally caught what she was saying, finally understood her mutterings.

"I can't." She licked at her dry lips and shook her head, her glazed eyes meeting his. The look in their amber depths—fear, anxiety, embarrassment—hit him with the force of a puck to the throat. "No insurance."

Mat curled his hand around the doorframe, surprised the metal didn't crumple under his grip. He leaned forward and brushed his lips against her forehead, hoping to reassure her.

"Don't worry, I'll take care of you."

Her eyes widened, just a fraction before her lids drifted shut and her head tilted to the side. Instead of looking reassured, she had looked frightened. Or maybe Mat was only imagining things. It didn't matter.

He closed the door and moved around to the other side of the car. He could worry about what he may or may not have seen in her eyes later. Right now, his first priority was taking care of Nicole.

Chapter Fifteen

"Are you out of your fucking mind?" Derek's usual grin was gone, his lips pursed in an angry line. Mat glanced around the bustling hall then stepped closer, ready to grab Derek around the throat, ready to tell him to keep his voice down. Better yet, to just keep his mouth shut.

But Bridget beat him to it, stepping closer to Derek's side and rubbing her hand along his back in soothing circles. At least, Mat figured they must be soothing because Derek calmed almost instantly, his mouth slowly relaxing, the color of his face fading from an angry red to a frustrated pink.

"Derek, not so loud." Bridget glanced around, her brows furrowed in concern before turning to Mat.

"Thanks, Bridget. At least you understand."

"But I don't, Mat. Not really."

Mat's jaw closed with a snap. He ran a hand through his hair then dragged it down his face. Stubble scratched his palm, the rasping sound echoing in his ear, reminding him that he hadn't shaved in more than twenty-four hours. Not since yesterday, before he left the house to pick Nicole up for their picnic date.

Had that been just yesterday? So much had happened since then, the hours warped in his mind from all the time they'd been in the hospital. He glanced at his watch, looking at it twice, his mind fighting to count the hours.

Had it really been that long? Yeah, it had been. Nearly eight hours had passed since he first pulled into the emergency room parking lot. They were upstairs now, a few feet away from Nicole's room, where she'd be spending at least one night.

She had been given some IV antibiotics and her arm had been cleaned in the ER—after waiting entirely too long to be seen. Nicole had barely been able to fill out the paperwork, she'd been so out of it with fever. So Mat had finished for her, asking the questions, waiting with infinite patience for each answer. And then they'd reach the part of financial responsibility, of who would be responsible for anything not covered by insurance. Nicole had simply looked away, shaking her head.

Mat didn't even hesitate, didn't think anything through, just entered his own personal information.

And then they waited. Nicole was finally called back and Mat went with her, standing off to the side of the cramped curtained cubicle. He'd been in a daze, his focus only on Nicole, on how she seemed to be getting worse before his eyes. He told himself that couldn't be possible, that it was nothing more than his imagination. And then he noticed the quiet murmurings, the intent looks being shot his way as one nurse helped Nicole into a hospital gown while the other examined her arm.

And then he'd been asked to leave, to wait outside.

The request was too short and authoritative to be anything but a command so he complied, his concern and confusion swirling and morphing into something else, something he didn't want to acknowledge.

But he knew, just knew, what was going through their minds. They thought he was responsible for what happened to Nicole. That he had been the one to hurt her. To grab her arm hard enough to leave angry bruises on her soft skin, to gouge her flesh with his nails, opening her skin, dirtying it to the point of causing an infection.

Mat had looked over at Nicole, at her flushed and restless body stretched out on the sterile hospital bed. His stomach lurched, filling with bile, the burning acid eating its way up his throat. He swallowed it back and turned away, his jaw clenched as he stalked from the cubicle.

Then he called Derek, not sure what else to do, only knowing he needed to talk to someone. Knowing he needed advice, needed a friendly face or a voice of reason or something.

Yeah, he probably shouldn't have called Derek. Kenny would have been a better choice, with his moments of silence and calm reassurance, with his ability to see things that others missed. But he'd called Derek, somehow knowing that Bridget would come with him.

Mat thought that maybe having Bridget here, that having a woman—someone who wasn't a complete stranger—might help Nicole. Except Bridget hadn't even been in to see Nicole. There hadn't been time, not until now, not with everything else going on.

The police had actually shown up, one officer disappearing behind the curtain while the other herded

Mat into an empty cubicle. The questions had come one after the other, over and over. Several questions were rephrased and asked again until Mat had even begun questioning himself, wondering if maybe he really had done something wrong.

Then the first officer, the one who'd gone in with Nicole, came back out. Some wordless communication passed between the two and then, just like that, Mat had been exonerated. But he still didn't know who had hurt Nicole, didn't even know if the officers knew.

And now Nicole was in her room with another bag of IV antibiotics and Mat was standing out in the hallway, completely speechless as Derek and Bridget studied him.

"What the hell were you thinking, man? You don't just agree to be responsible for someone like that!"

"Derek, keep your voice down." Bridget rubbed her hand along his back one more time, her eyes never leaving Mat. "Help us understand, Mat. I mean, what you did…"

"I just—" He stopped, ran a hand through his hair again, and let out a heavy sigh. He just—what? Yeah, he'd assumed financial responsibility. What the hell else was he supposed to do? No, he hadn't been thinking. But he'd do it again, no questions asked. "You're making a bigger deal out of it than it is."

"Are you fucking insane?" Derek repeated the question for what seemed to be the hundredth time but at least he wasn't shouting it. "I don't think you have any idea how much this shit is going to cost."

"You think I give a fuck about that? You didn't see her, dude. So don't fucking tell me—"

"Knock it off, both of you." Bridget stepped between them, fire flashing in her eyes. She brushed a thick strand of red curls away from her face then placed a hand on Mat's arm. "Mat, I know you meant well but I still don't understand why you would do something like that."

"Because I had to."

"You mean because you think you're in love and hearing wedding bells."

"Fuck you, asshole—"

Something hit him in the chest. Not hard, not painful, just enough pressure to cut off his words and stop him from going after Derek. He looked down, surprised to see Bridget squaring off with him and Derek at the same time, a hand planted firmly in the middle of each of their chests. But why should he be surprised? He knew how strong-willed Bridget was, knew how stubborn she could be.

He immediately took a step back, ready to apologize. But she waved it off, her glare warning both of them to behave.

"Neither one of you are helping anything by acting like this." Bridget leveled a meaningful glance at Derek, who let out a deep breath and stepped back. Mat didn't miss the expression of irritation and impatience that crossed his face but he didn't say anything.

"Mat, what do you need from us?"

He turned back to Bridget, not sure how to answer. How could he put into words the jumbled torrent of emotions running through him? Anger, rage, concern, guilt, exhaustion, worry. And so much more. And none of it made sense, no matter how he tried to sort through it. All he knew was that someone had hurt Nicole—and he was helpless to do anything about it.

He glanced over at Derek, taking in the man's irritation and clenched jaw, then turned back to

Bridget. "Could you—would you go in to talk to her?"

"And say what?"

"I don't know. You're a social worker, you have experience with this kind of thing. Maybe find out what happened. Find out..." Mat cleared his throat and looked away, no longer able to meet Bridget's clear eyes. Because she was watching him too intently? Because he was afraid of what she might see? Hell if he knew. He cleared his throat again. "Can you just talk to her? Please?"

Sympathy and understanding flashed in her eyes but she didn't move, not right away. A long minute went by, the silence agonizing. She glanced over her shoulder, her gaze on Derek, then she let out her own sigh.

"I can't force her to talk, Mat."

"No. I know that. But maybe...I mean—" He didn't know what he meant, not enough to put into words. But maybe she saw something in his eyes, or maybe she could just sense whatever he was trying to say, because she finally nodded and stepped away.

Then she stopped, fixing them both with a stern glare. "But you two knock it off. No more arguing. Go to the cafeteria and get something to eat, try to relax."

"Bridget—"

"I mean it. Go." She waved her hands in their direction, dismissing both of them. "Go talk about the wedding or training camp or something. I don't care what, just not about this."

She narrowed her eyes, giving them both one final warning, then headed down the hall to Nicole's room. She knocked on the door, waited a few seconds, then walked in without another look in their direction.

Mat held his breath, waiting. Wondering if maybe

she'd come back out and tell him Nicole wanted to see him. But the door remained closed.

Something tugged on Mat's elbow and he turned to see Derek standing beside him, his brows lowered in a frown.

"You need your fucking head examined, you know that, right?"

"I thought we weren't going to talk about it."

Derek grunted, the sound full of impatience. "Yeah, okay. Whatever." He rolled his eyes and grabbed Mat's elbow again. "Come on, let's go get something to eat."

"But what if—"

"Let it go, man. Bridget's in there. She'll call if she needs us to come back. But you need a break because you look like shit. And yeah, we're still going to talk." Derek tugged on his arm again. Mat finally followed him, telling himself not to keep looking back at Nicole's door. Bridget was with her, talking to her.

That was a good thing, right?

Chapter Sixteen

Nicole came awake with a start, the gasp catching in her throat. Her lids fluttered open, long enough for harsh light to sear her eyes, then closed again. The light was wrong, all wrong. Too bright. Too white and artificial. She wasn't in her room, where the most light she ever got was a washed-out dreary gray filtering through the small dirty window.

Where was she?

Fragments of memory flashed through her mind. Just glimpses, like she would see if she was reviewing pictures on her camera. They whirled in front of her closed eyes, moving too fast for her to make sense of them.

A flash of heat rushed over her, searing, followed by an abrupt chill that pebbled her damp flesh. Her hands closed over something both soft and scratchy. A blanket? It must be, but it wasn't hers. She didn't care, just pulled it over her, trying to get warm. Five seconds later another blast of heat washed over her and she pushed the covers away. Her left arm throbbed, the pain dull and muted.

Her left arm.

Donnie, grabbing her, his nails digging into her flesh.

Fireworks and laughter.

Sweet kisses and sweaty sex, daring, exciting.

Green eyes, deeper than any she'd ever seen, watching her. Filled with concern. With worry and anxiety.

The images, the memories, came back to her, fast and slow at the same time. Nicole remembered now. At least, bits of it. A vague recollection of Mat's concern, of him taking her...somewhere. Of being questioned, of being asked if Mat—

"No!" Nicole shot up, her heart pounding in her chest, her lungs freezing, unable to draw breath. She bent over, eyes closed as she gripped the railing, forcing air into her lungs.

"No, no, no." She repeated the words, over and over like a chant, hoping that if she said them enough, her fears would fall away.

A cool hand grabbed her arm and Nicole gasped, shaking it off and trying to scramble away at the same time. Her gaze skipped around the room, the disorientation dizzying until she saw the clear green eyes watching her.

But no, there were the wrong shade of green. Not forest green, not the green of a deep woodland lake or a mystical dragon. Nicole closed her eyes and took a deep breath, hoping the world would right itself, that the dizzying disorientation would disappear.

One more deep breath and she reopened her eyes, her gaze slowly sweeping across the room. A hospital room, small and sterile. Things were coming back to her now, the glimpses lasting longer, a little clearer. She turned, searching for those green eyes, and swallowed back the odd disappointment.

Not Mat's eyes—Bridget's.

The woman hovered near the bed, her feathered brows pulled down in a frown. Her thick red hair was pulled back in a careless ponytail. Several thick strands of curl had come loose and framed her face, the bright light catching in the red, turning the color to a deep vibrant flame. Her gaze met Nicole's, cautious, curious, maybe a little hesitant.

Nicole blinked and looked away, searching. But there was no one else in the room, just Bridget.

"How are you feeling?"

Nicole shook her head, not sure how to answer. But the woman kept watching her with that steady gaze, silently coaxing her to answer. Nicole reached for the blanket and tugged it over her shoulders again, ignoring the pinch of pain in the back of her arm, the small pull of the IV line in her hand. She shook her head again then shrugged.

"Tired. A little woozy."

Bridget nodded, like that made perfect sense. She stood there another few seconds, so still and watchful. Then she reached behind her for the lone chair in the room and slid it next to the bed, settling into it like she had no plans to leave.

"Is there anything you wanted to talk about?" Her voice was soft, not quite a whisper but not loud or intrusive. Relaxing, coaxing. Nicole opened her mouth, caught herself and snapped it shut again as memory came rushing back.

Bridget was a social worker. Or working on becoming one. Something like that, she couldn't remember. That was how Nicole knew her, through the work she did at the hospital. Did she only work with children? Nicole didn't know. She didn't know Bridget that well at all, certainly not enough to open up to her.

Especially when there wasn't anything to open up about.

"Not really, no." Nicole waited, wondering if she was going to be asked more questions, if she was going to be subjected to a repeat of the interrogations she'd had to suffer through more than two years ago. But there was only silence. Not accusing, not demanding, just...quiet.

Nicole looked over, saw that Bridget was just watching her. The other woman met her eyes and gave her a small smile. A real smile. Like they were friends or something. Like she was actually concerned. Why would she do that? They didn't know each other, not really. They were nothing more than friendly acquaintances and they certainly didn't run in the same circles. The day of the picnic and fireworks had been the first time they'd actually spent any real time together, getting to know each other. It had been a fun day, leaving Nicole wondering if maybe they could actually be friends. But it certainly hadn't been enough for Nicole to suddenly open up, not after—

She glanced down, frowning. Was she remembering right? No, she couldn't be. Had that just been yesterday? She closed her eyes, trying to remember. The picnic. Frisbee throwing and fireworks and music. Not wanting the night to end, not wanting to go home. Going to Mat's house instead.

Her face heated and she shifted as more memories came back, flooding her with warmth. No, she wasn't likely to forget any of her time with Mat. But after that…what had happened?

Bits and pieces floated, just out of reach. She squeezed her eyes closed, fighting through the thick haze that clogged her brain. God, it *had* been just yesterday. How could that be, when it seemed so long ago?

"Did you have fun yesterday?"

Nicole moved her head to the side, her eyes widening at Bridget's question. Was the woman reading her mind? But there was only curiosity in her face, in her eyes. Nothing sinister, nothing probing. Just an innocent question, like one friend talking to another.

"Uh, yeah." She cleared her throat and nodded. "Yes, I did."

"Me, too. Derek grumbled the whole way there, convinced he was going to be bored out of his mind." A broad smile lit the woman's face and sparkled in her eyes. "But he had fun in spite of himself. He likes to pretend things like that aren't his style. I think he gets that from where he grew up, just outside Boston. You could say he was a little spoiled growing up." Bridget chuckled, the sound clear and light and warm. Nicole watched her, not sure what to say. Her mind was still fuzzy, exhaustion pulling at her as another chill shook her.

"I know Mat had fun. But he enjoys things like that, more than Derek usually does. He's a great guy, by the way. He'd do anything for his friends. Someone you always want on your side, someone who always has your back."

Nicole nodded, afraid to speak even though she agreed completely. That was part of what scared her. Mat *was* a great guy, from everything she'd seen so far.

She'd known it that first night, in New Orleans. That's why she went back to his room. If she was going to have a one-night stand, a night to celebrate her new freedom, a night to remember, she wanted it to be with someone nice.

She'd never meant to see him again, never even considered the possibility. Because why would such a nice guy want anything to do with someone like her? Things like that didn't happen in real life. Not in the life she knew.

"Did you know they call him the Saint?"

"I'm—" Nicole shook her head, certain she had lost track of the conversation somewhere. "I'm sorry, I don't understand. Who do they call that?"

"Mat. I think Derek's actually the one who started the nickname, back when we first started dating. I still don't know the whole story."

"Oh. I, uh, didn't know that." And she would have never guessed it, not after their time together. A saint? Not from what she'd seen, not unless someone with the rugged beauty and sinful talent of a fallen angel could be called a saint.

"Yeah. Mat hates it so if you ever want to irritate him, just call him that." Bridget chuckled again then shifted in the chair. She looked down, her hand smoothing the patterned material of her leggings, her fingers picking at some imaginary spot. A few minutes went by before she looked back at Nicole, her eyes serious beneath her lowered brows.

"You know the police questioned him, right? About your arm. They thought he was the one who assaulted you."

Nicole's heart thundered in her chest. Another chill shook her, one that had nothing to do with whatever was wrong with her and everything to do with fear. *Assault.* She shook her head, her mind screaming in denial. But her voice was barely more than a ragged whisper when she spoke.

"Mat didn't hurt me. It was—" Her mouth snapped shut before she said anything else. Had she told the police? She had a hazy memory of them asking her questions, of clearly telling them it hadn't been Mat, that he would never hurt her. But had she told them who? She thought maybe she had but she couldn't remember. Not that it would have made a difference, not like anything would happen. It never had in the past, why would it now?

"Who was it, Nicole?"

"It doesn't matter. Not anymore."

Bridget watched her, her gaze clear, studying. Waiting. But not judging. Nicole didn't understand. Why did this woman care? There was no reason for her to care.

"Was it your ex-husband?"

Nicole wanted to look away but the other woman's gaze was too strong, holding hers, refusing to let go. Nicole chewed on her lower lip, her body shaking, her mind fighting each word that wanted to tumble from her mouth. Why? Why was she fighting so hard? What difference did it make? None. Not anymore, maybe not ever.

She dropped her gaze, no longer able to meet Bridget's, and slowly nodded. "Yeah. He, uh, he showed up when I left the hospital the other day."

She took a deep breath, each word a painful struggle as she told the other woman what had happened. Nicole ended with a short laugh, the sound brittle, almost desperate as she glanced at her arm. "Do you want to know what's funny? This is mild compared to some of the things he used to do. And I think this time really was an accident, that he didn't mean it. I don't think he even realized what he did."

"He grabbed you, Nicole. Put his hands on you. That's never an accident."

There was nothing Nicole could say, not with the thickness clogging her throat and the burning in her eyes. She ran a hand across her face then took a deep breath. There was no reason for her to act like this. It was over, done with.

She thought it had been over months ago. Years ago.

She took another deep breath, forced herself to sit up straighter. Swallowed once more and hoped her voice would come out stronger. But she kept her eyes focused straight ahead, her gaze on the scratched surface of the closed door. Hoping to hide her shame, her mortification. "Please don't tell Mat."

Silence greeted her but she couldn't look over, couldn't bring herself to see whatever expression might be on Bridget's face. So she concentrated on the hushed noises floating under the door. Muted voices, louder as they passed by her room, fading as the speakers moved away. Mechanical blips, their noise softened by distance. A disembodied voice, almost robotic, paging someone's name.

And closer, just off to her side, the gentle swish of material brushing together. The creak of a chair as Bridget shifted, followed by a heavy sigh.

"Nicole, he already knows."

Chapter Seventeen

Nicole jerked awake, that awful disorientation causing her head to spin. She blinked, her gaze sliding around the darkened room, her pulse beating heavy in her throat as the disorientation slid away.

But the fear, the embarrassment and shame, stayed with her. She rested her head against the thin pillow and pulled the blanket higher around her shoulders. The terrible chills, the burning flashes of fever, seemed to be gone. But the sterile air brushing across her arms chilled her, raising bumps along her flesh.

Was she feeling better? Maybe. Or maybe she was just kidding herself. She was tired. Tired and drained. And thirsty.

She turned her head to the side, looking for a glass of water, and felt her pulse kick up even higher. Mat was in the room with her, his large body folded in the small plastic chair. His arm was stretched out along the mattress, his head resting against it. His hand was loosely curled, so close to hers. Like he had been holding her hand, or reaching for her.

Tears burned her eyes and she blinked them back. Why was he here? He should be home, sound asleep in his large bed, curled under the soft warmth of the downy comforter. Not folded into a hard plastic chair that was too small for him, too hard and uncomfortable.

Why was here?

Nicole moved her hand, tempted to reach out and run her fingers through the thick softness of his dark hair, to brush the hair off his forehead. She wanted to stroke his cheek and see if the thick stubble that covered his jaw would tickle her palm with softness, or if would be sharp and prickly instead.

But she couldn't do any of that so she curled her fingers into a fist and moved her hand to her lap, away from temptation. No, she couldn't touch him. But she could watch him.

She had heard men referred to as beautiful but she had never seen one who could be called that. Not until Mat. He was beautiful in the same way the ancient sculptures she'd seen pictures of were beautiful. Hard, rugged, all sharp lines and curves. Chiseled. Yes, chiseled was the perfect word to describe him.

Her eyes drifted down to his hand, loosely curled near her leg. Such strong beautiful hands, with long fingers and neatly trimmed nails. A faint dusting of hair covered the backs of his hands, lighter than the hair on his head. Even his wrists and forearms strong, each line of muscle so clearly defined.

Strong hands, but gentle, too. So gentle, always careful. She couldn't imagine that his hands would ever be raised in anger.

And God, now she was just being silly, placing

importance on things she shouldn't be, getting worked up over nothing. She shouldn't be comparing, had no right to compare. Yes, she could appreciate them, marvel at their strength and photograph them—

Nicole sat up, her breath leaving in a rush. Mat jerked awake, his eyes immediately focused on her, concern flashing in his eyes and radiating from the stiff lines of his body. He reached out and took her hand in his, gently squeezed it.

"Nicole? Are you okay? What is it?"

"My camera. Oh my God, where's my camera? The pictures—" She couldn't even say it, couldn't put her fear into words. Mat just looked at her, his concern turning to confusion.

"Nicole, it's okay. Don't worry. Your camera's at my house. Nobody is going to touch it."

"No, you don't understand. It's not the camera. It's the pictures. The pictures I took. From the other night. I didn't erase them—"

"Shh. Nicole, it's okay." He stood from the chair and moved closer, resting his hip on the edge of the mattress next to hers. He leaned forward and brushed the hair from her face then pressed a kiss to her forehead. "Nobody is going to touch your camera. It's fine."

"But—"

"It's okay, baby. I promise. Nobody will see the pictures."

Nicole watched him, not understanding how he could be so calm. She finally eased back against the pillow, chewing on her lower lip as she looked over his shoulder, not quite able to meet his gaze.

"How are you feeling?" He ran the back of his free hand along her cheek and down to her neck. "I think the fever is gone. How's the arm? Better?"

"I—" Nicole swallowed, still unable to look at him. "Yeah. Yes, better."

"Good." He sat back, scooting a little closer on the bed, his thigh flush against hers. He adjusted the hold on her hand, threading their fingers together before raising their joined hands to his mouth. He dropped a kiss on the back of her knuckles, his lips soft and tender. So tender.

How could such a large man be so gentle? And why? Why would a man like him, a man who had everything, worry about her? Men like him didn't exist, not in her world. Tears came to her eyes and she blinked them back, not wanting Mat to see them.

Silence hung between them, thick and expectant. She waited, afraid Mat would ask questions, questions she didn't want to answer about things she'd rather pretend didn't exist. Her discomfort and anxiety grew as the minutes stretched between them but the questions didn't come.

Mat dropped their hands to his lap, his thumb rubbing gentle circles along her knuckles. She took a deep breath, working up the courage to look at him, afraid of what she'd see in his eyes. Pity. Anger maybe. Condemnation.

But all she saw was worry and relief and concern. And something else, something that warmed her and confused her and scared her all at the same time. How could he look at her like that? She didn't understand.

"You had me worried, you know? This morning. I—I didn't know what had happened, wasn't sure what to do."

"I'm sorry." And what a stupid thing to say. Empty words that meant nothing about something she couldn't control. Mat sat back, his brows lowering in a brief frown.

"Why are you sorry? You didn't do anything."

"I know. I mean—" What did she mean? She didn't know. "I didn't mean to worry you."

Mat laughed, the sound a short burst of noise that lacked any real amusement. He squeezed her hand, one corner of his mouth curling in a brief smile. "Yeah, I didn't think you did it on purpose. But you still freaked me out a bit."

"Why?" And oh God, why did she have to keep opening her mouth? She closed her eyes, wishing sleep would claim her. But she was wide awake, more awake than she wanted.

"Why?" Mat repeated the question. She could feel him watching her, feel the penetrating gaze of those deep green eyes. But she didn't want to see them, couldn't bring herself to look at him. She felt him shift, felt the heat of his body as he leaned closer to her. "Nicole, look at me."

She wanted to say no. Wanted to shake her head or feign sleep or just ignore him. But she couldn't, not when he said her name in his low voice, not when his breath whispered across her skin. She took a deep breath for courage and opened her eyes. Mat's face was inches from hers, his gaze never wavering as he watched her.

"Because I care about you, that's why."

"But you can't. You don't even know me."

"I know enough."

The answer scared her, because if their situations were reversed, she'd say the same thing. She knew enough. But how was that even possible? They didn't know each other, not really.

"But you don't. You just met me."

"Well, not really." He smiled again, that charming boyish smile that sent shivers of warmth through her. "Technically it's been almost two months."

A smile tugged at her lips at his attempt at humor. She opened her mouth, ready to correct his math, to tell him it had been more like six weeks, not two months. But she started crying instead, deep sobs that racked her body. She closed her eyes, mortified. Tried to pull away, to curl up into a ball when he called her name.

But he wouldn't let her.

Strong arms closed around her, pulling her close, holding her. And she kept crying, she couldn't stop, her tears soaking the front of his shirt, her shoulders shaking with the force of each sob. And he just sat there, holding her, his hands rubbing gentle circles along her back as he murmured soft words of reassurance in her ear.

Telling her it was going to be okay.

Reassuring her that she was safe.

Telling her that nobody would hurt her again, telling her he was there for her.

She wanted to believe him. As they sat there in the darkened room, with his arms around her as she cried senseless tears, she wanted to believe him. With all her heart. But she was afraid to, afraid to trust his words, afraid to trust what she felt.

How could she, when she knew that dragons weren't real?

Chapter Eighteen

Mat circled the block, his eyes searching for a parking space close to Nicole's home. He reached the corner, ready to make the turn to go around once more, thinking he'd just double-park if he had to. But Nicole tensed beside him, her hands clasped so tightly in her lap that her knuckles were white.

"You can just let me out here, that's okay."

"I'm not just dropping you off. I told you that already." He had, at least a dozen times since this morning, when they had started the discharge proceedings. Neither one of them had expected it to take so long, not with all the paperwork and forms and instructions. They were both tired and drained, and a headache was starting to form at the base of his neck. Nicole had to be feeling worse, after everything that happened the last two days. She hadn't said anything, not even a whimper of complaint, but Mat knew she was exhausted. Her complexion was too pale and there were smudges under her eyes. She needed sleep. And food. And uninterrupted rest away from any stress or worries.

He didn't want to drop her off here. Not just at the corner—he didn't want to leave her here, at her house, period. His protective instincts had been in high-gear since yesterday morning and they were only getting stronger. Was it a gut-feeling telling him something was wrong, or something more? He had no idea, but he wasn't going to second-guess himself, not on this.

But Nicole didn't want to listen to him. She had it in her head that she was going to go home—to her mother's house—and that everything would be fine. A stubborn streak had emerged in her and it was only getting stronger. Had it always been there? Probably. Any other time he would have admired it, but not now. Not where her health was concerned. Not just her health; her safety, too, whether she realized it or not.

Or maybe he really was overreacting, his instincts screaming for all the wrong reasons. No, not for the wrong reasons—for the right ones. Because no matter how little sense it made, no matter how foolish it sounded, Mat was pretty sure he was falling in love with her. He shouldn't be, not when they hadn't known each other that long, not when they hadn't spent that much time together.

But he knew his own heart, knew what he wanted. And he knew what he was feeling. He realized it last night, as Nicole cried in his arms, as he held her and comforted her, as she curled close to him and fell asleep in his arms, murmuring something about dragons not being real.

He circled the block, finally just double-parking in front of the weathered rowhome that was her mother's house. He cut the ignition but didn't make a move to get out. Neither one of them did.

They sat in silence for a few minutes, not looking at each other. Mat's hands clenched the steering wheel as he stared straight ahead, his mind racing. He took a deep breath and let it out in a rush.

"I really think you should come home with me." It wasn't a question, more like a plea. But Nicole shook her head and he already knew what she was going to say.

The same thing she'd said the last hundred times he had suggested it.

"I can't."

"Why not?"

"I just—I can't, Mat. You've already done enough. I can't just…" Her voice drifted off and she shook her head again. He watched her from the corner of his eye, saw her lips purse and her brows lower into a frown. Was she reconsidering? Having second thoughts? Or trying to talk herself out of saying yes?

Mat didn't want to push, afraid of scaring her, afraid of sounding like he was trying to control her. She didn't need that, which was something he completely understood. Probably too much, after the last thirty-some hours.

"I'm worried about you."

"I know. I'll be fine."

Mat wanted to argue but he bit back the words instead. He sighed, the sound ringing like defeat in his ears, then reached for the door handle. "I'll walk you in."

"You don't have to—"

"You're not the only one who can be stubborn." He fixed her with a steady gaze, letting her know he wasn't budging on this. She met his gaze straight-on, showing him another glimpse of her stubborn streak. Then she finally looked away, nodding.

He got out and hurried around to the other side, holding the door open for her and offering her his hand. She looked like she wanted to refuse then gave in with a weary sigh. Her hand was still chilled, a little damp and shaky. She needed to get inside, get some food, take her medication and lie down.

Mat grabbed her backpack and slung it over his shoulder, then led her to the door, his arm wrapped protectively around her waist. Her body stiffened when they reached the top step and he knew she was going to argue again, tell him he didn't need to come inside. He gave her a stern look and shook his head.

"I don't want to hear it. I'm making sure you get inside okay, making sure you do what the doctor said you were supposed to do. I'm not budging on this, Nicole, so you may as well give up now."

He expected to hear her argue, expected to see a flash of stubbornness in her eyes and the set of her chin. Instead he saw wariness and embarrassment. His heart skipped, twisting a little in his chest at the look in her eyes.

Mat reached up and cupped the side of her face, brushed his thumb along her lower lip. "Nicole, all I care about is you. Not your house, not what it looks like. None of it. Just you. Please don't shut me out. Okay?"

She chewed on her lip, like she wasn't sure if she should believe him or not. But she must have seen something in his eyes, or maybe it was just the words he spoke, because she slowly nodded and opened the door.

The interior was dim, cloaked in depressing gray

light. The linoleum floor in the entranceway was cracked and stained, the edges curling away from the wall and the base of the worn stairs. His gaze drifted to the living room, to the mismatched sofa and chairs covered in tattered sheets. Magazines and dirty dishes littered the table and floor. Cigarette butts floated in a few dirty glasses, like someone had used them for ashtrays.

Mat forced his face to remain expressionless, forced his body to remain relaxed. Not an easy task when all he wanted to do was pick up Nicole and take her back out to his car and drive, not stopping until they reached his house.

He felt her eyes on him, knew she was watching, waiting for some kind of reaction. He smiled, letting her know everything was fine, that nothing had changed his opinion or how he felt.

He motioned to the steps ahead of them. "Is your room upstairs?"

She looked away, a flush spreading across her pale cheeks. "Yeah, but you don't—"

"Nikki? Is that you?"

A voice called from somewhere in the back of the house, beyond the living room. Nicole jumped, the flush on her cheeks deepening, a harsh red against her pale skin. Her body stiffened and she threw a panicked look at Mat, her eyes wide. He grabbed her hand, threading their fingers together, offering her support. Her fingers were like ice, stiff in his hold despite their shaking. Tension thrummed though her, rolling off her in oppressive waves.

He squeezed her hand then brought it to his mouth, brushing a quick kiss along her knuckles. "You okay?"

"Yeah." Her voice cracked and she cleared her throat. "Yeah. Fine."

"Nikki?" The voice was closer now. A raspy smoker's voice, rough and abrasive. Mat turned as a woman walked into the room, her attention focused on lighting the cigarette hanging from pale dry lips. "Where have you been all night? You were supposed to be bringing dinner home—"

The woman stopped, her glassy eyes settling on Mat. Her gaze raked him from head to toe, judging him, sizing him up. She dropped a lighter into the pocket of her tattered robe, her eyes never leaving him. Then she took a long drag of the cigarette, its tip glowing as red as the flash of speculation in her eyes when she noticed their clasped hands.

"Who's this?"

Nicole shot him a look of apology before gently pulling her hand from his and turning back to her mother. "This is Mat. He—"

"So where were you? Did you stop to get any food?"

"Mom, I was at the hospital. I—"

"Yeah?" Her mother took another deep drag from the cigarette, her eyes raking Nicole this time. "What happened?"

"It was an infection. In my arm—"

"She was assaulted." The words came out clipped, cold. Mat didn't care, not when his anger was so close to the surface. He watched, waiting for her mother's reaction, thinking he'd see...something. Concern or worry or outrage. Something.

But all he saw was impatience and disbelief. Her gaze skimmed over him then shot back to Nicole.

"Assault? What happened?"

"Nothing—"

"No, not *nothing*." Maybe Mat was overstepping bounds, but he wouldn't let Nicole brush this away or downplay it. "Her ex-husband attacked her and shredded her arm so bad it became infected."

"You're saying Donnie did this?" Her mother frowned then looked away from Mat, her attention completely focused on Nicole. She took another long drag and blew the heavy stream of smoke in their direction. "What did you do to upset him this time, Nikki?"

"Excuse me?" The curt words fell from his mouth before he could stop them, before he even realized he was going to say anything. Had he heard her mother right? Was she really blaming Nicole for what happened? What kind of fucked-up twisted reasoning was that? "Maybe you didn't hear—"

Nicole reached for his arm, her hand shaking. "Mat, don't. Please. It's not worth it."

"But—" Mat didn't get a chance to finish because Nicole's mother kept on talking, acting like he wasn't even there.

"Well, I'm sure whatever you did, he's forgiven you. He came by last night, looking for you."

Nicole's hand tightened around his arm, squeezing, like a floundering ship that tossed an anchor overboard in order to stop and right itself. Her face paled, the color completely draining.

"Donnie was here? Again?"

Her mother nodded then lowered herself to the sofa. Ashes fell from the cigarette and landed in her lap but she barely looked at them, just brushed them off with a careless swipe of her hand. "Yeah. He waited around a while but you never showed up."

"Oh God. He was here? In the house?"

"Of course. You didn't think I'd make him wait outside, did you? I told him he could wait upstairs."

"Mom, no! Oh God, please no. He was in my room? You let him in my room?" Desperation was clear in her voice, in the tremors shooting through her. She turned and ran up the stairs, stumbling, saying "No" over and over again.

Mat didn't hesitate, just took off after her, the stairs creaking under his weight as he rushed up them. He caught himself, skidding to a stop before running into Nicole.

She stood just inside a tiny room, her shoulders slumped, her head hung low. "Oh God, no. No, no, no."

"Nicole, what is it?" Stupid question. Even from where he was standing, he could see what was wrong. A makeshift desk, nothing more than a piece of plywood propped on old plastic milk cartons, had been placed under a small dirty window. Pieces of a shattered laptop were strewn across the desk, along with broken pens and shredded strips of paper. The bed had been stripped, the sheets and blanket tossed in a pile on the stained floor. The mattress had been pulled from the bed and now rested at a crazy angle against the box spring.

Mat's fists clenched, anger searing his veins as he surveyed the destruction. Deliberate, malicious. His gaze stopped at the vile word hastily scrawled on the wall where a picture had once hung.

BITCH.

How could someone do something like this? What would possess someone to do something like this? Destruction like this, so deliberate and malicious and personal, was so far out of Mat's experience, he didn't know how to react.

But this wasn't about him, it was about Nicole. How she was reacting, what she must be thinking and feeling. He pushed back the anger, the sudden burning need for retribution. None of that would help Nicole. Not now. He stepped forward, ready to wrap his arms around her, ready to tell her things would be okay even though he knew they wouldn't. But she moved away, her breathing harsh as she hurried to the small closet.

She dropped to her knees, pulling things from the closet and throwing them carelessly behind her. Each short movement was choppy, desperate. Her fingers scratched against the floor, digging. Searching.

"Please. Please. Please."

Mat wanted to help her, wanted to ask what she needed, what she was looking for, but he didn't know if he should. He wasn't sure if she even knew he was there. He took a step into the room, one more—then stopped when she let out a small scream.

He didn't hesitate, just dropped to the floor behind her and wrapped his arms around her. "Nicole, what is it? What's wrong?"

"It's gone. All of it."

"What's gone?"

She laughed, the sound short and almost hysterical. She held up the box in her hand, one of those small metal cash boxes with a flimsy lock. The lock had been broken and the lid hung at an odd angle, one of the hinges busted. The box was empty.

"My money. All of it. Gone."

"Nicole—"

But she wasn't listening. Another short cry, more hysterical than the first, escaped her. She dropped the box and reached deeper into the closet, digging. A sigh of relief, too loud, echoed around him as she emerged with another metal box hugged to her chest. This one was thicker and sturdier than the first, similar to a security box of some sort.

Her arms tightened around the box, holding it even closer. She started rocking back and forth, her breathing harsh. Hair had fallen from her ponytail and hung in her face, hiding her eyes, her expression. Mat waited, not sure what to do, not sure what to say.

She finally looked at him, her eyes a little wild despite the relief he saw in their amber depths. "He didn't get this one. He didn't find it this time. He couldn't destroy them this time."

Mat couldn't stand it any longer. He wrapped his arm around her shoulder and pulled her close, holding her tight against him, like that would be enough to protect her.

"What didn't he get, baby?"

"My pictures. He didn't find them. They're safe."

He didn't ask Nicole to explain. He didn't have to because he instinctively knew what she meant. Mat closed his eyes, fighting against the emotions tearing him apart, focusing on the one that was most important: taking care of Nicole.

"You need to call the police. File charges—"

"No."

"Nicole, you have to. After what he did the other day? After this?"

She leaned back, sadness filling her eyes as she shook her head. "It doesn't matter. Nothing will happen. It never does. A month or two of jail time, maybe, but after that? Nothing. I can't do it again, Mat. I can't go through that again. It's over. He got what he came for: the money. That's all he wanted."

He wanted to argue, to convince her she was wrong, that she should call the police. But her silent plea tore at him, begging him not to push. He clenched his jaw, torn between doing what was right—or doing what was best for Nicole.

Mat finally swallowed his arguments and nodded. Nicole tried to smile but it wavered on her lips, dying away as she leaned against him, her eyes closed. He held her for long minutes, feeling her body slowly still, feeling some of the tension and desperation leave her. He dropped a gentle kiss on the top of her head then pushed to his feet, tugging Nicole with him.

"Come on, we're leaving."

"But—"

He placed his hands on either side of her face, tilting her head back so she would look at him. So she could see his eyes, see the emotions racing through them—through him.

"I am not letting you stay here. I'm not. I—" He swallowed, cleared his throat, started again. "I care about you, Nicole, and there is no way I'm letting you stay here. I wouldn't be able to sleep knowing you were here, knowing what could happen. Please. Come home with me. Please."

Could she see what else was in his eyes? Could she understand the words he couldn't say, not yet? Mat didn't know. And that was fine. It was too soon, she had so many other things to worry about it. But she had to know he cared. Didn't she?

Yes, she did. He could see it in her eyes, a spark of acknowledgement. And that was all that mattered.

Nicole pulled her gaze from his and slowly nodded. He breathed a silent sigh of thanks and pulled her in for a quick hug.

"My things—" She stopped, her shoulders slumping as she looked around at the destruction surrounding them.

"We'll figure something out, don't worry." He grabbed her hand and gently tugged, pulling her from the room. He needed to leave, to get her out of there as soon as he could. He wouldn't be able to breathe, to relax, until he did.

It would be a long time before he could relax at all, not after seeing all of this.

They reached the bottom of the stairs but Mat didn't pause, just reached out for the door handle. Her mother called out, her voice too loud, too scratchy.

"Nikki, where are you going?"

"She's leaving."

"Wait. You can't just do that! Where are you taking her?"

Mat looked over his shoulder, expecting to see Nicole's mother hurrying toward them in a fit of maternal outrage. But she was still on the sofa, a fresh cigarette held between her thin fingers as she leaned forward. Like she couldn't be bothered to get up, like it was too much trouble.

Mat clenched his jaw and stared at her, hiding nothing from his eyes, letting her see it all. His anger, his contempt, his willingness to do whatever was necessary to protect Nicole. She sat back with a gasp, her hand coming up and curling around the stained collar of the robe.

"I'm taking her somewhere safe." Mat pulled the door open, not caring that it slammed into the wall. He guided Nicole down the steps and out to his car, made sure she was safely buckled inside before moving around to the driver's side.

The engine roared to life and he stomped on the gas pedal, accelerating faster than needed as he sped away from the curb. He glanced over at Nicole, making sure she was alright, wondering if she would change her mind. But she simply sat there, not even bothering to look behind them as she reached over and curled her hand around his.

Chapter Nineteen

Nicole studied the image on the screen, squinting her eyes and tilting her head, checking it from different angles. A few more adjustments and she was done. She printed a copy then saved the final image, making a back-up as usual.

Except nothing was *as usual*. Not anymore, not for the last two weeks. She could deal with it when she was busy, when she was occupied with her pictures, her mind so engrossed that nothing else mattered.

It was when she wasn't busy that the whirlwind of changes hit her, overwhelming and dizzying to the point her stomach dipped and rolled and her lungs seized, fighting to draw breath.

She took a deep breath now and pressed a hand to her stomach, trying to control the flock of butterflies that had taken nest there. It was unreal, all of it, like some kind of hazy dream that kept playing out with no logical end in sight.

Nicole looked around, her gaze skimming over the room. No, not just a room. An office. Her office, to use as she pleased, with space to spread out, with amenities she had never imagined.

The desk with the built-in filing cabinets and drawers filled with every accessory she might need. The leather chair she was sitting in, overstuffed and soft, perfectly balanced. A state-of-the-art printer.

A brand new laptop loaded with every photo editing program she could ever want.

It was too much. Entirely too much. It didn't matter that the desk and chair and the other furniture had been here already. The laptop was new, and so was the printer. Mat had come home one afternoon, carrying the boxes upstairs and asking her if they would work for what she needed. No questions, no expectations.

It was too good to be true. Nicole knew what they said about things that were too good to be true. And she couldn't help but wonder if maybe she still hadn't learned her lesson, if the last two years fighting to get out, to find her own way, had been for nothing.

If she had moved from one abusive, controlling relationship to another.

Except the comparison wasn't even close. Mat was nothing like her ex had been, certainly not abusive. Definitely not controlling. He made sure she had her own space, encouraged her to do her own things, praised her photography. He opened his house to her, gave her a set of keys to his second car and told her she could use it whenever she needed. Told her to feel free to invite her friends over.

Except she didn't have any friends, not really, not since before Donnie. Not even the girls at the club could be considered her friends, certainly not enough to call or chat with after quitting. Not because of Mat, but because she couldn't handle the thought of going back there. Not when she hadn't enjoyed working there in the first place.

Mat had even gone to the hospital with her, when she went back to give Mia her pictures. And he'd surprised the girl with a small plush dragon with iridescent wings and a bright green body and glowing gold eyes.

Nicole brushed at the tears that came to her eyes, refusing to let them fall. Was it really too good to be true? Had she gone from one bad relationship to another?

Her heart told her no, she hadn't. Her heart told her Mat was the real thing. But her mind didn't want to accept it. How could she, after all she had been through? People like Mat didn't exist, not in her life. He smiled and laughed and gave, expecting nothing in return.

He hadn't even slept with her, not since bringing her home. He was affectionate, kissing her, holding her, cuddling with her while they watched television or just sat there and talked. About everything and anything, getting to know each other. But he hadn't pushed for sex, not once. They weren't even sleeping in the same room.

Part of her wondered if he was giving her space, making her feel comfortable, giving her time to adjust. Adjust to what? She didn't know, but something told her that she would have to be the one to initiate anything more.

Is that what she wanted? Yes. More than she wanted to admit. And that was the problem: she wanted so much more, and that scared her. What she was feeling scared her. Because she was very much afraid that she was falling in love—had already fallen in love with him—no matter how loudly her mind screamed that was a bad idea.

"Nicole, you ready?"

Mat's voice drifted into the room from the hallway. She swiveled in the chair, turning her back to the door and running her hands over her face, wiping at her eyes. She took a deep breath and pushed the hair from her face, trying to erase all traces of her thoughts and hopes and fears from her face.

She heard Mat behind her, felt his arms come around her from behind as he leaned in and pressed a kiss to her cheek. He stepped back and spun the chair around, the corners of his mouth tilted in a smile.

"The girls are downstairs, ready whenever you are."

Nicole tried to smile but it wavered on her face. She had been hoping to get out of the planned excursion but every excuse had been brushed off or waved away. Unless she was suddenly overcome with the flu or appendicitis in the next thirty seconds, she didn't see any way out of it.

She was doomed to go dress shopping. With Bridget and one or two other girls, wives or girlfriends of Mat's teammates. And she didn't want to go, not even a little bit. But she had to because Mat wanted her to go to his friend's wedding.

In two days.

Which meant she couldn't put it off any longer, couldn't make up excuses to reschedule.

Mat smiled again, no doubt knowing exactly what was going through her mind. He leaned forward, his mouth claiming hers for a searing kiss. Then he grabbed her hands and pulled her from the chair, walking backward toward the door.

"You're going to have fun."

"No, I'm not."

"Yes you will. This is a chance for you to get out, get to know some of the other girls, have some fun."

"This isn't a good idea, Mat—"

He stopped her with a kiss. Slow, deep. She sighed and leaned into him, wrapping her arms around his neck. His heat wrapped around her, filling her, chasing away some of the doubts and fears. But then he pulled away, leaving her breathless.

Leaving her frustrated and confused.

"It's a great idea. Give it a chance, you might surprise yourself." He smiled, that crooked boyish smile that made her toes curl, and reached up to tuck a strand of hair behind her ears.

Then he turned, leading her out into the hall and down the stairs.

Give it a chance, you might surprise yourself.

That's what she was afraid of.

Chapter Twenty

"You've lost your fucking mind, Herron. Completely and totally lost it."

Mat glanced in the rearview mirror, scowling at Kenny's reflection. He opened his mouth to respond but Derek jumped in, adding his own opinion.

"You can't lose what you never had to begin with."

"Fuck you, dude. All of you." Mat tightened his hands around the steering wheel, his knuckles turning white. For the tenth time in as many minutes, he questioned the wisdom of asking the guys along. Why had he bothered, when he knew this is what would happen?

"He's thinking too much with his dick, that's the problem." Harland leaned forward, pushing his head between the seats, his eyes still on his damn phone, doing who knew what this time. Facebook, Twitter, Instagram. He was into it all, always posting pictures or dry one-liners. A grin split his face, just for a second. The phone beeped with some kind of notification. Harland glanced at it, frowning, then lowered the phone and brushed the hair off his face. He chomped on his gum, the sound crackling in Mat's ear, and shook his head.

"Your problem is that you haven't dated enough. You're always waiting for the 'right one'." Harland's mouth twisted in a sneer as he made air quotes with one hand. "Now that you're getting it on a regular basis, you think you're in love."

Kenny gave a short bark of laughter and nudged Harland in the ribs. "So says the guy who can't get a real woman to look at him twice. You're so full of shit, Harland."

"Hey, I've got women. Lots of them."

"Yeah." Derek snorted. "Online, maybe."

"That's not—"

"Alright, knock it off. All three of you." Mat shot them each a look, his eyes narrowed, his jaw clenched. The glare didn't seem to faze any of them but at least they shut up. For now.

He rolled his eyes then glanced at the side mirror, checking for traffic before merging onto the exit ramp. Kenny leaned forward, pushing Harland out of the way, and pointed to nothing in particular. "Two blocks up and make a right."

Harland reached over and smacked Kenny's arm. "Get your fucking elbow out of my face, will you?"

"It's not in your face. And if you would fucking move, you wouldn't—"

Mat shot another glare toward the backseat. "Knock it the hell off! Christ, you're like a bunch of fucking two-year-olds back there."

Derek turned in the seat, laughing. "Yeah boys. Knock it off before Daddy turns the car around."

"You're not helping. You know that, right? Not

helping at all."

"Don't look at me that way. This was your idea, remember? Did you really expect anything different when you invited these two along?"

"Oh, and you're any better?" Mat snorted his disbelief. "Please. Don't kid yourself."

Derek rolled his eyes but didn't say anything— unlike Kenny and Harland, who were still bickering in the backseat. Mat moved into the right lane and stopped, waiting for the car in front of him to make the turn.

Kenny took a break from his shoving match with Harland and leaned forward again. "On your left, just after that next light."

Mat nodded, his eyes searching for the place. Derek shifted in his seat, his voice lowered so the other two wouldn't hear him. "Are you sure about this?"

Not really, no. But Mat nodded. "Yeah, I'm sure."

"I mean, like, really really sure? This isn't something you can change your mind about once it's done."

"Yeah, I know."

"You say that, but do you really? Because I don't think you do. I don't think you realize—"

"Dude, enough. I know what I'm doing. Okay?" At least the words sounded convincing, to Mat's ears at least. He cut across the two lanes of traffic and pulled into the parking lot, finding a spot close to their destination. He stared through the windshield at the storefront just off to his right, his damp hands still wrapped around the steering wheel.

Was he really doing this?

Yeah, he really was.

"Fifty bucks says he changes his mind." Harland

pulled some bills from his wallet and waved them around.

"You're on." Kenny pulled his own wallet out and thumbed through it.

"Nah, he won't change his mind. Like you said, Harland, he's thinking with his dick. But I got a hundred that says he cries like a baby."

"Fuck you, Derek."

"What? I told you, you have no idea what you're getting into." He pulled a crisp bill from his wallet and handed it back to Harland, placing his bet. Harland grabbed the money then climbed out of the car, joining Kenny on the sidewalk. Mat watched them for a few seconds then turned to Derek.

"What makes you say I'm thinking with my dick?"

"Because you are. It's like, now that you're getting sex on a regular basis, your mind has gone completely mushy."

"But I'm not."

"Yeah you are. Just being here proves your mind has turned—"

"Not that. I meant about the sex."

"What about the sex?"

"I'm not—" Mat snapped his mouth shut, wondering what the hell he was doing, why he was saying anything at all. Derek leaned back in the seat, studying him, confusion giving way to disbelief.

"You're not...what?"

"Nothing." He reached for the door handle but Derek grabbed his arm.

"Are you trying to tell me that you and Nicole aren't—"

"Just forget I said anything."

"No. Oh no." Derek grabbed his arm again,

stopping him from escaping. "Seriously, Mat? The girl is living with you, and there's nothing going on now?"

"No. I mean, it's not like that."

"Really? Then what is it? You take care of this girl, you're trying to keep her safe, bring her to live with you, and suddenly she doesn't want—"

"It's not her. It's me. I haven't—" Mat cleared his throat and looked away, his face burning in embarrassment. "I didn't want her to feel like she had to, you know? Didn't want her to feel like I was expecting anything in return. So I—I told her to take one of the guest bedrooms so she wouldn't worry and now—"

Derek burst out laughing, the sound too loud in the car. Annoying and abrasive. Mat pulled his arm away and thought about hitting him. Probably would have hit him if the wedding wasn't in two days.

Besides, if he hit him, Bridget would get upset and he didn't want that to happen.

"This is priceless. Absolutely priceless. Only you would do something so fucking asinine." Derek swiped a hand across his eyes, drying them. "You know, I meant that whole 'saint' thing as a freaking joke but now I know why it stuck."

"You're not funny. None of this is funny." Mat leaned his head against the seat and let out a heavy sigh, full of frustration and doubt. "And now I don't know what the hell to do."

"What do you mean, you don't know what to do? You just do what you did before. You know: a little wooing, some romance, making out, one thing leads to another—it's not fucking rocket science, you know."

"But I don't want her to think she owes me—"

"For fuck's sake. Mat, you were having sex with

her before she moved in, why would she expect things to be different now?"

"I don't know. I just thought—"

"You think too much, that's your problem. And now she's probably wondering what's wrong, why things changed. Smooth, Mat. Real smooth. For someone usually so smart about women and relationships, you really can be a dumb fuck at times."

He heard Derek's words, every single one of them, but he didn't want to believe they were true. They couldn't be. Could they?

Shit. Had he really screwed up? He closed his eyes and Nicole's face immediately came to mind. Her smile, her laughter, the way she curled against him when they were watching television. His chest burned with remembered warmth, that spot just above his heart where she always rested her hand. Like she needed to feel the beating of his heart, like it reassured her or anchored her or soothed her or something. He couldn't put it into words, only knew that he felt something similar, that feeling her hand resting there always filled him with a sense of peace, of belonging.

Another image followed that. Nicole's brows briefly lowered in a frown, confusion flashing in her eyes as she watched him.

When he pulled away or backed off. When he slowed and stopped their kisses, not wanting to push, not wanting her to feel like he was expecting anything from her.

Fuck. Was Derek right? Had he screwed up?

Yeah, he had.

Fuck.

He heard the car door opening, heard Derek step out. "Come on guys, we're going back."

Mat shot upright, his eyes popping open. He reached across and grabbed Derek, dragging him back into the car. "Dude, what the hell are you doing? We're not leaving!"

"You're still going through with this? After what you just told me?"

"Yeah, I am. Why wouldn't I?"

Derek held his hand out to Kenny and Harland, telling them to hang tight, then climbed back into the car and slammed the door. "Seriously? You still want to go through with this?"

"Yeah, why wouldn't I?"

"Holy shit, Mat. After what you just told me? I thought you were to the point where it was all roses and rainbow unicorn shit with Nicole, thinking you told her you loved her, that you were planning the wedding, you name it. That's why I thought you were doing this. And then you tell me you're not even sleeping with her? That you put her up in a spare bedroom?"

"I never said I loved her—"

"Yeah, obviously, if you're not even sleeping with her."

"That's not what I meant."

"Dude, don't lie to yourself. You are so in love with her, it's not even funny. Everyone can see it."

"But—" Mat snapped his mouth closed. But what? Nothing, that was what. Derek was right, whether Mat was ready to admit it or not. It didn't matter that any sane person would say it was too soon, it didn't matter what anyone else thought. It didn't even matter that he hadn't even been able to really admit it to himself, not in those words. But his heart knew what it wanted, knew what was right for him.

Nicole. All of her—past, present and future. It didn't matter. He loved her.

He loved Nicole.

Mat smiled, a huge grin spreading across his face as a weight seemed to lift from his chest. Everything felt right now, like he'd found the final piece of a puzzle and clicked it into place, only to reveal a picture a thousand times more spectacular than he thought it would be.

He loved Nicole.

Of course he did. Why else would he be getting ready to do what he was going to do? And now he knew exactly what he wanted, could see it so clearly in his mind. It was going to be perfect.

He opened the door and climbed out, humming under his breath. Not even Derek could annoy him any longer, not even when he voiced his opinion—loudly, for everyone to hear—as they walked into the shop.

"You're out of your fucking mind."

Chapter Twenty-One

The pain was driving him out of his fucking mind.

He knew it was going to hurt. Hell, he wasn't that stupid. But he never imagined the raw, searing, burning pain that was shooting through him now. His skin felt like it had been ripped off, put through a meat grinder, doused with alcohol, and shoved back in place.

How in the hell was he supposed to follow through with his plans tonight when all he could think about was the burning on his chest? He should have listened to the guys. Should have waited, or picked something a little smaller, or had it done in segments instead of all at once.

Fuck that. The idea of going back before it healed, of having new pain layered on top of old pain. No. No way in fucking hell.

He just wished it didn't hurt quite so much because it was screwing up his whole night.

"Are you okay?"

"Yeah, fine."

Nicole tilted her head, disbelief clear on her face.

She was curled up in the corner of the sofa, one arm draped over the edge, the other holding a throw pillow against her chest.

It wasn't just disbelief that he saw. No, there was confusion on her face as well. In her eyes as she watched him, like she didn't quite believe him, like she knew something was wrong but didn't know what. The confusion had been there for the last hour, ever since he'd bolted from the sofa and moved away from her, to the safety of the overstuffed chair. He hadn't meant to, hadn't even thought of what he was doing. They had been sitting there, talking about her day as she reluctantly admitted that she'd actually had fun shopping. The television was turned on, the volume down so it wouldn't interfere with their conversation.

Then Nicole slid closer to him, her eyes darkening as she leaned in and pressed her mouth against his. Warm, delicious. Needy. Mat had groaned, pulled her closer, thinking he shouldn't have worried about what he planned to do because maybe Nicole had the same ideas.

And then she put her hand on his chest, right above his heart like she usually did. Burning, searing pain shot through him and he jumped off the sofa so fast, he nearly knocked her over in his haste to get to the chair.

That's when she slid over to the corner and grabbed the throw pillow, holding it to her like some kind of shield. Except for grabbing the remote and nudging the volume up, she hadn't moved since. And Mat was still in the chair, his legs stretched out in front of him. He had shifted around so much he was actually sitting on the edge, in real danger of falling off. He didn't care, not when all he wanted to do was rip his shirt off and pile ice on his chest.

How the fuck was he supposed to know getting a tattoo would hurt so fucking much?

He pulled at the shirt, wincing as the material stuck to the raw skin for just a second before peeling away. What the hell was he supposed to do now? His mind was going a hundred miles an hour, trying to figure out how to salvage the night and put his plans in motion. There had to be a way for him to follow-through that didn't involve sheer agony and torture.

He shifted again, catching himself at the last minute before he fell out of the chair. Nicole looked over at him again, her brows lowered in a frown.

"Are you sure you're okay?"

"Yeah. Fine." Fuck. No, he wasn't fine. He needed to put more of that greasy lotion on his chest, maybe a cool washcloth, too. Kenny said that would help if he really needed it.

Yeah, right now, he really needed it. Maybe, once he cooled it down and put some lotion on it, got some of the stinging to disappear, he could focus on the rest of his plans for tonight.

He pushed out of the chair, wincing when his shirt brushed across his chest, then hurried to the stairs. "I, uh, I'll be back. I need to go do something."

Mat didn't even wait for Nicole to answer, just hit the stairs running, not stopping until he was in his bathroom. He ripped the shirt off, his arms tangling in the sleeves. He yanked on it, hard, and heard a tearing sound as he pulled it over his head. Then he reached for a washcloth and held it under the faucet. Why the hell was the water so warm?

He checked, making sure the faucet was turned all the way to cold. Yeah, it was. Shit. Usually it was colder than this, wasn't it?

Or maybe he was just doing some serious wishful thinking because right now, he wasn't even sure if ice would be cold enough to help.

He twisted the excess water from the washcloth then slapped it on his chest, praying for a miracle. One second. Two. Five…there, finally. Mat breathed a sigh of relief, the sound echoing off the marble around him. He sagged against the counter, closing his eyes as the stinging slowly, so slowly, eased up.

"Mat? I'm going to bed. Goodnight."

Nicole's voice drifted in, so faint against the running water that he almost missed it. He reached for the faucet, turning it off.

"Wait!" His voice came out as a croak. He cleared his throat and called out again, a little louder, hoping she'd hear him. "Nicole, wait. I didn't hear you."

"I just said I was going to bed. Goodnight."

"But it's still early." He glanced at his watch, just in case. It was only a little after nine. Later than he thought it was, but still too early.

"It's been a long day, I'm a little tired."

Her voice had faded. Was she moving down the hall? Moving toward her room?

No. No, no, no. This was not how the night was supposed to go. Not even close.

"Nicole, wait. Uh, could you come here for a minute?" Oh yeah, smooth. Real smooth. What was he going to do, try to seduce her in the bathroom?

He moved the washcloth from his chest and glanced in the mirror, did a double-take. Holy shit, was it supposed to be all red and puffy like that? He tilted his chin and looked down at his chest, just in case he was seeing things. No, the mirror didn't lie—his chest really was that red and puffy. And oozy. Shit. He touched it with the tips of his fingers then let out a loud hiss.

"Did you need something?"

"Uh, yeah." Nicole was in his room now, maybe two feet from the bathroom, judging by the sound of her voice. He reached back and nudged the door closed a little, just so she couldn't see in. Lotion. Where the hell did he put that lotion?

"Mat?"

"Yeah, just a sec." He reached for the tube, his fingers just brushing against it and knocking it to the floor. He bent over, banging his head against the counter in the process. "Fucking shit. Dammit."

"Mat? Are you okay?"

"Yeah. Fine. Hang on." Son of a bitch, that hurt. He'd be lucky if he didn't have a bump on his head in the morning from that one.

He grabbed the tube then opened it, squeezed some of the thick clear lotion onto his fingers. Now all he had to do was smear it over the tattoo.

Which meant he had to touch it.

Shit, this was going to hurt.

He closed his eyes, took a deep breath, and slapped his hand against his chest, thinking if he did it fast, it would hurt less. It was the worst thing he could do, touching his chest like that.

The breath rushed from his lungs in a sharp hiss. Loud, drawn out, like the air rushing from a balloon. Christ, he sounded like a fucking sissy but he couldn't help it. It fucking hurt. He'd rather take a puck to the throat or a stick to his arm or a blade to his face than deal with this.

"Mat? Are you okay?" Nicole's voice, full of

concern, was closer now, her steps just outside the bedroom. He saw her hand curl around the edge of the door, watched from the mirror as the door swung open. Slow, like she wasn't quite sure what to expect.

He wanted to slam the door shut but he couldn't do that, not with Nicole already standing in the doorway. He could move, turn so his back was to her, but even that wouldn't work, not with the mirrors surrounding him.

So he just stood there, the tube of lotion in one hand, the other hand smeared with the greasy stuff and hovering just above his chest. He tried to hide his disappointment, tried not to look deflated when she pushed the door all the way open, her eyes meeting his in the mirror.

He had wanted to surprise her, hoping she'd understand the significance, hoping it would mean as much to her as it did to him.

Hoping that it would make it easier to tell her what he wanted to tell her.

But he blew it. Yeah, some surprise. Some romantic he was.

He dropped his hands to his side and turned, facing her but not quite able to meet her eyes. "I, uh, wanted to surprise you but—I don't think it turned out like it was supposed to."

Yeah, that was putting it mildly. Not with all the red puffiness and raw skin and dots of oozing blood and splotch of greasy lotion.

Mat looked down at the tube in his hand, still not able to look at Nicole, not with her standing there, completely silent. Her silence was saying more than enough. He sighed and turned away, putting the lid back on the tube before tossing it to the counter. Now what? He was an ass, that's what. An ass with a raw, shredded chest.

"You got a tattoo." Nicole's shocked whisper echoed around him. He shrugged, not knowing what to make of the words, not understanding the tone of her voice.

"Yeah. This afternoon. While you were out shopping."

"It's—" Her voice faltered. Mat wished he could see her face but he couldn't look at her, not yet. "Oh my God, Mat. It's…it's…"

"Yeah. Pretty bad, huh?"

"Are you serious? It's beautiful!" Her voice cracked again, ending in a choked sob. Mat turned, saw the tears in her eyes and the small smile that trembled on her lips. He blinked, wondering if he was seeing things. She stepped closer, her hand reaching out, not quite touching his chest. Her fingers shook and she lowered her arm, curling her hand into a loose fist.

Then her eyes drifted up to meet his gaze. Beautiful amber eyes, lit from within, their color almost the same as the eyes of the dragon covering the left side of his chest, over his heart.

"I can't believe you did this. It's…Mat, it's beautiful. And…" Her voice cracked and trailed off again. Panic seized him when he saw the tear falling from her eye. Just a single tear, slowly tracing its way down her cheek. He reached out, wiping it away with his thumb.

"If it's supposed to be that nice, why are you crying?"

"Because—it's a dragon. A beautiful, wonderful, majestic dragon." She tried to smile but it wavered again, not quite blooming into the full smile he wanted to see, had hoped to see.

"Of course it's a dragon. You like dragons."

"You got this...you did this for me?"

"Yeah. I thought—I mean, I just wanted..." Why were the words so hard to find? They shouldn't be. He had this all planned out, had envisioned how the night was going to go, how he was going to surprise her.

Of course the words wouldn't come. Nothing else had worked out like he planned, why would finding the words be any different?

She reached out with her hand again, her trembling fingers tracing the intricate designs without really touching them. The rearing head, proudly held high. The wings, not quite extended for flight, a paler green than the dragon's graceful body. The long tail, trailing just a bit across Mat's ribs.

And the dragon's clawed hands, carefully folded around an amber heart, the color perfectly matching the eyes of the dragon.

She looked up at him, her trembling fingers still hovering near his chest. "I can't believe you did this. For me. I don't understand. Why would you do something like this?"

"You don't like?"

"No, I do. It's—" She cleared her throat, glanced back at his chest then met his gaze. "It's beautiful. You have no idea what it means. I just...I don't understand why."

Mat swallowed, searching for courage, praying the words would come out right. He grabbed her hand, holding it between his. "You said dragons weren't real. In the hospital. I thought—I just wanted—"

Another deep breath. But God, it was so hard to breathe, not when she was looking up at him like that, her beautiful amber eyes shining, filling with tears as she chewed on her lower lip. Waiting. Hoping? He didn't know, could only hope himself.

He took another deep breath, released it slowly as something warm and peaceful descended over him. This was right. What he was feeling was right. Being here, with Nicole, was right.

"I wanted to show you that dragons do exist. That you shouldn't give up on believing." He dipped his head and brushed his lips against hers, the touch feather light. He lowered his voice to a whisper, soft. "I love you, Nicole."

Her hand tensed, her grip tight against his. He felt her shift, felt her try to take a step back. Mat closed his eyes. He'd blown it. He shouldn't have told her, not yet. It was too soon. She probably thought he was crazy, was probably wondering how soon she could pack and leave and—

"You love me?"

"Yeah. I'm sorry, I shouldn't have said—" His words were cut-off, stopped by the press of her lips against his. Soft, warm, tender. Mat sighed and pulled her closer, teasing the seam of her lips with his tongue until her mouth opened under his. And then he was kissing her, losing himself in her sweet fire, drinking her surrender even as he offered her his own.

But then she pulled away, her face flushed as she stared up at him.

"You love me?"

"Yeah. I—"

"I wasn't sure. I was scared, thinking it was too soon, thinking that maybe I was crazy but I wasn't. I'm not. It's not."

"It's not?"

Nicole shook her head, her hair tumbling around her shoulders as a bright smile lit her face. "It's not. Too soon, I mean. Because I love you and I thought I was just crazy and—"

This time it was his turn to interrupt her, to kiss her senseless until she melted against him, until her arms wrapped around his neck and she pressed her body against his. Close, so close, like she couldn't bear to be apart from him.

Burning seared him, the sensation stealing his breath. But it was a different kind of burn, the kind that made him suck in a sharp breath and ease Nicole away from him with a small groan.

"Mat? What is it? What's wrong?" Her eyes narrowed in concern as she studied him, her hands gliding over his face, down to his shoulder, down to his chest.

He gasped again and grabbed her hands, taking a step back until he was leaning against the counter. Christ, he was a fucking idiot, to stop her like that, when he wanted nothing more than to hold her in his arms, to feel her body against his.

To lose himself inside her and tell her, over and over, that he loved her.

Mat shook his head and tried to grin, to ease her worry.

"I'm fine. My chest is just kind of on fire right now, though, and it feels like ground meat."

Nicole's eyes widened. She glanced at his chest then covered her mouth with her hands. Her shoulders started shaking, just a tiny bit as she laughed. The sound was musical, echoing around them like an angel's voice in a cathedral. He didn't want her to stop.

But she did, all too soon. Her gaze met his again,

filled with amusement. She dropped her hands then placed a quick kiss against his chest, just above the fresh tattoo.

"I'm sure it does. You had a lot of work done, a lot of line work and detail." Her fingers hovered over the tattoo, tracing the air just above each line and curve. "It really is beautiful. I can't believe you had them do it all at once."

"Yeah. I, uh, didn't know that you could do it over time. I wasn't thinking. Besides, I wanted to surprise you."

Her eyes lit up again, so soft and warm. "You did. Thank you. But let's get you fixed up."

"Fixed up?"

"Yeah." She grabbed his hand and led him to the large tub, motioning for him to sit on the edge. Then she went back for the washcloth, soaking it in cold water before ringing it out.

Her hands were gentle, soothing, as she placed the cloth against his chest, holding it there until the stinging faded away. All Mat could do was watch her. The way she tilted her head, the light catching in her hair when it fell over her shoulder. The tiny movements of her hands as she moved the washcloth and uncapped the lotion. Each detail burned into his mind, forming a picture he would recall for years to come. Even her small laugh when he gasped and tried to pull away when she spread a thin layer of the lotion over the tattoo. All of it. All of her. Picture after picture of future memories, sealed away forever. In his mind. In his heart.

He reached for her, scooping her up in his arms and carrying her to the bed. His mouth closed over hers, claiming, possessing. Being possessed in return.

Their clothes disappeared, the last barrier between them. Then Mat leaned back on the bed, pulling her on top of him, settling her against his body.

"I love you. God, I love you so much." He pulled her down for a kiss, his hands touching her, gliding over her skin, memorizing each inch of her body. She pulled away, pushing to a sitting position as she straddled him, a smile on her face.

"I love you, Mat Herron. Always." Then she lowered herself on him, her eyes never leaving his, and he lost himself.

No, not lost. He found himself. In her touch, her smile, her body. Her heart. Found himself over and over.

Chapter Twenty-Two

It was a dream. It had to be, because Nicole had never felt this way before. Like she was floating. No, not floating. Flying. Being carried away on the back of her very own dragon, safe and protected high above the clouds where nothing could touch her. Nothing except her exquisite, beautiful dragon.

She frowned. Right now, her exquisite beautiful dragon was standing next to the car, his brows lowered in fierce concentration as he ran his hand over his chest. Back and forth, over and over.

"Stop scratching."

"It itches."

"That's because it's healing. Now stop." She moved to stand next to him, reaching up to adjust the crisp square of blue linen peeking from the pocket of his tux. She pressed a kiss against his chest, just because she could, then stepped back. Heat filled her at the look in his eyes. Warm, loving, wrapping around her until her toes curled and she wanted to do nothing more than grab his hand and run off somewhere so they could be alone.

How had it happened? What had she done to deserve a man like him? She still couldn't believe it, was still afraid that this was nothing more than a dream. That she'd wake up to her old life and realize she had only imagined this.

But it wasn't a dream. She knew, because Mat kept reassuring her it wasn't. Or he'd laugh and smile that silly crooked smile and tell her if it was a dream, it was one they were dreaming together. As long as they were together, it didn't matter.

And he was right.

He smiled at her now, heat flaring in his deep green eyes as his gaze slowly traveled over her. "You are so beautiful."

Nicole blushed but she didn't deny it. How could she, when she saw it so clearly in his eyes? And she felt beautiful. Not just from the look in Mat's eyes, although that would be more than enough to do the job. It was the dress and heels, the entire outfit.

Bridget and Kayli had picked it out, oohing and ahhing over it when she tried it on. Nicole had seen it on the rack and fell in love with it but didn't think it would like right on her, didn't think someone like her could wear something so beautiful. But the women—her new friends—had insisted. Nicole was glad she had listened to them.

The dress hugged her to her hips then fell in a graceful flare to just above her knee, flowing as she walked. The material was a rich green, deep and vibrant, the two thin straps that held it up made of a slightly iridescent material that shimmered in the light. The dress had a matching wrap, with that same iridescent material woven through it. Wearing it made her feel…magical. Which was such a silly way to feel just because of a dress, but she couldn't help it.

It was all part of that dream, the dream she was now living.

Mat reached for her hand and brought it to his mouth, his lips brushing across her knuckles. He tucked her hand in the crook of his elbow then led them away from the car, toward the large cedar-sided house. The late afternoon sun sparkled on the water behind the house, shooting rays of gold all around them.

Both the wedding and the reception were being held here, in the back yard of the groom's house. Mat had told her the arrangement was a compromise, that the bride had wanted a simple outdoor wedding. The groom was the one who insisted on formal attire for the ceremony—which is why Mat was carrying her backpack, so they could change into different clothes later if they wanted.

Looking at Mat now, so handsome and regal in the fitted tux, Nicole wasn't sure she wanted him to change. Maybe she could convince him to put it back on later, once they got home.

"Wait. My camera—"

"It's in here, don't worry."

"Okay." She took another two steps then paused. "Did you grab the extra memory cards?"

"Yes. Stop worrying, I took care of everything."

"Are you sure you grabbed the right ones?" She had lost track of time, trying to get her hair and make-up just right, so Mat had gathered the camera and other accessories for her. She just hoped he grabbed the right things.

"Yes, I'm sure." He squeezed her hand and led her

through the house then outside to a large deck. The yard stretched out before them, a blanket of thick grass that ended at a stone bulkhead. Beyond that was a small strip of sand, dipping down to the water's edge. A pier led out into the water, two jet skis tied at the end, bobbing on the gentle waves.

An arch had been placed at the end of the yard, decorated with an abundance of flowers and garland. White chairs were lined up in uniform rows on either side of a wide aisle but nobody was sitting in them, not yet. People were milling around, talking in small groups, holding glasses or plates or both in their hands.

Nicole stopped, her hand tightening around the edge of the wrap as she stared in shock. She had never seen so many gorgeous men in one place. So many large men. Ever.

"Your mouth is hanging open."

"What?" Nicole turned to face Mat, saw him grinning at her shocked expression.

"Everyone is so...so—" She didn't know what to say, couldn't find the right words.

"It's a little overwhelming at first, isn't it?" She heard Kayli's voice behind her, felt something like relief go through her when she saw Kayli and Bridget walking toward them—until she saw the two men following behind them. Her relief floundered, just a little. She knew the one man, had already met Derek. But she didn't know who the other man was. Her hand tightened around Mat's and she thought she might have taken a step back, she wasn't sure.

Kayli stepped closer, a welcoming smile on her face. "Nicole, this is my husband, Ian."

"Nice to meet you." He reached out, his hand swallowing hers when he shook it. The corners of his eyes crinkled with his smile, his teeth white against the dark hair of his neatly-trimmed beard.

She muttered hello then glanced over at Mat, felt herself relax when he smiled and winked at her.

Kayli leaned forward, like she was ready to tell a dark secret. "Don't let their size fool you. They're all just a bunch of big teddy bears."

The three men immediately started denying it but their objections didn't sound very convincing. Nicole looked around again, taking a closer look. She would love to get her camera out right now, just start shooting. There were so many interesting faces, all sharp angles and lines.

"These are your teammates?"

"Yeah. Most of them. Come on, I'll take you around and introduce you—"

"Mat! Uncle Mat!"

A young girl, maybe eight or nine years old, came running out of the house, heading straight for them. The wreath of flowers covering her light brown hair slid forward over her face, covering her eyes when she slid to a stop in her bare feet. She scowled then pushed the wreath back with an impatient hand, muttering under her breath.

"Hey, Squirt. Are you supposed to be out here yet?"

"No but I heard you so I had to come say hi." She wrapped her arms around Mat's waist for a big hug then stepped back and gave him a high five. The girl laughed when Mat shook his hand, pretending her slap had hurt. Then she looked at Nicole, her head tilted in curiosity.

"Hi, I'm Taylor. Who are you?"

"Nicole."

The girl nodded then turned back to Mat. "She's pretty."

Mat winked at the girl then turned to Nicole, heat in his eyes. "Yes, she is."

A woman came out, dressed in a simple pale blue sheath that accented the soft waves of her short blonde hair. She frowned, frustration evident in the faint lines that feathered out from her stormy gray eyes and bracketed her mouth. Her coloring was different from the young girl's but Nicole could see the other resemblances. It was there, in the shape of their faces, the slightly tilted nose and stubborn chin.

The exasperation in her voice when she spoke left no doubt in Nicole's mind that this was the young girl's mother. "Taylor, get back in here. And where are your shoes? JP is having a big enough meltdown, he doesn't need to see you out here in your bare feet on top of everything else."

"Why is JP having a meltdown?"

"Because there's no formal photographer. He thought he had confirmed one but he didn't. So now he's inside, convinced he's a failure and everything is doomed while Emily is trying to tell him she didn't want all this fuss to begin with."

"It's funny, Uncle Mat. He's completely forgetting to speak English and Aunt Emily keeps laughing because he's saying all the bad words."

The woman who had come out placed her hands on her hips and gave Taylor a stern look. "And just how would you know he's saying the bad words?"

Taylor's mouth dropped open and she shuffled from foot to foot. "Oops." She grinned and shrugged. "I need to go get my shoes on."

She spun on one heel and flew back into the

house, the wreath sliding sideways as she disappeared inside. The gathered crowd laughed, and even Nicole couldn't help but smile. Some of the tension eased out of her and she felt herself relax. She leaned against Mat, his hand warm and comforting as it settled around her waist.

Until he spoke.

"Nicole could be the photographer."

She stiffened, tension shooting through her as everyone on the deck turned and stared at her. She shook her head, ignoring everyone else as she threw a frightened look at Mat.

"No. I can't. I couldn't—"

"Yes, you can. Nicole, I've seen your stuff. Your great at it."

"Mat, no." She looked around, trying to ignore the curious glances, then leaned closer to Mat, lowering her voice so only he could hear. "I've never done anything like this. This is too important, I couldn't."

"Why not?"

"Because I can't. What if I mess something up?"

He dropped a kiss on the tip of her nose, his smile reassuring. "You won't mess up."

"You know, Mat's right." Bridget stepped closer and placed a reassuring hand on Nicole's arm. "I've seen your work, Nicole. Don't underestimate yourself."

Nicole shook her head, trying to deny it, trying to convince everyone that she couldn't do it. But Mat pressed another kiss to her cheek and stepped away, heading for the door.

"Perfect. I'll go tell JP, talk him down from the ledge."

"But I can't. What if I mess up?"

But her objections fell on deaf ears as Mat

disappeared inside, as everyone else started talking again, the conversations so wide and varied, Nicole couldn't keep up.

She stared down at the camera Mat had thrust into her hands, looking at it like she had never seen it before. Why wasn't anyone else worried? A wedding was so important, a lifetime event full of promise and new beginnings. What if she messed it up? What if she missed something?

Nicole closed her eyes, an image of Mia coming to mind. Promises and new beginnings. Isn't that what she did at the hospital? No, it wasn't exactly the same, not really. It was a different kind of promise, a different kind of new beginning. And its own way, maybe more important.

Nicole took a deep breath, her hand folding around the camera, her fingers tracing the familiar lines. Okay, she could do this. It was just pictures, something she did all the time.

She could do this.

She hoped.

Chapter Twenty-Three

Mat raised his hand, ready to scratch at his chest. But his gaze caught Nicole's and he lowered it. She watched him, a smile on her face, her eyebrows raised, letting him know she knew exactly what he'd been ready to do. He grinned then rolled his shoulders, trying to convince himself that might help with the itching even though he knew it wouldn't.

Lotion would help. Nicole rubbing the lotion on his chest, her fingers so light and soft against his skin, would help even better. He'd have her do just that, as soon as he went in to change out of his tux. JP had a few extra rooms. Mat could take her into one, let her rub that lotion on him, finally feel her hands on his bare skin. Maybe convince her he needed lotion on places other than his chest—

He swallowed back a groan and shoved thoughts of getting Nicole naked from his mind. Not an easy thing to do, not when that's all he could think about every time she looked at him, when he saw his own hunger reflected in the depths of her amber eyes.

But there was something else he needed to do first, something more important. He pulled his gaze away from Nicole and looked around, searching. His eyes came to rest on Alec's wife, AJ, standing off to the side, talking with Bridget and Kayli and Emily. Mat made his way over to them, his eye catching AJ's.

"Did you want to take a look now?"

"I can look, Mat. But no guarantees. I don't have much say in that, you know that."

"I know, but it wouldn't hurt, right? And then if something comes open, or if you need a quick fill-in or something." Mat stopped rambling and shrugged, trying not to get his hopes up. AJ was a sports reporter for the local paper. He was hoping that maybe she could put a word in, see if the paper needed a photographer for anything.

And yeah, he knew it was pretty far-fetched, knew that nothing would come of it, but it didn't hurt to try. "She's good, AJ. Really."

"Are you talking about Nicole?"

Mat turned to Bridget, nodding. "Yeah. I want AJ to look at some of her stuff, see what she thinks."

"Mat's right, AJ. I've seen the work Nicole does for the patients. She has a real talent, a real knack for capturing things you wouldn't think you could see."

"I'm sure she does. I just don't know if I can help." AJ smiled, softening the sting of disappointment Mat felt at her words.

He turned and headed over to where Nicole was sitting, her gaze focused on her camera as she placed a new memory card in it and studied the small screen. He saw her start, saw her body jerk just the tiniest bit before she straightened and looked around. Her eyes widened when they settled on him, a small flush coloring her cheeks. He couldn't help his answering grin, thinking maybe she had been having the same thoughts he'd been having, that maybe convincing her to follow him into one of the spare rooms wouldn't be as hard as he'd first thought.

But first he wanted her to show AJ the pictures she'd taken. She'd probably argue, would probably be too bashful to show them off, but Mat was prepared for that. He glanced behind him and saw that Bridget and Kayli and Emily had followed him as well. This was even better. How could Nicole refuse to show the pictures to the bride? She couldn't.

Mat grinned, coming to a stop in front of Nicole. She looked up, her body tensing, vibrating with wariness. She stood up, her eyes meeting his before darting to the women behind him. And already she was lowering the camera, trying to hide it behind her back. Almost like she knew what he was going to do before he even did it.

He grabbed her free hand and tugged her closer, his arm sliding behind her. "Nicole, this is AJ. Alec's wife. She's a reporter."

Nicole's eyes darted to his, curiosity clear in their depths. She turned to AJ, smiling in greeting.

"You should show her your pictures. She might be able to help get you some work or something."

"Oh. Uh—" Nicole tensed, shooting him a panicked look as she pulled the camera further behind her.

"Like I told Mat, no guarantees. But I can look. There might be some freelance opportunities available, I'll have to check with my editor. And the team's blog always needs pictures. They don't pay, of course, but it's a way to get some photo credits."

"Wow. Thank you. That would be—" Nicole shot him another look, some of the panic leaving her eyes, then turned back to AJ. "That would be great, thanks. I can send some over—"

"No, show her the ones you took today."

She turned, still trying to hide the camera. "I don't think—"

But Mat had been expecting that. He snatched the camera from her hand, grinning at the shocked expression on her face when he handed it to AJ.

"Mat, no!" Nicole reached for it with a surprised gasp but it was too late, AJ already had it, raising it up so the other girls could see, too.

"Oh my."

"Wow."

"Um, yeah. Wow."

Mat watched them, studying their reactions, waiting to hear how impressed they were with what Nicole had done. He wrapped his arm around her waist and pulled her close, feeling the tension and anxiety running through her. Of course she was anxious but that would change, as soon as she heard how impressed everyone was.

"What do you think? I told you they were good."

"Yeah, they're uh—" AJ cleared her throat, a slow smile spreading across her face. Bridget placed her hands over AJ's, moving the camera closer so she could see better.

"No, wait. Flip back, I want to see that one again." She smiled, her eyes darting to Mat's before moving back to the camera. "Oh yeah. These are definitely better than what I was expecting."

He tightened his arm around Nicole, giving her a reassuring squeeze. "Relax, baby. They like them. I knew they would."

"Mat, I don't think—"

"What are you guys looking at it? Are those the pictures from today?" Derek moved behind Bridget, leaning over her shoulder to get a better look.

"Yeah. I thought—"

"No, they're not." Nicole's strangled words cut him off. He looked down at her, confused, not understanding why her face had gone from pink to an alarming red.

"What's not what?"

"The, uh, the pictures." Nicole inched closer, her face practically buried in his chest now, her voice muffled. "They're not from today."

"Oh." He shrugged. "Well, that doesn't matter. They can still see—"

"Holy shit. What the fuck? Give me that." Derek grabbed the camera from the women, his hands fumbling with the buttons before he finally just shoved it at Mat. "What the hell are you trying to do, Herron? Christ, you don't just…and then…and you…really? You? Of all people? What the fuck?"

"Dude, what's your problem? They're just pictures."

"I don't give a fuck. You don't go showing your shit around like that. What the hell's wrong with you?"

Mat narrowed his eyes at Derek, wondering why he was cussing like that in front of the women. That wasn't like him, not at all. "Dude, seriously, you need to watch your language."

"You're going to jump on me about my language after that—that—" Derek swallowed, glanced around at the women, then looked back at Mat. "That *stuff* I just saw? I need bleach for my eyes now."

"I don't know, I liked them." Kayli's clear voice was tinged with laughter and appreciation. Her eyes met his, raked down his body, looked away.

"Oh yeah, definitely." Emily looked straight at him, her eyes bright.

Bridget laughed, ignoring the outraged look on Derek's face as she gave Mat a sly playful smile. "Definitely a side of you I've never before."

"A side we never expected to see," AJ added. The four women looked at each other, wide smiles on their faces, then started laughing.

Discomfort settled over Mat, coupled with a niggling feeling that something wasn't quite right. He glanced down at the camera in his hand, suddenly afraid to look at it. It didn't help that Nicole was glued against his side, her eyes squeezed shut, her face a bright red.

"Uh—" He swallowed and looked down at the camera again. Against his better judgment, he brought it up to his face and thumbed the power button on, then groaned when he saw the screen.

No, the pictures definitely weren't from today. They were from the other night, picture after picture. Of him. Posing. Playing. Full body shots and close-ups. Close-ups of everything, from his eyes—all the way down to his hands, wrapped around his cock.

Mat powered the camera off, his face burning when he realized what the four women had been looking at. He shifted and looked around, not quite able to meet anyone's eyes as embarrassment surged through him.

Well hell. What should he do now?

Because it wasn't embarrassment surging through him. Embarrassment had never caused his cock to harden and throb with need.

And there was no doubt Nicole felt it. How could she not, pressed against him as tightly as she was? He felt a shiver go through her, felt her body soften and warm in response. He eased away, just enough so he could claim her mouth in a searing kiss that left them both breathless.

"Really, Herron?" Derek repeated, his voice a little strangled. "You need a new nickname, because you sure as hell aren't a saint."

He looked over at Derek, a slow smile spreading across his face. "You're right, I'm not." Mat wrapped his hand around Nicole's and turned, heading back to the house.

"Where are you going?" Derek's voice could barely be heard above the feminine whistles and catcalls that followed them.

Mat didn't bother looking back when he answered, didn't even break stride. "Inside. For another photo shoot."

Epilogue

Nicole sat back in the chair, studying the picture, her mind's eye choosing and rejecting different edits. It was an action shot, a close-up of Kenny Haskell boarding a player from Colorado in the Banners' last pre-season game. His face was twisted in fierce concentration, the camera capturing the stark lines of his cheeks and jaws, the sharp curves of his mouth above his opponent's shoulder, shoved up against the glass.

Nicole shook her head. The picture didn't need any edits. It was perfect just as it was. She saved it in her game picture file then opened her email program, surprised to see she had so many new emails. They could wait, at least until she got this one sent out first.

She composed a quick email, adding a few lines of text to accompany the picture, then hit send. Accomplishment filled her and she smiled, still not quite able to believe all the changes that had happened so quickly.

AJ had given her the name of the team's blog,

Banners Bytes, an unofficial online blog that covered the team's practices and games and everything else in between. She had sent them a few pictures and quickly received an invitation to submit whatever photos she had relating to the team. Mat had arranged for her to attend the open sessions of training camp, where she received a quick and brutal lesson on the game itself, on the physical demands made of the players.

And she had captured it on camera, focusing on what the other photographers there seemed to miss. It had been enough to secure her a spot as a permanent contributor to the blog.

No, it didn't pay. But she was doing what she loved and getting credit for it. She couldn't ask for more.

Her laptop beeped, signaling another email. They'd been coming more frequently as people wrote to her, commenting on her photos. Some of them were a bit disturbing, like the ones from some women asking for pictures they had no right to be asking for, as if Nicole somehow had full behind-the-scenes access to the showers and locker rooms. Mat had just laughed and told her to ignore them, explaining that all the players received requests like that—or worse.

So that's what she did. Ignored and deleted.

She opened the latest email, wondering if it was going to be more of the same. Her eyes skimmed it but the words didn't make sense. Not at first.

She squeezed her eyes, thinking maybe she'd been at the computer too long, that she was seeing things. She read the email again, then read it a third time, her heart thundering in her chest.

The door downstairs opened and she heard Mat call her name. Nicole jumped from the chair and raced downstairs, almost slipping on the last one. Mat caught her just before she would have fallen, his arms strong around her waist as he swung her against him.

"I got it. I got it!" She wrapped her arms around his neck and pressed her mouth to his for a quick kiss.

"Got what?"

"A chance at freelancing. I just got the email. They saw my pictures on the blog, want to see what else I have."

"That's fantastic! I told you that you could do it." Mat pressed his mouth to hers, the kiss a little longer, a little deeper this time.

"Yes, you did." She kissed the corner of his mouth, down along his jaw, the stubble tickling her lips. "Thank you."

"For what?"

"For believing in me. For telling me I could do it." She pressed herself even closer, feeling his body respond against hers as she dragged her mouth along his neck, nipping at the corded muscle.

"I love you, Nicole. Of course I believe in you." His voice had lowered, becoming a little thicker, a little hoarser as she dragged her hands down his chest and grabbed the hem of his shirt, lifting it up so she could place a kiss on his chest, over the exquisite dragon tattooed there. Over his heart.

"I love you, too. So much."

Mat leaned forward, his mouth claiming hers, hot, spicy, full of need and desire. But then he pulled away, his small groan echoing hers, and grabbed her hands, tugging her into the living room. "This calls for a celebration."

"Oh yeah? What do you have in mind?"

"Close your eyes."

She raised her brows, silently asking why. But he shook his head, a grin on his face, so she did as he asked. She heard him move, heard paper rustling and what sounded like plastic or metal clicking. Curiosity pulsed through her and she squeezed her eyes tighter, not wanting to spoil whatever surprise he had planned.

Especially not when his surprises generally left her gasping for air and screaming his name as pleasure ripped through her.

"You ready?"

"Hmm, yeah." God, was that her voice, so husky, filled with need? Yes, it was. Only Mat did this to her, made her feel this way. Needy. Alive, special. Cherished. Loved.

"Good." He stepped closer, the heat from his body reaching out, caressing her skin. "Go ahead, open your eyes."

She did, expecting…she wasn't sure what. She blinked, her eyes trying to focus on the object Mat was holding out to her. Recognition slowly dawned and she looked up at him, her mouth parted in surprise. He couldn't be serious.

Could he?

"Since you're becoming a hotshot photographer now, I thought maybe you should expand your horizons, learn how to work with video." A shy grin spread across his face, along with the barest hint of a blush. "What do you think?"

Nicole answered his grin with one of her own then reached for the video camera he was holding. His eyes darkened, the green becoming even deeper, fluid and enchanting, cloaking her in sorcery. In desire.

Then he stepped back, waiting as she brought the camera to her eye, learning the controls, adjusting the

271

focus.

Zooming in on his hands, closer as he reached for the button of his jeans, as he tugged at the zipper, each movement slow, deliberate. Enticing. Promising.

And Nicole wondered, not for the first time, how anyone could have ever confused her dragon for a saint.

*****

SHOOT OUT

Lisa B. Kamps

ABOUT THE AUTHOR

Lisa B. Kamps is the author of the best-selling series *The Baltimore Banners*, featuring "hard-hitting, heart-melting hockey players" (USA Today), on and off the ice. Her newest series, *Firehouse Fourteen*, features hot and heroic firefighters and launched with ONCE BURNED.

Lisa has always loved writing, even during her assorted careers: first as a firefighter with the Baltimore County Fire Department, then a very brief (and not very successful) stint at bartending in east Baltimore, and finally as the Director of Retail Operations for a busy Civil War non-profit.

Lisa currently lives in Maryland with her husband and two sons (who are mostly kinda-sorta out of the house), one very spoiled Border Collie, two cats with major attitude, several head of cattle, and entirely too many chickens to count.

Interested in reaching out to Lisa? She'd love to hear from you, and there are several ways to contact her:

Website: www.LisaBKamps.com
Newsletter: www.lisabkamps.com/signup/
Email: LisaBKamps@gmail.com
Facebook: www.facebook.com/authorLisaBKamps
Twitter: twitter.com/LBKamps
Goodreads: www.goodreads.com/LBKamps
Instagram: www.instagram.com/lbkamps/

Lisa B. Kamps

ONCE BURNED
Firehouse Fourteen Book 1

Michaela Donaldson had her whole life planned out: college, music, and a happy-ever-after with her first true love. One reckless night changed all that, setting Michaela on a new path. Gone are her dreams of pursuing music in college, replaced by what she thinks is a more rewarding life. She's a firefighter now, getting down and dirty while doing her job. So what if she's a little rough around the edges, a little too careless, a little too detached? She's happy, living life on her own terms--until Nicky Lansing shows back up.

Nick Lansing was the stereotypical leather-clad bad boy, needing nothing but his fast car, his guitar, his never-ending partying, and his long-time girlfriend--until one bad decision changed the course of two lives forever. He's on the straight-and-narrow now, living life as a respected teacher and doing his best to be a positive role model. Yes, he still has his music. But gone are his days of partying. And gone is the one girl who always held his heart. Or is she?

One freak accident brings these two opposites back together. Is ten years long enough to heal the physical and emotional wounds from the past? Can they reconcile who they were with who they've become--or will it be a case of Once Burned is enough?

Turn the page for an exciting sneak peek at ***ONCE BURNED.***

"Oh shit," Mike repeated under her breath, too horrified to do anything more than force herself to breathe. Not an easy task, considering she was literally frozen to the spot. The air was thick with heated tension and the buzzing in her ears made it impossible for her to hear anything. She willed herself to move, to do something.

Shit, it's Nicky. Shit, it's Nicky. The phrase kept spinning through her mind until she thought she'd be sick with the dizziness of it. Her chest heaved with the effort to breathe and her pulse beat in a tap dancer's rhythm.

Did anyone else notice the sudden change in the room? Mike forced herself to look away from that face from her past and quickly glanced around. Four sets of eyes fixed on her with varying degrees of bewilderment. She could still feel *his* eyes on her, too, filled with stunned disbelief.

Feeling like she was trapped in a nightmare where everything moved with the speed of molasses, Mike pushed away from the counter and walked across the room, straight past the frozen figure of Nicky Lansing and through the swinging door. She turned a corner and rushed through a second door that opened into the engine room, not stopping until she reached the engine on the far side, where she promptly collapsed on the back step.

Heedless of the dirt and grime, she let her head drop against the back compartment door, ignoring the length of hose line in her way. Her breathing came in shallow gasps that did nothing to help the lightheadedness that caused black dots to dance across her closed lids.

Hyperventilating. She was hyperventilating. The

calm, rational part of her—she was surprised she still had one—told her to lean forward, to get a grip on herself and her breathing. Now bent over, sitting with her head between her knees, Mike grabbed the running board with both hands and concentrated on the feel of the diamond plate cutting into her palms.

The spots faded away and her breathing slowed to something closer to normal. One last deep breath and she straightened, only to choke on a scream when she came face-to-face with Jay, his brows lowered in a frown as he studied her with concern.

"Jesus! Don't scare me like that!" She pushed him away then stood, only to sit back down when she realized how bad her knees were shaking.

"Scare *you*? What is wrong with you? Are you okay?"

"I'm fine. I couldn't be better! Don't I look fine?"

"You look like you're ready to pass out. What the hell is going on? Do you know that guy? He looks like he's seen a ghost!"

"He probably thinks he has." Mike moved over and motioned for Jay to sit down, ignoring his scrutiny as he twisted sideways and continued staring at her.

"Are you going to explain that?"

"No." She ran her hands through her hair, muttering when she pulled a thick hank of it loose from the pony tail. Sighing, she reached back and pulled the elastic band loose, then quickly rearranged her hair into a more secure hold. Jay watched her intently then nudged her leg with his when she continued to ignore him.

"Well?"

"Well nothing. He's just somebody I used to know, that's all."

Jay snorted. "Bull."

"Okay, fine," she conceded grudgingly. "He's also somebody I never wanted to see again." Mike reached down and gingerly touched her right side, trying not to remember but unable to forget. If Jay noticed the motion, he didn't say anything.

They sat in silence, the familiar background noises of the station virtually unnoticed. A few minutes went by before Jay spoke again. "You sure you don't want to talk about it?"

Mike shook her head, ready to make a sarcastic reply when the sound of footsteps echoed through the engine room. The steps paused, then changed directions and hesitantly walked around the side of the engine. Mike knew without looking who it was: the steps were those of a stranger, someone who didn't know his way around.

Nicky stopped at the back of the engine, not saying anything as Jay slowly stood and positioned himself slightly in front of Mike, shielding her. She touched his arm briefly, in a gesture both of thanks and of reassurance that she was alright. Jay looked back at her, one brow cocked in question, then reluctantly walked away at her nod. Mike didn't see where he went but knew that he would be close by in case he was needed.

She stood slightly, leaning against the running board, then crossed her arms in front of her, covering the jagged scar that ran along her left forearm. The stance was as close to aloof and detached as she could manage considering her insides were making a milkshake of her early dinner. Too late, she remembered the sunglasses hanging around her neck and wished she would have thought to put them on to hide any emotion in her eyes.

With an effort that took more strength than she wanted to admit, she let her eyes slowly, coolly rake the man in front of her from top to bottom.

Dammit. The Nicky Lansing from her past had been ruggedly handsome with dark looks and boyish charm; this Nick Lansing was dangerously gorgeous. A little taller than she remembered, he stood just over six feet, and was definitely broader through the shoulders and chest. The boy she remembered had finally filled out, to all the best advantages.

The long hair of his past was gone, cut to a length that brushed just past the collar of the light blue shirt he wore. Still too long to be squeaky clean, but short enough by today's standards to be rated as acceptable. His eyes were the same, though. A dark chocolate brown framed in long lashes, they invited a person to swim in their depths and lose their soul without a second thought.

She would know, since she had done just that.

*****

Lisa B. Kamps

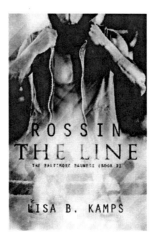

Amber "AJ" Johnson is a freelance writer who has her heart set on becoming a full-time sports reporter at her paper. She has one chance to prove herself: capture an interview with the very private goalie of Baltimore's hockey team, Alec Kolchak. But he's the one man who tries her patience, even as he brings to life a quiet passion she doesn't want to admit exists.

Alec has no desire to be interviewed--he never has, never will. But he finds himself a reluctant admirer of AJ's determination to get what she wants...and he certainly never counted on his attraction to her. In a fit of frustration, he accepts AJ's bet: if she can score just one goal on him in a practice shoot-out, he would not only agree to the interview, he would let her have full access to him for a month, 24/7.

It was a bet neither one of them wanted to lose...and a bet neither one could afford to win. But when it came time to take the shot, could either one of them cross the line?

Forensics accountant Bobbi Reeves is pulled back into a world of shadows in order to go undercover as a personal assistant with the Baltimore Banners. Her assignment: get close to defenseman Nikolai Petrovich and uncover the reason he's being extorted. But she doesn't expect the irrational attraction she feels—or the difficulty in helping someone who doesn't want it.

Nikolai Petrovich, a veteran defenseman for the Banners, has no need for a personal assistant—especially not one hired by the team. During the last eight years, he has learned to live simply...and alone. Experience has taught him that letting people close puts them in danger. He doesn't want a personal assistant, and he certainly doesn't need anyone prying into his personal life. But that doesn't stop his physical reaction to the unusual woman assigned to him.

They are drawn together in spite of their differences, and discover a heated passion that neither expected. But when the game is over, will the secrets they keep pull them closer together...or tear them apart?

Kayli Evans lives a simple life, handling the daily operations of her small family farm and acting as the primary care-taker for her fourteen-year-old niece. She knows the importance of enjoying each minute, of living life to its fullest. But she still has worries: about her older brother's safety in the military, about the rift between her two brothers, and about her niece's security and making ends meet. And now there's a new worry she doesn't want: Ian Donovan, her brother's friend.

Ian is a carefree hockey player for the Baltimore Banners who has relatively few worries—until he finds himself suddenly babysitting his seven-year-old nieces for an extended period of time. He has no idea what he's doing, and is thrust even further into the unknown when he's forced to participate in the twins' newest hobby. Meeting Kayli opens a different world for him, a simpler world where family, trust, and love are what matters most.

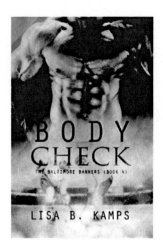

Baltimore Banners defenseman Randy Michaels has a reputation for hard-hitting, on and off the ice. But he's getting older, and his agent has warned that there are younger, less-expensive players who are eager to take his place on the team. Can his hare-brained idea of becoming a "respectable businessman" turn his reputation around, or has Randy's reputation really cost him the chance of having his contract renewed?

Alyssa Harris has one goal in mind: make the restaurant she's opened with her three friends a success. It's not going to be easy, not when the restaurant is a themed sports bar geared towards women. It's going to be even more difficult because their sole investor is Randy Michaels, her friend's drool-worthy brother who has his own ideas about what makes an interesting menu.

Will the mismatched pair be able to find a compromise as things heat up, both on and off the ice? Or will their differences result in a penalty that costs both of them the game?

Jean-Pierre "JP" Larocque is a speed demon for the Baltimore Banners. He lives for speed off the ice, too, playing fast and loose with cars and women. But is he really a player, or is his carefree exterior nothing more than a show, hiding a lonely man filled with regret as he struggles to forget the only woman who mattered?

Emily Poole thought she knew what she wanted in life, but everything changed five years ago. Now she exists day by day, helping care for her niece after her sister's bitter divorce. It may not be how she envisioned her life, but she's happy. Or so she thinks, until JP re-enters her life. Now she realizes there's a lot more she wants, including a second chance with JP.

Can these two lost souls finally find forgiveness and Break Away to the future? Or will the shared tragedy of their past tear them apart for good this time?

Valerie Michaels knows all about life, responsibility--and hockey. After all, her brother is a defenseman for the Baltimore Banners. The last thing she needs--or wants--is to get tangled up with one of her brother's teammates. She doesn't have time, not when running The Maypole is her top priority. Could that be the reason she's suddenly drawn to the troubled Justin Tome? Or is it because she senses something deeper inside him, something she thinks she can fix?

On the surface, Justin Tome has it all: a successful career with the Banners, money, fame. But he's been on a downward spiral the last few months. He's become more withdrawn, his game has gone downhill, and he's been partying too much. He thinks it's nothing more than what's expected of him, nothing more than once again failing to meet expectations and never quite measuring up. Then he starts dating Val and realizes that maybe he has more to offer than he thinks.

Or does he? Sometimes voices from the past, voices you've heard all your life, are too strong to overcome. And when the unexpected happens, Justin is certain he's looking at a permanent Delay of Game--unless one strong woman can make him see that life is all about the future, not the past.

Sometimes it takes a sinner...

Nicole Taylor has been fighting to get on the right side of the tracks all her life, but never as hard as the last two years. Finally free from an abusive relationship, her focus is on looking forward. Her first step in that direction? A quick get-away to immerse herself in her photography--and a steamy encounter with a gorgeous green-eyed stranger.

To love a saint...

As a forward for The Baltimore Banners, shooting fast and scoring often is just part of the game for Mathias "Mat" Herron. Off the ice is a different story and this off-season, he has a different goal in mind: do whatever it takes to rid himself of the asinine nickname he was recently given by some of his teammates. An encounter with a beautiful stranger helps him do just that.

And life to teach them both what's important...

When reality collides with fantasy, will passion be enough to see them through? Or will it take a shoot-out of another kind to show them what matters most?

Jake Evans has been in the Marine Corps for seventeen years, juggling his conflicting duties to country and his teenage daughter. But when he suffers a serious injury and is sent home, he knows he'll be forced to make decisions he doesn't want to. Battered in spirit and afraid of what the future may hold, he takes the long way by driving cross-country.

He never expected to meet Alyce Marshall, a free-spirited woman on a self-declared adventure: she's running away from home.

In spite of her outward free spirit, Alyce has problems of her own she must face, including the ever-present shadow of her father and his influence on her growing up. She senses similarities in Jake, and decides that it's up to her to teach the tough Marine that life isn't just about rules and regulations. What she doesn't plan on is falling in love with him...and being forced to share her secret.

Michaela Donaldson had her whole life planned out: college, music, and a happy-ever-after with her first true love. One reckless night changed all that, setting Michaela on a new path. Gone are her dreams of pursuing music in college, replaced by what she thinks is a more rewarding life. She's a firefighter now, getting down and dirty while doing her job. So what if she's a little rough around the edges, a little too careless, a little too detached? She's happy, living life on her own terms--until Nicky Lansing shows back up.

Nick Lansing was the stereotypical leather-clad bad boy, needing nothing but his fast car, his guitar, his never-ending partying, and his long-time girlfriend--until one bad decision changed the course of two lives forever. He's on the straight-and-narrow now, living life as a respected teacher and doing his best to be a positive role model. Yes, he still has his music. But gone are his days of partying. And gone is the one girl who always held his heart. Or is she?

One freak accident brings these two opposites back together. Is ten years long enough to heal the physical and emotional wounds from the past? Can they reconcile who they were with who they've become--or will it be a case of Once Burned is enough?

Angie Warren was voted the Most Likely to Succeed in school. She was also voted the Most Responsible. And responsible she is: she made it through college on a scholarship and she's even working her way through Vet School. She has an overprotective older brother she adores and a part-time job tending bar that adds some enjoyment to her life. In fact, that's the only pleasure she has. She's bored and in desperate need of a change. Too bad the one guy she has her sights set on is the one guy completely off-limits.

Jay Moore knows all about excitement and wouldn't live life any other way. From his job as a firefighter to his many brief relationships, his whole life is nothing but one thrilling experience after the other. Except when Angie Warren enters the picture. He's known her for years and there is no way he's going to agree to give her the excitement she's looking for. Even Jay knows where to draw the line—and dating his friend's baby sister definitely crosses all of them.

Too bad Angie has other plans. But will either one of them remember that when you're Playing With Fire, someone is bound to get burned?

Dave Warren knows all about protocol. As a firefighter/paramedic, he has to. What he doesn't know is when his life became nothing more than routine, following the rules day in and day out. Has it always been that way, or was it a gradual change? Or did it have anything to do with his time spent overseas as a medic with the Army Reserves? He's not sure, but it's something he's learned to accept and live with—until a series of messages upsets his routine. And until one spitfire Flight Medic enters his life.

Carolann "CC" Covey has no patience for protocols. Yes, they're a necessary evil, a part of her job, but they don't rule her life. She can't let them—she knows life is for the living, a lesson learned the hard way overseas. Which is why her attraction to the serious and staid Dave Warren makes no sense. Is it just a case of "opposites attract", or is it something more? Will CC be able to teach him that sometimes rules need to be broken?

And when something sinister appears from Dave's past to threaten everything he's come to love, will he learn that Breaking Protocol may be the only way to save what's really important?

CPSIA information can be obtained at www.ICGtesting.com
Printed in the USA
LVOW11s1744200916

505434LV00001B/31/P